TIFFANY SLY LIVES HERE NOW

DANA L. DAVIS

TIFFANY SLY LIVES HERE NOW

HARLEQUIN® TEEN

Recycling programs
for this product may
not exist in your area.

ISBN-13: 978-1-335-99413-4

Tiffany Sly Lives Here Now

This edition published by arrangement with Harlequin Books S.A.

For questions and comments about the quality of this book, please contact us at CustomerService@Harlequin.com.

Printed in U.S.A.

For Uwe,

Because you believed in Tiffany…

And you believe in me.

TIFFANY SLY LIVES HERE NOW

1

"You did good, miss. You can open your eyes. We're landing."

I nod, eyes sealed shut. *We've landed.* That's what I'm waiting to hear. I tighten my grip on the armrests, as if somehow this plane landing safely is contingent upon the act. The man beside me gives my shoulder a gentle, reassuring squeeze.

"It's so loud," I whisper. "Is that normal?"

"Perfectly." His voice is calm and composed despite the fact that we're defying gravity, soaring through the air in a fancy-shaped tin can with wings. "I never did catch your name."

"It's Tiffany," I mumble, lowering my head, bracing myself for impact. "Tiffany Sly." What if the plane skids off the runway and catches fire? That happens. I saw it once on CNN. A commuter plane skidded off the runway, rammed into a chain-link fence and struck a tree. The tree ripped off the propeller. The propeller…*exploded.* I should've listened to the captain's speech. Now I don't know what to do in case *our* propeller explodes.

"How old are you, Tiffany?"

"I'm—" I pause. The plane's vibrating and shaking now. "Did you feel that? Is *that* normal?"

The gentleman's heavy hand rests on my shoulder just long enough to give it another comforting squeeze. "Completely. We're landing. Only a minute more."

"But I think something's wrong." I contemplate opening my eyes. I need to see the looks of terror on the other people's faces. Then it would all make sense—this intense foreboding bubbling inside my chest, in rhythm with the beat of my heart.

Thump-thump, thump-thump: *We're not landing.*

Thump-thump, thump-thump: *We're crashing!*

"How old are you?"

"I'm…fifteen. I mean, sixteen. Today's my birthday."

"How wonderful. Happy birthday, Tiffany. First time flying?"

"Yes… I mean, no. I flew once…when I was a kid. But… I don't remember. I was with my mom then."

"And where's your mom today?"

"*Omigosh!* Shouldn't we be slowing down? It feels like we're going faster. Is that normal, too?"

"It only *feels* that way." His voice is so serene. Like he's totally unaware that if I let go of these two armrests, this plane would essentially veer off course and explode. "In a few seconds, the wheels of the plane are going to make contact with the ground. Have you ever been on a roller coaster, Tiffany?"

"I hate roller coasters." I lurch forward. "What just happened?" I plant my feet in front of me and push back so that I'm pressed firmly against the seat.

"Tiffany, we're on the ground. Seconds more and you can breathe easy."

The whooshing sound of the airplane as it speeds across

the runway pavement both comforts and terrifies me. Only a moment more and I can stop desperately clutching these armrests and all these people will owe me a big fat thank-you.

Thank you, Tiffany, they'll all exclaim. *If you hadn't kept your eyes shut this entire flight and squeezed those armrests the way you did, we would never have made it into Los Angeles.*

"Open your eyes," the man says softly. I hear the captain's voice through the airplane speakers over the rustle of passengers shifting about. "We're here."

I open my eyes and sigh inwardly. The plane is still moving but slowly. We're on the ground—alive. None of us will be on tomorrow's news as the unlucky bunch aboard the doomed 747 from Chicago to Los Angeles. There won't be an article with photos of smiling people and short descriptions of lives tragically cut too short trending on Facebook.

I turn to the man who was gracious enough to relinquish his armrest for our four hours together, truly seeing his face for the first time. His bright blue eyes are an alarming contrast to the tiny portion of night sky I can see through the small plane window. And his face matches the tone of his voice, warm and wise.

"I'm sorry," I say. "Hope I didn't ruin your flight."

He smiles. "You did *very* good, Tiffany. Now, better call your mom and let her know you arrived safely."

I nod graciously as the plane comes to a halt, standing to gather my carry-on luggage from the overhead space, feeling so damned lucky to be alive.

"Grams, I'm here. I'm in LA." I clutch my cell in one hand as I weave through the hundreds of travelers moving through LAX, my well-worn guitar case decorated with old '80s rock band stickers slung over my shoulder, dragging my small carry-on behind me.

"See? God is good. I was praying for you the whole time, Tiff."

I'm glad Grams can't see me roll my eyes.

"How was the flight?"

Awful. "Nice."

"I bet it was. How did you like first class?"

Not sure. My eyes were closed the whole time. "Classy."

"Don't be intimidated by all that class. Just be yourself."

"Grams, who else would I be?"

"The Tiffany I know is funny and brave and..."

While Grams drones on and on about how awesome she thinks I am, I imagine my new dad standing at the base of the elevator. He'll be waiting with a bouquet of roses to whisk me away so we can do father-daughter things like, um, whatever it is that fathers and daughters do, I guess.

My phone vibrates and I see *My New Dad* scroll across the caller ID. I nearly jump out of my Converse sneakers. "Shoot. It's him. Grams, I'll call you when I get to the house." I tap the button to switch calls before Grams has a chance to respond. "Hey!" I hop onto the escalator, my stomach an epicenter of nervous energy, butterflies dancing wildly. "Are you here?"

"Tiffany. I—I'm so sorry. I have to make an emergency run." His voice is deep and husky just like I remember from our last phone conversation. *Such* a dad voice.

"That's okay. I don't mind waiting."

At the base of the stairs, I notice men in black suits holding up strips of cardboard or iPads with names on them. One of the men holds a strip of paper with my name. We make eye contact and he smiles.

"It would be too long. I had to send a driver," he explains. "I feel terrible."

"No, no. It's okay. Not a big deal." I try to focus on happy thoughts like my therapist told me to do when disappointment arises.

Skittles.

Rainbows.

Care Bears.

Popsicles dipped in sugar.

"This shouldn't take long, Tiffany. I can't wait to see you."

"Me, too..." I pause. Why can't I say it yet? *Dad.* The word sounds so foreign rolling off my tongue, like an exotic language I've learned but haven't earned the right to speak yet. "I can't wait."

"It's a long drive to Simi Valley from LAX. I'll definitely make it home before you get there."

"It's long?" I swallow. "How long?"

"I'd say about an hour at least. Depending on traffic, maybe two."

Two *hours*?

"Tiffany, is that okay? Because if it's not I can—"

"No, it's fine," I lie. "Not a problem at all."

"Great. See you soon."

I stuff my cell into the back pocket of my jeans and take a frustrated step off the escalator, moving toward the man who holds my name on a strip of paper. He's short and round with jet-black hair and dark eyes.

"Tiffany?"

I nod and exhale. He looks safe-ish.

"Wow," he declares, looking up at me since I'm kinda towering over him. "How tall are you, anyway?"

"I'm five-eleven."

"That's pretty tall. Or maybe I'm just pretty short." He cracks up at his own joke. "Name's Juan. You got more luggage?"

"Nope. This is it."

"Cool. You hungry? Wanna stop and get a burger or somethin'?"

I shrug.

"How 'bout some In-N-Out?"

"What's that?"

His face lights up like a cherub. "What's In-N-Out?" He lifts my carry-on like it weighs half a pound. "C'mon, kid. Your life will never be the same after today. Want me to take the guitar, too? I don't mind."

I run my fingertips over one of the Rolling Stones stickers displayed on the plastic case and pull protectively at the strap. "Nah. I got it."

He nods. "Follow me."

I stuff the last handful of greasy, salt-sprinkled fries into my mouth, then slowly sip from a straw, letting the icy-cold vanilla shake linger on my tongue for a bit, afraid to swallow for fear of officially ending my first In-N-Out experience.

"How you doing back there?" Juan asks as he weaves through heavy Los Angeles traffic.

"Hmm?" I say sleepily, deep in an In-N-Out-induced state of euphoria.

Juan laughs. "See? Told ya. Life changed forever."

My phone chimes. A text from my best friend, Akeelah, says: You is kind. You is smart. And you is important.

I text back: And you is a dork.

"You from Chicago, kid?" Juan asks.

"Yes, sir."

Juan whistles. "Chi-Town, eh? How long you stayin'?"

I shrug. "Forever, I hope."

Another text from Keelah: I Googled your new school. It's less than 1% African American. Doooood. WTF does that even mean? What if you're the only black girl there? #weaksauce #yournewschoolsucks.

I text back: I'm not black. I'm brown, you moron.

"I lived in LA my whole life and ain't no place better," Juan testifies, swerving onto an overpass. Within a moment we're on the freeway, speeding across pavement so fast the foreboding returns.

Thump-thump, thump-thump: *This guy is not a good driver.*

Thump-thump, thump-thump: *You'd be better off in a tin can with wings.*

I grip the side of the car door as another text from Keelah comes through: Brown's boring. You're a mocha Frappuccino.

Me: More like a shot of espresso.

Akeelah: LOL. Then I'm a double shot!

"You ever been to Simi Valley before?"

"No." I look up and notice Juan's hands are not at ten and two like universally suggested. More like one hand at six o'clock, while the other hand sort of hovers in midair, fiddling with buttons on the dash. He's also not a safe distance away from the car in front of him. I check out the speedometer. Seventy-five miles per hour and tailgating. Dread crawls up my spine. What if the car in front of him slams on the brakes?

Thump-thump, thump-thump: *We're going to crash for sure.*

Thump-thump, thump-thump: *You might make tomorrow's news, after all.*

I picture a beautiful newscaster. Hair freshly straightened and superpolished under studio lights. Makeup so perfectly applied she looks like a sculpture from a wax museum: *"A sedan crashed in Los Angeles last night, killing a sixteen-year-old girl. Thankfully, the driver survived uninjured."* Then she'll smile. *"And in other news, the Powerball is up to a billion!"*

"You excited?" Juan snaps me out of my morbid fantasy.

"A little." He switches lanes again, rapidly accelerating to tailgate a new car. "I think I'm more nervous than anything."

"Why you moving all the way to Simi Valley? It's freakin' hot out there, man."

"I'm moving in with my...dad."

"He a nice guy?"

I glance out the window, palm trees whizzing by in a dark blur as we speed along. I check the speedometer again. Eighty mph! "I dunno. I never met him. Hey, could we slow down?"

I see Juan's big brown eyes expand in shock through the rearview mirror. "Never met your dad? You shittin' me?"

"It seems like we're going really fast." I close my eyes and grip the handle on the car door. Not like I'm gonna open it and jump out or anything. I mostly do it in hopes that it will slow the insane rhythm of my heart so I won't have a heart attack and die. But with my eyes closed and my hand clenched tightly around the door handle, the car feels like it's moving faster than ever. "Omigosh, please slow down, sir. *Please!*" I'm screaming. I'm aware. The cat's out of the bag. I am officially no longer a supercool black girl from Chicago who can play the shit out of the guitar slung over her shoulder. I am now, officially, a freak.

He slows down enough to make me exhale appreciatively. "There. I'm doing fifty-five. Better?"

I grab my head to dull the ache. Deep breath in. Hold it. Exhale.

Puppies.

Fairies.

Samwise Gamgee.

"You okay, kid?"

I pop open an eye to see Juan's concerned face through the rearview mirror. Actually, less concerned, more… WTF is wrong with this kid. "Sorry. I get scared in cars."

"Man, that's an understatement! But check it. Never had an accident if that makes you feel better."

"It does."

"Where's your mom?"

Back home, everyone's been supercourteous, avoiding the M-word like the plague. I contemplate making up a story. She's an astronaut in cryo on a two-year mission to Saturn? A sniper on a covert operation for the US government?

Juan leans on the horn, then throws both hands in the air in frustration, leaving the steering wheel completely unmanned, causing the car to veer ever so slightly to the right. I grip the door handle once again. "Get off your damn phone!" Juan screams through a closed window. "Freakin' smartphones gonna be the death of everybody." He settles on a station and rap music blares through the speakers. "What's your favorite kind of music?"

"I dunno." Of course I know my favorite kind of music. But how can I think straight and form clear sentences when Los Angeles's all-time-worst driver is at the wheel. I only wanna make it to Simi Valley. *Alive.* That's my favorite kind of music—the kind you listen to when you're not dead.

Juan places one hand back at six o'clock and I breathe a sigh of relief. "You like Rihanna? Or Katy Perry or somethin' like that?"

Not really. "Sure, that's fine."

He settles on a new station. Sia's sultry belt blares through the speakers and Juan bobs his head and sings along to the hit song "Chandelier."

I ponder swinging from a chandelier. Has Sia tried it? Probably not. I'm pretty sure any attempt at swinging from an actual chandelier would result in a broken neck. A text comes in from Akeelah: All jokes aside. You're my best friend and I know you're gonna be okay.

I want to tell Keelah the truth. To explain to my best friend in the world the secret that's ready to burst out of me and erupt like a spray of confetti from a confetti cannon. She's my best friend. She wouldn't judge me, *or* my mom. She'd understand. She'd comfort me. Know all the right things to say. The words to soothe my soul. I desperately want to confide in her, but I text a bunch of smiling poop emoticons instead.

He said the court order would be delivered on October 14. That's seven days from now. I've got seven days to come clean to my new dad. Seven days to tell the truth. I think back to Xavior—to the moment he showed up at our door and shook up my already very shaken-up world.

I was pulling a sweatshirt over my head and getting ready to head over to Keelah's house when there was a knock on our apartment door.

"Who is it?" I asked, skirting around the mounds of stacked moving boxes in our unit. Searching for my metro pass among the mess.

"Xavior Xavion," the deep voice said from the other side of the door.

"Who's that?" I peeked through the peephole and saw a kind-looking black man on the other side, clutching a bouquet of sunflowers. He looked sane enough, so I opened the door. "Yeah?" He was tall. Basketball-player tall. The kind of tall where you have to lower your head so you don't bump it on entryways when you move from room to room.

He beamed. Like he was gazing upon a bright, shiny new BMW. "Hi, Tiffany. Do you remember me?"

"Um..."

"We met at your mom's funeral?"

"Oh! That's right. Nice to see you again." I didn't remember him. There were so many people I met on the worst day of my life. I glanced at the clock on the wall. I needed to hurry up if I wanted to catch the 12:20 bus.

"Would it be okay if I came in?" He handed me the flowers.

"Thank you." I set them carefully on a counter by the door. "But my grams is at church and—"

"Say no more. I should come back when she's here. In fact, that would be better. That way I can speak with both of you."

I raised an eyebrow. "Speak with us about what?"

Xavior paused for a moment and rubbed his bald head. "Tiffany, I think I might be your father."

My jaw dropped. Like literally. And I stood there for a few seconds with my mouth hanging open, staring at him, probably almost drooling on myself. "Are you crazy?" I finally managed to ask.

He laughed and said, "Probably," in a way that was so similar to me it made my entire body tense. His skin was dark brown. Just like mine. In fact, he sort of reminded me of...me.

"Your mother and I. Well, we dated. I mean, we dated about sixteen years ago."

"So? That doesn't prove anything."

"We *dated*." He sighed. "It might not prove anything but it certainly begs the question. Wouldn't you agree?"

I did agree. A fact that made me wanna slam the door in Xavior's face and run around the apartment wailing at the top of my lungs like Harry Potter's spoiled cousin, Dudley Dursley. I didn't want to be a victim of some sort of cliché, baby-daddy, *Maury Povich*–esque DNA testing. My mom was better than this. *I* was better than this.

"Look, I can come back when Juanita's home."

"No! Don't come back here. You can't say these things to my grandma. She'd have a heart attack and die."

"I thought you'd be happy."

"Why did you think *that*?"

"Don't you want to know who your father is?"

"Pretty sure you're confused. I already know who my father is. Anthony Stone is my father. That's what my mom told me, so that's the story I'm sticking to. And I'm moving in with him. *Tomorrow.*"

He rubbed his head again, then held up an envelope. "Tiffany. There are letters, pictures—it proves your mother and I were a couple. The dates match up. Look, I'll come back. I want to speak with Juanita about you and me taking a DNA test. I already spoke with a lawyer and—"

"Omigosh! You seriously can't just show up here like this, with an envelope of photos, and expect me to go take a DNA test with you."

"Tiffany, please understand."

"Dude, stop calling me Tiffany. Stop acting like you know me or something."

"If you don't do it, my lawyer will *make* you. On October 14, Juanita will be served court documents. You'll be *required* to submit to DNA testing. Look, I'd really like to speak with her. I'll come back later."

"No!" I grabbed my head for fear it would spontaneously combust and Grams would find my exploded head guts in the hallway when she came home from Bible study. "This would… I mean… Mom just… Grams is a wreck, okay? Please. This would *destroy* her. Do you really want to destroy an old lady who's mourning the loss of her only child? Can't you just go away? Like forever?"

"I want to know if you're mine, Tiffany. I deserve to know. Deserve the opportunity to be a father. I think I'd be a good one."

I snatched the envelope from his hands and ripped it open. Pictures of Xavior and my mom. Holding hands. Kissing. Wrapped in a loving embrace. Laughing together.

I leaned against the doorway for support, fearing my knees would buckle and I'd fall backward. "My mom's not here to defend herself. Do you understand how unfair this is?" I asked so softly I wondered if he could even hear me.

Apparently, he did hear me because he replied, "I know it's unfair. But what should I do, Tiffany? Tell me what to do."

I looked up at him standing so tall and statuesque and adult, asking teenage me what he should do. How the hell should I know?

"I'll take your stupid test." I handed him back the envelope and photos. "My grandma doesn't need to know about this."

"You're a minor. You'll need to be accompanied by your legal guardian. We should let my lawyer facilitate."

"Anthony is my legal guardian. What if I gave you his info?" I pulled nervously at my braids and wondered how this would play out if I gave Xavior fake info. Like the number and address to the Walmart on North Avenue. "You can serve him instead. Save my grandma all this drama."

Xavior nodded. "That's fair. I can do that, Tiffany. On October 14. That's seven days from tomorrow."

I nodded and repeated to myself, "Seven days."

"You seem awfully quiet back there. You okay, kiddo?" Juan asks, snapping me back to my current reality. Sia has been replaced by a new singer. I don't know who it is, but the lyrics, about a bash and some cash and…a hash? It's making my head spin.

"I'm okay," I reply. "But is there any way you could change the station?"

"I asked what kind of music you like. You never answered."

"I like Black Sabbath, Deep Purple, Led Zeppelin, Jimi Hendrix—"

"Sweet." Juan nods. "Rock and roll it is."

Traffic is getting much heavier now, so the SUV is slowing to a crawl, saving both our lives for sure. Pearl Jam's "Jeremy" blasts through the car speakers. Nice. I lean my head back against the seat and close my eyes.

2

"Wake up, kiddo. Almost there."

I yawn lazily and rub my tired eyes.

A young security guard steps out of a guard gate as Juan pulls up to the entrance of what appears to be a large gated community.

"Dropping off," Juan says to the security guard, handing him his driver's license.

The guard takes a moment to check his computer. He hands Juan back the driver's license, glances at me through the lowered window and waves. I wave back.

"Enjoy your day, sir," the security guard says as the tall wrought iron gates slowly open.

I peek out the window and catch my breath, mesmerized by the extravagance of the houses. Correction: these aren't houses—they're *mansions.*

Juan whistles, looking just as mesmerized as I am, slowing the SUV while scoping out the expensive homes. "Your dad a doctor or somethin'?"

"Actually, yeah. He is."

"Doctor, lawyer, oil tycoon, czar. Gotta be *something* fancy to live in a place like this."

We continue on, deeper and deeper into the elaborate housing development, finally turning into a large cul-de-sac. Juan pulls into one of the driveways and clicks off the engine.

I stuff my hand into my front pocket and grab my tiny box of wild berry Tic Tacs, shake a few into my mouth and yank my long braids out of the bun on top of my head, pulling them neatly over one shoulder. Juan heads toward the trunk of the car and I smooth out my gray Guns N' Roses T-shirt, leaning forward to check my face in the front mirror, suddenly regretting my decision not to wear makeup today. Everyone always tells me my dark brown skin doesn't need makeup. But still, what if my dad doesn't think I'm pretty enough? I dig around the other front pocket for my tube of cherry-scented lip gloss, add a quick coat, reach over to free my guitar from where it's strapped into the seat beside me and carefully sling it back over my shoulder before hopping out onto the cobblestone of the massive driveway.

"Dropping your bag off inside!" Juan hollers over his shoulder as he casually moves toward the front door.

A surprising burst of loneliness creeps into my heart as I allow the evening breeze to warm my skin, icy cold from the air-conditioning that was blasted in the car. This place is classy. Fancier than anything I've ever been privileged to. Shouldn't I be happy? It's like I've won the jackpot. Plucked from the inner cities of Chicago and flown first-class to high society and all I can think about is my neighborhood back home. We lived in a high-rise apartment building with a smelly, wonky elevator in desperate need of a safety inspection. Every day after school, I'd risk my life in that stupid thing, cuz there was no way I was climbing twelve flights of stairs, and then I'd walk across a faded and dirty carpet in a poorly lit hallway to apartment 1203. Mom was sometimes home from work. She'd be yapping on the phone, greet me with a cheerful wave and point to a plate of snacks she'd left for me on the table. And even though she'd turn her back to me, a clear signal that she was deep into conversation and didn't want to be bothered, I'd hug her and lay my chin on her shoulder and ask, "Did you miss me?"

She'd laugh and reply, "Tiffany, my dear, how can I miss you when you're always here?"

I picture myself back in Chicago, stepping out of the cold into a local 7-Eleven. I'd approach a clerk, safe behind thick bulletproof glass.

"Here you go, sir." I'd slide my winning ticket under the opening in the glass.

He'd scratch his head in confusion as he read the numbers. "Miss, you just won ten million dollars."

I'd nod, well aware. "You can keep it. I'm going home."

I smile at the thought. Across the street, a black Hummer is parked in a fancy, lit-up driveway, with a bumper sticker that reads My Kid Gets All A's at Curington College Prep for Boys and Girls… What's Yours Do?

Curington College Prep—it's the name of the school I'm set to attend. I got good grades at my last school. Mostly As. A few Bs. But that was only the neighborhood public school on the west side. Not a private college *preparatory*. Though Akeelah says that all high schools are college preps and Curington only has a long, pretentious name so rich people will feel better giving them all their money.

"Think about it, though," she explained to me while helping me pack a few weeks ago. "For forty thousand dollars a year, you ain't gonna send your kid to a school called West. Trust me, all the high schools with one-syllable names…free. Them expensive schools got long-ass names."

I inhale, drinking in the sounds of the peaceful neighborhood: crickets chirping from somewhere deep in the bushes, the beep-beep of a truck some distance away, the yap of an angry, undoubtedly harmless puppy.

"Well, well, well…look what the cat dragged in straight from LAX."

I turn to face a young, smiley-faced girl with a mouth full of silver braces and pale blue eyes. She has very light brown skin and wild, curly hair pulled into a bouncy ponytail. She wears a beautiful yellow tunic dress that cuts off an inch or two above her knees, showing off her long legs and bare feet.

"Excuse me?" I'm suddenly self-conscious about my casual attire: boot-cut jeans with strategically placed holes in the knees, brown leather wraparound bracelets on both wrists and scuffed black-and-white Converse sneakers.

"Cool hair." She reaches out and grabs a few of my braids, massaging them curiously with her fingers. "Are these extensions?"

"They are, yeah."

"Sweet! I've always wanted extensions but my dad won't let me." She smiles as she scans my wardrobe with a slightly judgmental smirk. "Guns N' Roses? Shouldn't you be wearing, like, a Lil Wayne T-shirt?" She giggles. "Totally kidding.

I'm Nevaeh. It's *heaven* spelled backward, which I personally think is so dumb. Why would anybody spell *heaven* backward, right? People think it's pronounced Nah-vee-ah. But it's Nah-vay-ah. I'm only twelve now, but when I get older, I'm legally changing my name to something simple like Jane. Do I look like my name could be Jane?"

My eyes bulge. Nevaeh talks *fast.* "I'm sorry…what?"

"Hey? Do you need a tip or something?" Nevaeh calls out as Juan exits the house and moves toward the SUV. "I can run in and get some cash from my mom. She's out back setting up."

"Already included with purchase." Juan tosses me another toothy grin. "Triple five. Eleven, eleven."

"Huh?" I reply.

"My number. Easy to remember, right? You find yourself needing a ride, don't hesitate to dial it. Oh, and every time you eat an In-N-Out burger, remember it was me who gave it to you first. Good luck to you, kiddo."

He hops into the car and backs onto the street, leaving Nevaeh and me standing alone on the cobblestone driveway underneath the light of the full moon.

"In-N-Out?" Nevaeh frowns. "Don't tell my mom you already ate. She'll freak. She cooked a feast."

"Who's your mom?"

"My mom?" She raises an eyebrow. "My mom is Dad's wife."

"*My* dad's wife?"

"*Our* dad."

I try not to show my surprise, though it's a weak effort

at best. Did Grams know my new dad had a *wife*? Another freakin' *kid*?

"I don't really see the resemblance," Nevaeh declares with a shake of her head. "I mean…not just cuz you're dark…"

My eyes narrow. "I'm not *dark*. I'm dark-*skinned*."

"Oh, shiz! Did I offend you?"

"No, no," I mumble, realizing by the apologetic tone of her voice that offending me truly wasn't her intention. "It's fine. I don't like the word, is all. There are negative connotations attached to it in regards to African Americans. Like, dark is the opposite of light and associated with evil and—"

"Whoa." She raises a hand to stop me. "Trust me, I get it. Sometimes people call me a mixed breed and I'm all—do I look like a puppy? Do I bark? I mean, I *am* a mixed breed. Of the humanoid species. But aren't we all? Oh, and seriously. I really am sorry if I offended you. I want us to be more than sisters, you know? We should be friends." She beams. "Isn't this wild, though? The craziest thing to happen to our family, like, ever. And it's your birthday! Omigosh, happy birthday! Can I hug you?"

She lurches forward and pulls me in for a hug.

"Give her some air, Nevaeh. God."

Another girl moves across the driveway with a face that matches Nevaeh's. She's got the same braces, light skin, blue eyes and wild, curly hair pulled into a ponytail. A realization quickly sets in—they're twins. Identical twins. I might have identical twin *sisters*?

"This is Heaven." Nevaeh rushes to meet her. "Get it? Heaven and Nevaeh? So lame." She groans. "Why couldn't our parents have named us Mindy and Pindy or Lisa and Pisa?"

"Pindy and Pisa? Those aren't even real names." Heaven rolls her eyes. "I happen to like my name."

"I like your name, too. It's not spelled *backward*." Nevaeh turns to me. "We have another sister. She's fifteen and her birthday is exactly two months after yours. Isn't that so awkward? Dad knocked up two women at the exact same time!"

"*Another* sister?" I croak.

"Nevaeh, shut *up*." Heaven elbows her in the side. "You can't get two women pregnant at the exact same time. It's physically impossible." She turns to me. "I'm so sorry about her. She has Tourette's. And she never stops talking, so I hope you brought earplugs."

"I do not have Tourette's and I do so stop talking. I gotta sleep, don't I?" Nevaeh says seriously. "Besides, I'm just stating the facts. Dad was *obviously* some sort of Casanova sixteen years ago. A real *ladies'* man." She makes a thrusting movement with her hips and Heaven covers her face in embarrassment.

Two women pregnant at the same time? *Three* sisters? What the hell did I just walk into? "I'm superconfused, you guys."

"Of course you're confused." Nevaeh casually wraps her arm around Heaven's shoulders like they're the best of friends, which I imagine they are. "I told Mom sending a car was rude and would confuse you. But Dad was supposed to pick you up and then he couldn't and Mom didn't want to leave the party prep."

Heaven elbows Nevaeh. "It was supposed to be a surprise! You ruined it!"

"Ruined what? We weren't gonna jump out from behind furniture and scream, 'Happy birthday.'"

A party? Now Nevaeh's fancy dress makes sense. And Heaven is dressed up, too. Sort of. An ankle-length blue cotton tank dress blowing ever so softly in the evening wind.

As if reading my mind, Nevaeh grimaces. "You should change. Dad's weird about holes in your clothes. In fact, I'd hide those jeans if I were you. Dinner attire is always Sunday chic. It's the house rule."

"We have lots of house rules," Heaven adds.

I pull the leather strap on my case to take some of the weight off my shoulder.

"Cool guitar case. Is there a guitar inside it?" Nevaeh asks.

"Why would she be carrying an *empty* guitar case?" Heaven replies.

"It could be, like, a suitcase or something… I dunno. Whoa!" Nevaeh jumps excitedly. "You know who you look like? Janet Jackson!"

I sigh. It's like I'm watching the twin Olympics and Heaven and Nevaeh are going for the gold. Can't they be quiet for, like, one second so I can figure out what the hell is happening here?

"Janet Jackson is short and sporty. Tiffany's tall and thin," Heaven states simply. "She looks more like Kelly Rowland."

"Holy shiz, you're right!" Nevaeh squeals.

"Stop cussing!"

"I said *shiz*, Heaven."

"Whatever. *Shiz* is stupid. You sound moronic."

"Do you see the resemblance?" Nevaeh asks Heaven, sizing me up once again as I stand awkwardly in front of them.

"Totes," Heaven replies, matter-of-fact. "The height. Thin like all of us. An air of awesome. I totally see it."

Nevaeh nods. "Yeah, yeah. I see it now!"

They stare at me with matching smiles and a glorious moment of silence passes. I seize my opportunity to get a word in. "Just curious but…where is, um…?"

"Dad?" Heaven saves my lips from having to form the word on their own.

"Yes. Where is he?"

"Emergency C-section." Heaven tosses out the words like it's as normal as a walk in the park. "He'll be home soon. Hopefully. *Maybe.*" She rolls her eyes.

"She ate In-N-Out," Nevaeh whispers.

"Don't tell my mom that. She'd die. She's been cooking since 5:00 a.m."

My phone buzzes in my back pocket. I grab it and check the caller ID. "It's my grandma. Sorry, could you guys give me a second?"

Heaven pulls Nevaeh by the arm. "Take your time. We'll see you inside, okay? Then we can show you your room. And you can change. And meet Pumpkin."

"Pumpkin?"

"Yeah. Our sister." Nevaeh smiles.

"Oh, right. Gotcha. Our…sister."

I wait until the girls have disappeared inside the house and take a few steps toward the street as I swipe across the screen. "Did you know Anthony has other kids?" I whisper angrily into the phone. "He has *kids*!"

"So I'm assuming you made it safely?"

"Grams, did you hear me? I have sisters!"

"Sisters? I only knew about one, Tiffany. I swear. I only knew about London."

"*London?* Who is that?"

"That's the sister I knew about. London. She should be about your age."

Then who the hell is Pumpkin? It hits me. "Oh, my *gosh*! Grams, there must be four!" I contemplate slamming my phone down onto the cobblestone driveway and watching the glass screen shatter into a hundred pieces, but that would only tame my rage for a few seconds and then, of course, leave me with a broken phone. Maybe there's not four. Maybe London's *nickname* is Pumpkin. But why would London's nickname be Pumpkin? Maybe she looks like a Pumpkin?

"Tiffany, you have to believe me. I only knew about the one."

"So why didn't you tell me *that*? Would've been a nice heads-up!"

"It wasn't my place to tell you."

"Yes, it was!" My eyes burn as hot tears form. "You had *no* right to keep this from me. I feel totally blindsided." I wipe a tear. What did I expect? That Anthony Stone would be sitting in a giant empty house waiting for me all by himself, feeling the way I've felt for all these years—incomplete? How could he possibly feel incomplete with a wife and *four* daughters? And how will he feel when he discovers I may not be his? With four daughters and a wife, my guess is...*relieved*.

As I'm pacing, the door to the house across the cul-de-sac swings open and a teenage boy steps out onto the neighboring driveway. He's wearing a sweatshirt with the hood pulled low, concealing his face.

"Tiffany," Grams says with a tired sigh. "Get to know your father. It's his job to tell you the truth. The whole truth. You deserve it."

"Grams—" I'm distracted as the boy looks up and our eyes meet. The sight of his face literally takes my breath away. It's covered in some sort of heavy white makeup, pasty and drawn, his green eyes almost glowing under the light of the full moon.

"Yes, Tiffany? What's going on? You all right?"

"Look… I'm here. I made it safely."

"Please don't be mad at me. I'm already hurting so much. I can't have you mad at me."

"I'm not mad. I'll talk to you later." I hang up before she has a chance to respond, my heart pounding, my mind a jumble of confusion.

The boy with the white face is still standing there, staring. He smiles and raises a gloved hand to wave at me. More than a bit spooked, I timidly wave back, then spin around and run inside the house.

3

Something's attached itself to me.

I look down to see tiny hands wrapped around my leg and enough wild, curly hair to open up an exclusive wig store. "Um, excuse me? Hi."

An adorable face emerges from the mass of auburn-tinted curls. She's got pouty full lips, light brown skin and the same pale blue eyes as Heaven and Nevaeh.

"I Pumpkin. I two! Birthday, December 19."

"Hi there, Pumpkin," I say weakly as I realize Pumpkin *wasn't* a nickname for London and there actually *are* four sisters. "I'm Tiffany." Pumpkin's wearing a pretty pink dress with lots of ruffles. She looks like a porcelain doll. Like she should be on sale at Toys R Us.

"I Pumpkin. I two years old."

"Oh. Okay. I'm Tiffany. Again. I'm sixteen."

"I Pumpkin! I two!"

"I'm sorry. She'll do that all night." A woman has emerged from around the corner. She quickly peels the little tyke from my leg and scoops her up. "*Tiffany.* Oh, it's so nice you're here!" she gushes. "I'm Margaret Stone. Anthony's wife." She leans forward to embrace me warmly and when she pulls away Pumpkin is attached to my hair, her tiny fingers gripping a handful of braids gleefully.

"Pumpkin! Let go! Sweetie, it's not nice to pull hair," Margaret scolds, and Pumpkin releases my hair. "Say sorry."

"It's okay. Didn't hurt." I fold my arms under my chest and hunch over, wishing for a moment I could be swallowed up by the shiny white marble floor of this massive foyer. I look around in awe, taking in the splendor of the mansion. There is a curved staircase, a stunning, three-tiered crystal chandelier as big as me and ceilings so high not even a long ladder on top of another long ladder could help you get anywhere close to the top.

"Pumpkin, say sorry," Margaret says again, this time more sternly.

"I sorry!" Pumpkin shouts with a smile.

"Inside voice, Pumpkin." Margaret gives me an apologetic tilt of the head. "I'm sorry, too."

"No worries. It's very nice to meet you, ma'am."

"No, no. Please don't call me ma'am. It makes me feel a hundred years old. Call me Margaret."

Margaret's white and maybe in her forties. She's not really pretty as much as she is *very* put together. Conservative and classy looking with the kind of clothes that look expensive and meticulously tailored. A pearl-white, high-waist pencil skirt, silky black blouse and matching heels. Certainly not the kind of lady you'd find in my neighborhood back in Chicago.

She's got brown shoulder-length hair and dark eyes. Wait—*dark* eyes? Shouldn't they be blue, like all the girls?

"Are you my sister?" Pumpkin screams.

"Pumpkin, not so loud! *Inside* voice." Margaret turns back toward me. "This is Pumpkin. We call her Pumpkin because she was born with this wild auburn hair. Some sort of recessive gene, I guess." She laughs nervously. Actually, *nervous* is an understatement. Margaret is literally shaking. "Your dad just called. Surgery went well. He should be home soon." She sets the squirmy two-year-old down and Pumpkin races off around a corner like a magical gnome. "We're going to eat on the terrace to celebrate. Made a cake from scratch. Got the fancy dishes out and everything." I notice Margaret eyeing my attire.

"I didn't know about the dinner. Sorry. I would've worn something nicer. I swear."

"Oh, it's fine. We bought you some *beautiful* dresses."

"You guys bought me dresses? You didn't have to do that."

"Are you kidding? It's so our pleasure. Do you like Anthropologie?"

I look into Margaret's eyes. Stretched wide, furrowed brows, pained expression. Crazy eyes for sure. There's also something about her that comes off as not quite genuine. She's got a syrupy sweet voice and that polite tilt of the head. I imagine she's one of those "nice" people that have a special way of getting on my nerves. Disgustingly polite, when you know, somewhere deep inside, they're screaming, *Fuck this shit!*

"Never trust a person who's *always* smiling," Mom used to say when I was small.

"How come?" I'd reply in confusion.

"Because, Tiffany," Mom said seriously. "Smiling is the easiest way to lie. And nobody, not even Jesus Christ himself, was always walking around happy and smiling."

I shift, suddenly uneasy in Margaret's presence. "Anthropology? Isn't that the study of humans?"

Margaret smiles. "Oh, my goodness. How cute are you? No, no. The clothing store."

"Oh!" My cheek starts to twitch and I scratch at it to hide the tremble. "Yeah, yeah. No doubt." I make a quick mental note to Google Anthropology the *clothing* store.

"Can I get you anything to drink before dinner?"

"Pop? That'd be cool."

"Pop?" Margaret gives me another polite tilt of the head. "I'm sorry?"

"That's how they say *soda* in Chicago." Nevaeh appears on top of the long, curving staircase, leaning casually over the railing, her voice echoing in the giant space. "But we don't drink soda, Tiffany. Mom says it's too much sugar."

"It's Pumpkin," Margaret explains. "She's on the autism spectrum and the sugar…it makes her a bit off balance."

"It makes her crazy," Nevaeh explains seriously. "I mean, she's already crazy but sugar makes it worse."

"Nevaeh, don't say that. Please don't refer to Pumpkin as crazy."

Nevaeh shrugs. "Come up, Tiff! I can give you a tour of the house."

"Sweetheart, I actually need you to help me set the table out back. Besides, Tiffany needs a chance to breathe and settle in. Right, Tiffany?"

A chance to breathe and settle in. I exhale appreciatively. "Yeah. That's cool."

"How about a tea? We have herbal tea," Margaret offers. "It's a rooibos and chamomile blend. It's *very* nice."

"Mom," Nevaeh declares with an exasperated sigh as she moves down the staircase. "You think she wants a hot cup of herbal tea? She's moving in, not retiring."

I bite my lower lip to conceal a smile that's trying to form. "Water's good. I'll take water."

Margaret exhales, relaxing somewhat. "I'll have one of the girls bring a bottle up to your room. I hope you like your room. And listen." Margaret wrings her shaking hands together. "I'm so sorry about your mom."

I lower my eyes again, pulling tightly on the strap of my guitar case, desperately hoping this part of the conversation ends quickly. "Yeah."

"Me, too," Nevaeh adds. "How did she die?"

"Nevaeh, sweetheart. That's not polite."

"*Mom*, omigosh! You say everything's not polite. It's a simple question."

"Sorry," I interrupt. "You say the room is upstairs?"

"Up the stairs, turn right. At the end of the hall. I had the driver put your carry-on right outside the door." Margaret smiles brightly again. "I'm so glad you're here, Tiffany. We're so lucky to have you." She gently grabs Nevaeh by the elbow and they both disappear around the corner.

My room. I blink in disbelief. It looks straight out of the pages of a Pottery Barn catalog. And bigger than our entire apartment back home. The floor is dark mahogany wood, and there's a narrow wrought iron spiral staircase leading to a loft area. A loft. An actual loft in my bedroom. I slide my guitar off my shoulder and set it carefully beside the wall.

The room is almost in perfect symmetry. Two full beds with matching white upholstered headboards. Two white bureaus set on opposite sides of the room. Two nightstands with matching lamps shaped like pretty sunflowers that emit a soft, golden glow of light.

One bed is decorated with gray bedding: duvet cover, fluffy throw pillows and sheets. The other bed has yellow-colored bedding. I assume the gray side of the room is mine since gray is my favorite color. Like the Chicago sky. A city shrouded by a blanket of silvery gray clouds eight months out of the year.

"I love when the sun disappears," I would tell my mom every October when the weather would start to turn. "Don't you?"

But Mom would shake her head in horror. "Girl, please. When we win the lottery, we're moving to Hawaii, where there is no winter."

"No," I'd plead. "When we win the lottery, let's move to Ireland!"

Mom would scoff. *"Ireland?"*

"We'll move to the countryside!" I'd say dreamily. "Have an herb garden and eat cakes and custards and take long walks in the rain!"

Mom would laugh. "Okay, Tiff. When we win the lottery, we will officially be the only African Americans living in *Ireland*. Lord help us."

I run my fingers across the duvet cover. The bedding has that fresh-out-of-the-box look. Pristine and untouched. Like someone took a hot iron to each sheet and pillowcase. At the far end of the room are stunning glass French doors. I move toward them and stop to catch my breath. Our room is overlooking a tennis court. These people have a *tennis court* in their backyard?

I open one of the doors and step out onto the small balcony, admiring the nighttime view. The house is nestled at the base of a hill of giant boulders so the entire backyard perimeter is enclosed and completely private. To the left of the tennis court, I see a hint of their pool that seems to be cut from stone so it looks like it's blending in with the rustic scenery of the hills. Bright fuchsia and purple lights glow from somewhere deep within the water and there's a water slide! *Amazing.* This is better than the houses I've seen on *MTV Cribs.* How can they be this rich?

I step back inside and notice a vintage record player set beside a wicker basket filled with records on top of my dresser. I move to it and sort through the music.

Pink Floyd.

Led Zeppelin: *Live at the Royal Albert Hall.*

Jimi Hendrix.

James Brown.

Stevie Wonder.

The Rolling Stones.

The Beatles.

It's almost *all* of my favorites! I flip open the Pink Floyd: *The Dark Side of the Moon* record and my jaw drops. A first-edition vinyl in almost perfect condition! It must've been so expensive and tough to find. I carefully set the record back among the others and run my trembling fingers across the antique record player.

"Be careful with that stuff."

I turn. London? She's got the same soft hair as Heaven and Nevaeh. Only hers isn't in tight ringlets like theirs; it hangs in soft waves down her back. She's also got a beautiful coffee-with-cream complexion, and the eyes—strikingly blue. I fidget with my leather bracelets, super-self-conscious. With full lips and that gorgeous black hair, all she needs is a pair of wings and a runway and she's Adriana Lima.

She tosses me a cold bottle of water and I catch it clumsily. "Those records are my dad's and so is the player, so please be careful."

"Oh. I thought they were for me."

"To *borrow.* My dad wouldn't give them to you. Those are all his favorites."

I'm stunned speechless for a moment and not because of the way she keeps stressing *my* dad. As if he's hers and hers alone. It's the music. All the music I've grown up listening to and loving. It's proof! Of course he's my dad. We like the *same* music? Genetic taste buds! I smile. Like really smile for the first time in a long time. Only London doesn't smile back. She frowns. Deep and almost threatening.

She's dressed in leggings and an oversize green sweatshirt that says Curington Girls Basketball in bright gold letters. She tosses her backpack onto the floor and pulls off the sweatshirt in one fell swoop, flinging it onto the bed, not even a trace of modesty as she stands before me in her pink cotton bra, showing off what probably doesn't come from my dad's side of the family: giant boobs.

"Sorry I'm late. I was studying for the SATs with a friend. So exhausting."

"SATs? Isn't it kind of early?"

"It's my senior year."

"You're a *senior*? I thought you were fifteen?"

"I am. I skipped a few grades."

"Oh. I didn't know people could do that."

"People skip grades all the time."

"I guess. But I mean…you must be supersmart to do something like that."

She shrugs as if yes, she is, but also, it's not very interesting. "Dad says your transcripts were mostly As."

"But I'm not all that smart. I study a *lot*." I'm trying my hardest not to gape at her way-too-big-for-a-fifteen-year-old breasts. In fact, I'm focusing so intently on her eyes, my own are starting to cross, and now my vision is blurry. I've never given my A cups much thought. Every so often Keelah would tease me and declare that one day my children would starve to death if I didn't find some sort of miracle grow, but it never much bothered me. Until now. In the presence of my new half-dressed, half-naked half sister, I suddenly feel inadequate and quite frankly…underdeveloped. Why *are* my boobs so freaking small?

"Weird you had to study so much. You went to, like, a basic, public school, right?"

Like a reflex, my face twists into a scowl. Basic? Who is she calling *basic*? "I'm not sure what you mean by that."

"Curington's upper-class curriculum is college level. No offense or anything. Don't feel bad if your GPA drops."

I untwist the cap off my bottle and take a tiny sip, swallowing hard as if I'm drinking a clump of sand. There doesn't seem to be a lot of pretense with London. No polite tilts of the head. No syrupy sweet voice to match. Could she be my new mean girl?

I had a plan for this new phase of my life. It definitely included a mean girl who hated me but I wasn't supposed to meet her until I started school on Monday. She'd call black people "coloreds" or "those people" as if we were a strange species from another planet and she'd ask me offensive questions like "What's it like having nappy hair?" and "Can the sun make your skin darker or is that as dark as it gets?" And then she'd ask me if she could touch it.

"Hey." I smile, attempting to lighten the sour mood. "I saw this boy outside—"

"Let me guess. White face, weird, serial-killer vibe?"

"*Yeah.* Does he always look like that?"

"Even at school. They tried to suspend him until he took it off, but his mom hired some fancy lawyer. Sued the school and won." She rolls her eyes. "So, as long as girls can wear makeup, then Marcus McKinney can look like a crazed maniac."

"Why does he wear it?"

"Lots of theories but no one really knows for sure. I think he wishes he was white or something. The whole family is weird. He has two moms. And they're always having barbecues with their 'hood-rat relatives and blasting annoying music. Did you talk to him?"

"No. He only waved at me."

"Seriously? *Creepy.* He never talks. I think he's half-mute or something. One of his moms won the lottery. That's the only reason they can afford to live here and send him to Curington. Curington's expensive. I mean, now that Heaven, Nevaeh *and* you are at Curington—"

"Heaven and Nevaeh? They go to Curington, too?"

"It's sixth through twelfth grade. You didn't know that?"

"I didn't."

"Anyway. Now that you're going, too, Mom and Dad are under a financial strain."

"That makes me feel really bad."

"I didn't mean to make you feel bad," she says with a half smile that gives me the feeling she really *did* mean to make me feel bad. She turns and unhooks her bra, tossing it onto the bed with a simple flip of the wrist as she heads toward a door under the spiral staircase and emerges a moment later wearing a fluffy white robe. "I'm gonna take a quick shower. Apparently, we have to dress up for this thing."

I take another sip from my sand water.

"And some of the boxes you had shipped are in the closet. Could you unpack them? It's giving me claustrophobia to be in there. So cluttered."

"As soon as I can. Sorry to invade your room this way."

"That's life."

She quickly pushes through another door in the room. I imagine it's a bathroom because within seconds I hear the shower running.

If Mom were alive and I told her about my first run-in with London Stone, she would probably say, "At least she's honest, Tiff. It's the people who are always smiling. Those are the ones with all the problems. Give her some time. She'll come around."

I glance at our matching beds, an area rug separating the space between them.

Time. Perhaps we'll have plenty of that.

Or maybe just seven days.

4

He's here. Omigosh, he's here. My hands are trembling as I swipe across my phone and scroll through my favorites list. I press the icon for *Keelah Bo Beelah.*

"Thank you for calling the Center for Disease Control. What horrible disease do you think you've contracted?"

"Akeelah!" I whisper. "Help me."

"Why you whisperin'? Your new dad lock you in the basement?"

"I'm in my closet. I'm hiding." I nervously flip my braids over my shoulder and yank on them.

"*Weird.* Did you forget to take your anxiety medication today or something?"

"No. I took it."

"Then why you hiding in the closet?"

"I'm scared. Talk me through this. He's home. He's downstairs. I can hear him with the other kids. I hear him!"

"What other kids?"

"I have siblings. I think."

"The *fuck*? What do you mean, you think?"

"Keelah. Help me out of the closet!"

"Girls or boys?"

"Four girls."

"Dang! How come nobody told you that you had *sisters*?"

"Keelah, focus!"

"But I'm sayin'. Four sisters and nobody told you? That's so *lame*."

"*Keelah!* I'm crouched in a closet hiding from this man! Help me."

"Oh! Okay, I got something that can help. Remember that episode of *Maury Povich* where the girl thought her baby-daddy was between her cousin, her boyfriend's brother and her boyfriend? And remember how happy the boyfriend was when he found out the baby was his?"

"Are you serious?"

"Yes, girl! I love that one. That's how happy your dad is gonna be when he sees you for the first time. He's gonna be like that baby-daddy. He danced all over the stage and did a backflip."

Unless he's *not* the father. And suddenly all I can picture is the episode of *Maury Povich* I remember very clearly. Not the one Keelah's talking about. In this one, Maury opened up a manila envelope and said, "Lula-Mae. Jim Bob is *not* the father." And then Lula-Mae fell on the floor and started crying and Jim Bob screamed, "Fuck all y'all!" and ran off the stage.

"Keelah, I'm hanging up now."

"Wait!" Akeelah exclaims. "What do your sisters look like?"

"They're mixed."

"*Mixed?* With what?"

"White."

"Does that mean you have a *white* stepmom?"

"I guess so."

There's a long pause.

"Hello?" I whisper.

"Sorry. I'm, like, trippin'. White stepmom? What if she hates black people?"

"She has black kids!"

"Half. Not the same thing. You're all black. She might hate fully black people. She might Cinderella you, Tiff. Be careful. You'll be sleeping in the attic with the rats."

"Her husband's all black! Uggh. You're not helping. I'm hanging up on you!"

And I do, angrily tossing the phone into the opposite corner of the closet. I scratch my back. This stupid Anthropologie dress is making me itch like crazy. I do *not* like Anthropologie. I look like Suri Cruise in this getup. I almost passed out cold when I saw the price tag Margaret must've mistakenly left on it. Four hundred and fifty *dollars*. For *one* dress?

I hear a knock coming from the bedroom. I stand, smooth out my study-of-humans dress and push through the closet door and back into the Pottery Barn room. Another soft knock and I'm stuck in an Edgar Allan Poe poem with someone faintly tap-tap-tapping gently at my chamber door. 'Tis maybe my dad and nothing more.

I clear my throat. "Come in."

The door opens and suddenly he's here. He doesn't do a backflip or anything. He only stands there looking at me. He's really tall and thin but sadly the similarities between us end there. He's *light-skinned*. And the eyes. Fuck my life, for real. They're *blue*.

"Tiffany Sly. You look so much like your mom. It's as if I've gone back in time."

I barely hear him. I'm too busy looking at his hair. It's cut short but the texture looks soft and wavy. It couldn't be possible, could it? He's mixed?

He moves into the room and sits uncomfortably on the edge of the bed. "Tiffany, I owe you an apology."

I can't even muster up a sound. I can only manage to stand, frozen in place, staring at this man that I'm most certain is definitely, probably, maybe *not* my real dad.

"When your mother contacted me and told me she was sick, that was the first time she told me about you. I should've flown to Chicago right then to meet you."

I've still got nothing. Still standing as frozen as an ice sculpture.

"But she made me promise. She had a plan, I suppose. Told me to go through with DNA testing but I didn't want you to endure the stress of that process. I didn't think it was fair. I *know* you're mine. I don't need some DNA test to prove that."

"She asked you to take a *DNA* test?" So did Mom know? Is there really a possibility Anthony Stone is not my real father?

He nods. "Sometimes you know things. The heart doesn't lie. I knew. I know. Jehovah knows I know."

I raise an eyebrow. *Jehovah?*

"Right away I hired a lawyer. Right away I started making arrangements for you to be here with us after your mom passed away. It was what she wanted. It was what I wanted, too. And so here we are."

"Yes." I look down at the floor. "Here we are." Then I cover my face with my hands and burst into tears.

"Please don't cry, Tiffany," Anthony begs. He stands and pulls me toward the bed and we sit side by side.

I wipe my eyes and runny nose with the back of my hand. Feeling so snotty and gross next to my statuesque-looking possible father. Cheeks twitching like crazy, palms sweaty, throat aching from all the guttural sobs.

"When did you find out about me, Tiffany?"

"Right before Mom moved into hospice care. She told me then. She said when she died she wanted me to live with you."

"But before that. What did she tell you about your father?"

"Artificial insemination. She said she wanted a child and that's how I was conceived. All my life that's what I've thought."

He lowers his head into his hand, rubbing his temples, and I take a quick moment to study his hair again. That soft, silky mixed-people hair. Not like my kinky hair, not even close. He looks up and his bright blue eyes stare into my dark brown ones. Uggh. We don't look *anything* alike.

"We have to find a way to move on from here." Anthony places a hand on my knee and I instinctively jerk away. He looks stunned. "Tiffany, I apologize if that made you uncomfortable."

"I'm nervous," I admit, feeling terribly guilty for shutting down his first attempt at affection. "I'm really sorry."

"Would it make you feel more comfortable if Margaret were here with us? She wanted to give us privacy but I can have her come sit here while we talk."

"No, no. I'm not scared of you or anything like that. I'm

just…" *Afraid you're not my real dad.* That's how I'd like to end that sentence.

"I'm actually from Chicago, you know," he says with a hint of embarrassment in his voice. Like being from Chicago is equivalent to being from Mordor. "Born and raised in Englewood. We moved to California when I was thirteen."

I give him a curious look. Englewood has to be one of *the* worst neighborhoods in Chicago. Anthony doesn't strike me as the Englewood type.

"Do you have any questions for me?" he asks. "Anything at all."

Only about a thousand. I decide to start with one of the dumbest questions I can think of. "How come you're so light-skinned? Are you mixed with something?"

"My mother is white, Irish American. Yes. And your grandfather, my father, is African American."

"Omigosh. Are you serious?" I cover my face with my hands again, a fresh eruption of tears wetting my face. "I'm sorry I'm crying. So, so sorry."

"Stop apologizing, Tiffany. This must be terribly confusing for you."

He's right. This is terribly confusing. Oh, why did I come here? Why didn't I just take the stupid DNA test with Xavior? What am I supposed to do *now*? "What…do you want me to call you?"

"You can call me Anthony if that feels comfortable. I'd prefer you to call me Dad. I'd really like that." He reaches out and touches my hair. "Are these extensions?"

I look up. My vision blurry through my tears. "Um, yes."

"If you're going to live here with us, Tiffany, then I will

treat you like I treat my other daughters. Same rules. You understand?"

My heart nearly stops, but I nod in understanding.

"I don't allow extensions. You'll have to take those out. Will you be able to have that done before school on Monday?"

"But—" I got my extensions fresh back in Chicago two days before I left. They took seven hours to put in and Grams paid nearly three hundred dollars. Plus, I can't wear my real hair. Not yet, anyway. It's just starting to grow back. It was about two months after Mom got her diagnosis when I got my own special diagnosis.

"Alopecia," my longtime pediatrician, Dr. Kerstein, explained to my mom with me sobbing by her side. Beanie pulled almost to my eyes to cover all the bald patches on my head. I was rocking the sideways comb-over like the middle-aged white men do when they start to go bald. But underneath the sideways swoop of hair I looked like I had donated my head to a science experiment.

"Alopecia?" my mom replied in horror. "How in the world she get something like that?"

"Stress," Dr. Kerstein replied sympathetically. "My instinct says it's psychosomatic. Understandable, considering."

After that, Mom made some changes at home. She no longer talked about her condition or all the chemo she had to endure that was making her so sick. In fact, no one was even allowed to speak the word *cancer.* There was a designated "crying" room because tears were no longer permitted in the main areas of the apartment. No sad movies or slow music or even regular TV. Mom mostly kept the TV on Disney Junior. Grams and I watched so many episodes of *Mickey Mouse Club-*

house that we started to have existential debates about Mickey and his friends. Did Mickey age? Did his mouse parents already die? Or were they all eternal?

"Tiffany?" Anthony repeated. "Do you think you can have those braids out before school on Monday? You can't go to school like that."

"Could you maybe make an exception for me?" I plead. "My hair—"

"Absolutely no exceptions. I'm sorry. Rules are rules."

Thump-thump, thump-thump: *But he's not even your real dad!*

Thump-thump, thump-thump: *And you're gonna look like a troll doll without braids!*

"I have alopecia," I whisper. As if whispering can somehow cover my shame. "You know what that is?"

"Tiffany, I'm a doctor."

"I know. Right. So you understand why I can't take them out?"

"Perhaps I'm not communicating clearly. I don't allow extensions. You *must* take them out."

"That seems *unreasonable.* What about the bald spots on my head? The braids are placed strategically to cover them up. It's no one's business that I'm sick."

"Alopecia's not a terminal illness, Tiffany. We'll get you on a vitamin therapy and we can schedule an appointment with the girls' beautician. She'll come up with a style you're comfortable with."

"You mean a style *you're* comfortable with? I'm already comfortable." I stand and move toward my new dresser. Staring blankly at the collection of music "gifted" to me.

"Tiffany—"

"Look, I'll take them out tomorrow."

"Good. Do you have a phone?"

"It's in the closet." I wipe my nose again, my back still turned to Anthony. "Do you want me to get it?"

"You can give it to me tomorrow after you've programmed your numbers into your new phone and I'll send the old one back to your grandma."

I sigh. Uggh. This is getting complicated. I spin around. "I just got that phone. It was a birthday present from Grams."

"Margaret and I got you a phone. That's the one you'll be using from now on. You're on the family plan. Only texting and phone calls allowed. No internet. And you have to hand it over every night. We keep the phones in our room so we can monitor them. That means we have all passwords. And we do read texts, so keep it PG." He rubs his forehead in that way grown-ups do when they seem stressed or overworked. "We're Jehovah's Witnesses. Did you know that? Did your grandmother tell you?"

"You're what?"

"Jehovah's Witnesses."

I remember Jehovah's Witnesses knocking on our door once in Chicago. They had a pamphlet and on one of the pages were cartoon images of very happy, smiling people walking away from a burning city. At the top of the page, it said, Get Ready for Armageddon. Grams was nice, but told them proselytizing wasn't allowed in our particular apartment complex before she swiftly shut the door. When I asked her what *proselytizing* meant, she said it was "when people who think they know everything annoy everybody around them."

"As you might know," Anthony continues, "Jehovah's Witnesses don't celebrate birthdays or holidays."

"Oh. So why are you having a birthday party for me?"

"It's a family reunion. Margaret made a cake and...we want you to feel at home here. This *is* your home, after all, Tiffany." He stands. "Is it just me? I feel like we may have gotten off to a bad start."

"Yeah, me, too." I turn back toward the dresser and pick up a copy of The Jimi Hendrix Experience. "One of my all-time favorite songs is 'Bold as Love.' So cool you have this. It's got to be one of the most beautiful things ever—"

"Let's join the others downstairs and talk more later. Okay? We don't want to be rude and stay away from the family too long."

I scratch at my trembling cheek. They've been around him their whole lives; I've only had five minutes, but, "Sure. Yeah."

"You'll want to wash your face a bit?"

"O...kay?" Rude much? I wipe at my runny nose again, self-conscious and majorly uncomfortable. "Can I ask you one more question please?"

"That's fine."

"Why do you think my mom wanted you and me to take a DNA test?"

"Legal reasons, I suppose. I told her there was no need for any of that, though."

"What did she say?"

"What do you mean?" He looks more than slightly frustrated.

"I mean, when you told her there was no need for a DNA

test, was she all 'Oh, okay, great'? Or was she like…? I mean, what did she *say* after that?"

Anthony folds his arms across his chest. "She thanked me for trusting her." He smiles. But it's not a happy smile. More of an I'm-done-talking-about-this smile. "May I hug you, Tiffany?"

I nod and he steps forward to embrace me. He smells like hospital soap and laundry detergent and his arms feel strong and defined. Like, this is a doctor who hits the gym before *and* after he delivers babies. But more important…they feel stiff. This time I don't jerk away like a crazy person, but the hug still feels cold. It's about as comforting as being embraced by the principal at my old school. And I hated that guy.

"We're so glad to have you here. It's a blessing to have my family all together. A real blessing."

He leaves the room and I stand for a long moment feeling as if I've arrived at Disneyland to find out the whole park is closed for repairs. Or worse. Like I'm a millionaire stepping out of the Dublin airport. The sky is bright blue, and it's a hot, sunny day.

"G'day, miss," one of the locals would say. "Dinna unnerstan this weather, aye? So lovely. Forecast says no rain in sight. Not for a long, long time."

5

Patio terrace: what *they* all keep calling it.

Backyard wonderland: what I'm calling it.

Stuff rich people have: what Keelah would probably call it.

Anyway...that's where we all are and, whatever you choose to call it, it's pretty amazing. Aside from the pool, fire pit, outdoor kitchen and full-size tennis court, there are also lots of colorful stones, granite and ultramodern furniture all around.

There's a small lounge area facing a ginormous mounted flat-screen television and a dining table set with dishes, silverware and glasses. And not the normal glasses you get in a box at Target like we had back at home. These glasses have designs cut into them and gold rims. The sort of glasses that if you broke one it would probably be, like...bad.

Finally, there are strings of soft white fairy lights strung across the ceiling of the outdoor kitchen, and wrapped meticulously around the trees, and perfectly manicured bushes in the yard. It all feels very enchanting and not like anything I've ever seen in real life.

Margaret sets down a glass pitcher of water with floating slices of lemon, lime and…*leaves*?

"Those are mint leaves," Margaret explains, catching me eyeing the pitcher. "Do you like mint?"

"Oh, yeah." Not entirely a lie since I like thin mint Girl Scout cookies.

"Then you'll find this refreshing." She gives me her signature polite tilt of the head and I wonder if her neck hurts at the end of the day. It's gotta.

On my left, and at the head of the table, is Anthony. No longer in hospital scrubs, but in a pair of dark jeans, a black shirt and a blazer. Looking not like a dad at all, but more like one of *People* magazine's 50 Most Beautiful People. On my right is Nevaeh. Across from me is a very conservatively dressed London, a stark contrast to the nearly naked London that greeted me upstairs in our shared room. She's dressed in a white blouse that is buttoned to the collar, dress pants and strappy sandals. Her pretty black hair is hanging neatly over her shoulders. Beside her is Heaven. Margaret and Pumpkin are at the opposite end of the table.

"We always thank Jehovah before we eat," Anthony explains, taking my hand and bowing his head as everyone else joins hands, too, and I wonder who exactly this Jehovah person is. For some reason I picture a red-faced man with horns and a pitchfork but wait…no, that's the devil.

"Jehovah," he starts. "We give You honor and great thanks as we sit before this meal. Thank You for safe travels for Tiffany and for blessing us with a complete family. We praise Your holy name and give You honor and glory above all things. In the name of Christ Jesus. Amen."

"Amen," everyone repeats except for me.

"Tiffany," Margaret starts, "now we go around the table and say something we're grateful for. Why don't you go first?"

My stomach drops. "Um, I'm grateful I didn't die on the way here."

Everyone sort of stops cold; an array of disturbed looks are tossed my way. *Shoot!* What was Grams thinking telling me to be myself?

"Was there some sort of accident or something?" Margaret asks quizzically. "On the freeway?"

"Yes," I lie. "We barely missed it, thank goodness."

"Thank *Jehovah*," Anthony states seriously.

There's that Jehovah guy again. Who *is* this man?

"Can I go next?" London asks with a quick raise of the hand.

"Absolutely, honey. What are you grateful for?" Margaret replies.

"I'm grateful that I could be Curington's valedictorian and give the graduation speech. That's a huge honor. I'd be the youngest valedictorian in the history of Curington."

"What about Marcus McKinney?" Nevaeh asks.

London scowls. "What about him?"

"He beat you out for the Young Scholar Award *and* the Minority High Honor Award for the eleventh grade last year. Let's just be real. He'll probably beat you out for valedictorian, too."

London turns to Anthony. "*Dad.* Can you please tell Nevaeh not to interrupt what I'm grateful for? That's so rude."

"Nevaeh, don't interrupt what London's grateful for," Anthony replies as if on dad autopilot.

"I'm stating the facts. Besides, how can you be grateful for something that hasn't happened?" Nevaeh asks.

"It's called faith," Anthony replies. "The evidence of things not yet seen."

"But that would be like me saying I'm grateful I might *maybe* be valedictorian, too," Nevaeh explains. "In six years. That's stupid."

"Yeah, that is stupid because you get Cs," London replies smugly. "You'll never be Curington's valedictorian."

"That's stupid," Pumpkin squeals.

"London and Nevaeh. Sweethearts," Margaret cuts in calmly with her polite head tilt, "that's a bad word for Pumpkin."

I look over at Pumpkin, whose mass of curly hair is approximately three times bigger than her head. The plate in front of her is plastic and instead of a fancy, gold-rimmed glass she's got a Tinker Bell sippy cup, which she suddenly hurls through the air. I watch it soar before it splashes down into the pool. Man, that kid's got an arm on her.

"Yay! Fun!" Pumpkin claps.

Anthony waves his hand at Margaret. "*Don't* get it. Let her learn. You throw your cup, you don't have anything to drink."

Margaret nods.

"I'm grateful I might be valedictorian, too," Nevaeh says. "In six years. When I graduate. That's what I'm grateful for. I have faith."

Anthony rolls his eyes. "Heaven? What are you grateful for?"

"I'm grateful our first scrimmage game is next Friday."

"Finally, right?" Nevaeh says. The twins bump fists across the table.

"Sixth-grade basketball." London rolls her eyes. "How droll."

"Tiffany, do you play ball?" Anthony asks. "I would imagine, with all that height."

"No. Not since I was four and had one of those plastic basketball hoops attached to the bathtub."

"Tiffany plays the guitar, Dad!" Nevaeh exclaims excitedly. "She brought a guitar case with an actual guitar inside."

Anthony's brow furrows. "Well, that's a shame about not playing basketball. With all that height? We gotta get you on the court. Basketball skills run in the Stone family."

A sport played by two teams with five players each on a rectangular court: how Wikipedia describes basketball.

Something fun to watch or play: how most people describe basketball.

Sweaty athletes exhausting themselves while running around and throwing an orange bouncy ball back and forth until a winner is declared and the madness ends: how I describe basketball.

"You should see if you can try out for Curington's team!" Nevaeh suggests. "Stone house rules say you gotta play a sport. Why not basketball?"

"I have to play a sport?" Dread crawls up my spine. "Why?"

Instead of answering my question, Anthony nods and says, "Good idea, Nevaeh."

"But, Dad," London cuts in. "JV team is suspended this year for hazing. And varsity tryouts are over."

Anthony shrugs. "I'll talk to Coach James. See what we can do. She's a transfer. She deserves a shot."

I picture myself on the court, braids out, hair in a Buckwheat-style 'fro with tiny bald patches peeking through. Gripping the ball, running across the court in tears. The referee blowing his whistle at me. The other girls on the team hurling profanities my way. Crowd hissing and booing. Cheerleaders standing in disgust, arms folded, refusing to cheer.

"Margaret, babe. What are you thankful for?" Anthony asks.

"I'm thankful Pumpkin's doing so well. Her behavior therapist thinks she might not even have the diagnosis by the time she's ready for kindergarten."

"See, honey? I told you not to worry so much. It's all about intervention with autism."

"Our hard work is paying off. Finally." Margaret turns to Pumpkin. "And what are you thankful for, Pumpkin, my love?"

"You thankful?" Pumpkin replies.

"No, honey. I'm asking you. Tell us what you're thankful for. Or maybe just something that makes you happy. What makes you happy?"

Pumpkin grins and looks my way. "Hi. How you?"

"Me? Oh… I'm…fine?"

"Pumpkin, tell us what you're *thankful* for," Nevaeh insists.

"I sick!" Pumpkin suddenly wails. "I hun-gee."

"So then you can be thankful for food," Nevaeh says kindly. "Say you're thankful for food so you don't have to be hungry."

"*No!* I mad," Pumpkin wails. "I so fus-tated!" She picks up her plastic plate and hurls it across the table, narrowly missing Anthony's head. "I very not happy!"

"Pumpkin!" Anthony bellows. "That is inappropriate behavior. You do not throw your plate!"

An epic-size shriek escapes from Pumpkin's tiny, little body. She kicks at the table. Beautiful, expensive dishes wobble dangerously as she thrashes about in her chair. "Leave me 'lone! I sad!"

Margaret tosses Anthony a worried look. "I don't think she gets *thankful* yet. It's making her upset. Can we let this one go? Please?"

"No," Anthony replies sternly. "Bedtime. Take her now."

Pumpkin's eyes fill with tears and she immediately calms down. "No! I so sorry. I so sorry, Daddy."

"Thank you for saying sorry, Pumpkin," he replies. "But you still have to go to bed. Your behavior is very bad and Mommy and Daddy are very sad and frustrated."

"I am bad! I am bad girl!" She screams as Margaret rises and grabs the toddler in her arms as she flails about. "Bad behavior! Bad!"

"Can we give her something to eat first?" Margaret shouts over Pumpkin's screams, struggling to tame the redheaded beast of a child. "She hasn't eaten since noon."

"Don't care. She ain't gonna starve," Anthony declares with a dismissive wave of his hand. "Good night, Pumpkin. Everybody say good-night to your sister."

Nevaeh happily throws up the peace sign and Heaven and London mumble something that sounds similar to good night, but feels more like good riddance.

"I apologize for Pumpkin's behavior, Tiffany," Margaret says without actually looking at me, and, with Pumpkin thrashing about in her arms, excuses herself. A moment later I can still hear Pumpkin shrieking from somewhere deep inside the house.

Nevaeh whistles. "Get that kid a prescription. Stat."

"*Can* you get her a prescription?" Heaven adds. "She doesn't seem to be getting any better."

"And Mom seems miserable," London adds. "It's not fair."

Nevaeh nods. "We need to take a family vote. Pumpkin's out of control. She needs medication."

"She needs exactly what she's getting," Anthony states angrily. "Besides, *no* child of mine is going to be a victim of some whacked psychiatrist pushing pills."

I swallow nervously.

"Now—I'm thankful for each and every one of you." He smiles. It's less of an *I'm happy* smile and more of an *I'm done talking about this* smile. "Let's eat."

"Babe, you outdid yourself this time." Anthony exhales, pushing his empty plate away.

"Yeah. That was good," I add as everyone else gives their personal praise for Margaret's meal.

It actually wasn't. There was a vegetable salad with some sort of brown tart dressing that gave me killer heartburn. Little brown pellets that everybody was calling keen-wah. I never had keen-wah before and I hope to never have it again after tonight. The grilled chicken wasn't *too* bad, but it had pineapple *salsa* on top of it. *Strange.* And the pineapple mixed with the keen-wah, mixed with the In-N-Out burger I ate earlier made my stomach bubble. There was also fish soup that tasted like…well…fish. So many chunks of unknown stuff floating around in that bowl it took all my strength not to throw it all up. And I'm pretty sure I saw a fish eyeball in there. And for dessert we all had an un-birthday cake. Margaret bragged that it was gluten free. In fact, the whole meal was gluten free. Apparently, gluten is something else Pumpkin can't have. No idea what gluten even is, but the cake tasted like coconut-flavored dirt balls, so my guess…gluten free is not a good thing. Mostly I'm glad this house comes with seven bathrooms because I am gonna need a toilet… soon. What if that wasn't a meltdown Pumpkin had? What if she planned her *escape*?

"Play us a song on your guitar, Tiffany," Heaven urges as we all make our way to sit around the glowing fire pit.

"Really?" I ask, surprised. "You guys want me to play?"

"Not if it's gonna be 'Hot Cross Buns' or 'Twinkle Twinkle Little Star,'" Anthony jokes, and London cracks up like it's the funniest thing she's ever heard as she snuggles up beside Margaret on one of the couches surrounding the fire pit.

"I can go get your guitar for you," Nevaeh offers.

"No, no. That's okay. I'll grab it."

I excitedly race inside the house and up the stairs; within a minute I'm back, Little Buddy slung over one shoulder. I call my Gibson guitar Little Buddy. A four-thousand-dollar acoustic Grams bought me when I was twelve. Normally, we wouldn't have been able to afford something so expensive, but Grams dipped into her retirement money and gifted me the fancy instrument. Mom was livid.

"A four-thousand-dollar guitar for a twelve-year-old?" Mom growled when I opened it on Christmas.

"It's my money," Grams replied with a wink in my direction. "Last time I checked, I was way past grown."

"But, *Mama*," Mom replied in frustration. "Tiffany's not responsible enough for something like this."

Only, Mom was wrong. I took extra special care of Little Buddy and was so enthralled with its magnificence I started practicing more and more and my skill level advanced exponentially. I even started teaching Mom some of the advanced techniques I was learning from YouTube. After I spent hours helping her un-learn some of her bad picking habits, she finally apologized to Grams and declared the guitar was the best thing to ever happen to our family.

Anthony brought a chair from the table, so now I'm seated in front of all of them, finally feeling at ease. When Little Buddy is in my hands, I'm not anxious or worried or sad. I'm my old self. The way I was before Mom got sick. Before she came home that fateful day and told me quite frankly: "Tiffany. I'm going to die." Back when life seemed full of promise and happiness, where moms and daughters were best friends and never a lie was shared between them.

"What are you gonna play?" London asks incredulously with a bored yawn.

"Whatever you want. My favorites to play are probably the Beatles or—"

"Wait a second now. You can play the Beatles?" Anthony raises an eyebrow. "Get outta town."

"What song is your favorite—" *Dad*. Uggh. Still can't say it.

"'Yesterday.'" He exhales and leans back. "Love that song."

"That's so cool," I reply. *What are the odds?* "That's my favorite, too." Another coincidence? Genetic taste buds?

He winks at me. "Great minds think alike."

I give my strings a quick strum to tune and smile, wondering if it's more like fathers and daughters think alike.

"Don't you need a guitar pick?" Heaven asks.

"Not for this song. It's called fingerpicking." I do a quick demonstration, slowly playing five chords arpeggio-style. "See? Like that."

"That was awesome!" Nevaeh exclaims. "Your fingers moved so fast. Do that again, Tiffany!"

"Nevaeh." Heaven elbows her sister on the lounge chair they both share. The orange hue of the fire reflects off their matching set of silver braces. "Be quiet. Jeez. Let her play the song."

I smile and slide my fingers up and down the fret board a few times. Something that makes me feel connected. It's not a guitar when it's in my hands. It's more like a body part—a perfect extension of Tiffany Sly. (If I were made of mahogany wood and steel.) I begin softly at first, allowing the words of the song to dance across my mind as the notes float out and soar into the air. Then I close my eyes and lower my head, not wanting the emotion of the lyrics to overtake me as it oftentimes can when I play. Suddenly, a beautiful tenor voice rings out in the backyard space, singing along with the notes I play. I look up. The glow of the fire dances in Anthony's blue eyes as he sings along. He can sing. I mean, he can really *sing.* I continue to play, but now with an even greater passion, as if the chords on their own can tell the sad story resounding in Anthony's hauntingly beautiful voice. The song continues on until I play the final chord, my fingers still moving on the fret board to create the vibrato as the music slowly fades away into the starry night.

"Tiffany!" Nevaeh's voice pierces through the magical moment, snapping me out of the special connection between Anthony and me. "You're like a superstar on that thing."

She claps and everyone joins in.

"That was lovely!" Margaret exclaims. "You're a real talent, Tiffany. Anthony, we have an artist in the family now."

He smiles proudly. "Where'd you learn to play like that?"

"My mom. She played. Did you know that?"

The chirp-chirp of a dozen crickets pierces through the uncomfortable silence as everyone turns to him.

He shifts. "I—I did know that about your mother. Yes."

"Yeah, she played. She gave lessons at Guitar Center. I'm gonna study music in college like her."

"So you can work at Guitar Center?" London asks.

"Nothing wrong with working at Guitar Center." I shrug. "But no. I wanna study music so I can be a songwriter. I can write really catchy songs. I wrote a commercial jingle for a local mattress company back in Chicago. They paid me and everything."

"You should have a plan B," London's quick to reply. "It's tough to make it in artistic career fields, huh, Dad?"

Anthony nods in agreement. "Maybe you can minor in music, Tiffany. Keep it as a hobby. You're good, but lots of people can play the guitar and write music. Best to choose academic career paths. Something stable so you can have a chance at a good life."

It's as if a giant vacuum dipped out of the sky and sucked up all the beauty of the night and then a separate giant leaf blower dipped out of the sky and blew crap in my eyes. Music—a hobby? Music is my passion. It's my connection to the world.

"Play us a song you wrote!" Nevaeh cries. "Please, Tiffany. Play the mattress jingle!"

"No, no. It's getting late," Anthony declares. "Time for you girls to go to bed."

"But, *Dad*," Heaven whines. "It's Saturday. Can we please hear a song Tiffany wrote?"

"Church in the morning," he replies. "Nothing's changed. You girls know the drill. We leave at seven thirty to make Bible study."

Church? *Bible* study? I grimace.

"Does Tiffany have to go?" London asks. "We have Witnessing tomorrow. She can't do that. She's not a part of our church."

"But she will be," Anthony states without even looking in my direction.

"What do you mean I will be? I'm *not* a Jehovah's Witness." I don't care who I offend. If I was going to pretend to be religious again, I'd pretend to be Christian. Like my mom was. No way I'm joining up with him and all the Witnesses.

Margaret looks down uneasily while the girls all turn to Anthony to see what his response will be. Rather than reply he says, "It'll be a long day, Tiffany. Church is in Malibu. We usually get home around five."

"What about my braids? That won't give me enough time to take them out. It's gonna take me hours and hours. And I have to wash my hair and try to fix it. Or something."

"You're right." He takes a moment, thinking. "Getting those braids out is a top priority. We can introduce you to the congregation *next* Sunday."

"But that means Tiffany will be here all by herself, Dad,"

Heaven points out. "We can't leave her alone. That would suck."

"Heaven, please. I know Pumpkin's asleep, but we have to watch our words."

"Sorry, Mom," Heaven replies respectfully.

"Tiffany's sixteen." Anthony gives the same dismissive wave he gave to send a screaming Pumpkin off to bed early and hungry. "She can stay here alone. Now up. Let's help Mom clear the table and clean so we can all get some sleep."

"What does your hair look like, anyway? Your *real* hair?" London asks, holding back as everyone returns to the table while I put Little Buddy away in his case.

A little like Stewie. A little like Donald Trump. A little like a nightmare. "I dunno. Regular, I guess."

"Can't wait to see it." London groans. "I *hate* my hair. I wish it was supercurly like Heaven and Nevaeh's. It's so boring the way it is."

I look at her wavy black hair hanging almost to her waist. The kind of hair I used to close my eyes and pray for when I was a little kid and thought praying to an invisible man actually produced results. Mixed-girl hair. Soft and silky and good to the root.

Dear God, I'd pray. *Please let me have pretty hair. Please make my hair long and nice. When I open my eyes, okay, God? Gonna count to three. I'll have nice hair, right, God? Please, God. Please.* But I'd open my eyes and my hair would still be a nappy mess.

"Your hair's perfect," I admit with a twinge of jealousy.

London shrugs as if yes, maybe it is, but also she couldn't care less. Like amazing hair is about as normal to her as a toe.

"Too bad about church tomorrow. I always learn something new at church. Like a supervaluable life lesson. Sorry you can't go."

"It's okay." *Because I will never be a Jehovah's Witness, anyway.* "I'll be here when you get back."

"Yeah." She sighs. "I guess you will."

6

A year ago, Akeelah and I won tickets in a radio contest to a Zayn Malik concert. Neither one of us actually listens to Zayn, couldn't name a song if we wanted to. But rather than sell the coveted seats, we decided to go. We'd planned to make fun of all the screaming ten-year-olds at Chicago's United Center Stadium and take pictures of the ones sobbing uncontrollably. We were also going to start an Instagram page to upload the photos and call it @ZaynMalik_LostConsciousness. But here's what ended up happening instead—some older girls sitting next to us smuggled in water bottles filled with vodka and Keelah and I got crazy, stupid drunk with them. The kind of drunk where your speech is slurred and you can't walk straight. And then you get sick and vomit. A lot.

Not only was I grounded for weeks when Mom picked us up and watched us clumsily stumbling to the car, I discovered something much worse than throwing up all night hovered over a toilet. The day *after* throwing up all night hovered over a toilet. My hangover was so bad Mom had to rush me to Urgent Care for dehydration. But she wasn't angry. Instead, she calmly explained (while I was clutching my stomach in the fetal position) that life has a special way of giving you exactly what you've earned.

But if Mom was right and life gives you what you earn, what on earth did I do to earn this? Because here I am alone, in a big new, cold house that is maybe not even mine, sitting on a towel on the hard floor, surrounded by piles of extension hair. Thirty braids taken down and about one hundred left to go.

Dear Life, please help me earn something better.

"Keelah? Did you hang up?"

"I'm still here. Googling."

"What'd you find out?"

"Dude. Jehovah's Witnesses believe some weird stuff."

"Like?"

"Well, for starters, they believe only people God approves of get eternal life."

"That leaves you out."

"Please. You'll be burning in hell right along with me."

"Ahh, yes, the fiery pits of hell. Just down the road from Mount Doom."

"Also, Christ is Michael the Archangel."

I finish unraveling a new braid and toss it onto the floor with the rest. "What's that mean?"

"Like I know? Tiff, why didn't you Google your new dad before you flew a billion miles away to live with him?"

"I wanted to be surprised."

"Well, surprise. You've just joined a cult."

"It's not a cult! Besides, I'm not joining their church." I

unravel another braid. "Hey. Can you Google Xavior Xavion for me?"

"Who is that? The cult leader? I saw a documentary once about a crazy man who made all his cult members drink poisoned Kool-Aid. Don't drink any Kool-Aid at their church."

"Keelah." I toss the unraveled braid onto the floor. "Just see if he has a Facebook page. Xavior Xavion."

A moment passes before Keelah says, "Got him. Is he related to you or something? He sorta looks like you."

My head instantly aches. I grab it to dull the pain. "For real? You really think that?" The sound of the doorbell rings loudly, echoing throughout the house. I snatch my cell from the floor and take Keelah off speakerphone. "It's the doorbell."

"Oh. Call me back."

"But my hair? What if it's somebody important?"

The doorbell rings again.

"Girl, go answer the door! Throw your towel around your head and go. Call me back." She hangs up.

I toss my cell onto the bed and stand to brush the hair from my Grateful Dead tank and yellow shorts. The doorbell rings again. I grab the towel from the floor and shake off more hair. Gonna have to find a vacuum before everybody gets home. I picture how Margaret would react if she saw her clean wood floors at this very moment. She'd politely tilt her head; her crazy eyes would get crazier. "Tiffany, sweetheart, my dear, my love," she'd say with eerie calm. "We do not put fake extension hair on hardwood. That's a bad image for Pumpkin."

I wrap the towel around my head turban-style and quickly head downstairs.

"Who is it?" I peek through the tiny hole on the door in the foyer and see an eye staring back at me.

"Nevaeh? Heaven? Is that you?"

"No. Sorry. It's… Can I help you?"

"I got a bunch of your mail by accident again. Can you open the door? Is that London? It's Jo McKinney from across the street."

I nervously unlock the door, slowly pulling it open to see a nice-looking black woman with supershort, perfectly styled hair. She's dressed casually in yoga pants, a loose-fitting shirt that hangs off one shoulder and flip-flops.

"Who are you?" she asks warmly. "Look at that skin. You're *adorable*."

Her skin is dark brown like mine, but made up with lots of perfectly applied makeup: thick foundation, eye shadow, cheeks dusted with pale pink, long lashes and gloss heavily coated on top of her full lips.

"Thanks." I fidget, uncomfortable. Whenever people call me pretty I honestly wonder why. I'm not like London. The kind of girl guys go out of their way to talk to and compliment. No guys ever compliment or even *try* to talk to me. Last year a bunch of people of color with first honors and academic excellence had to attend a special dinner with the principal. And one of the boys—I think his name was Devin Doheny or Devin Doohickey—anyway, he declared Alaysia Miller the prettiest girl at the table and all the other boys agreed. Alaysia Miller's mixed. Light-skinned, with long curly hair. But then Shante Peterson, who's dark brown like me, told Devin if Alaysia Miller is the prettiest at the table, then he's the ugliest and should shut the hell up before she punched him in the throat.

"What's your name, sweetie?"

"Tiffany." I see the pile of mail she has in her hands. "I can take that." She reaches out to hand me the mail but somehow during our exchange it all slips, splaying onto the concrete of the front doorstep. "No worries. I'll get it." I bend to retrieve the mail and my towel unravels and slides off. Braids tumble loosely around my shoulders. "Omigosh!" I try to grab the towel as quickly as I can but she's stepping on part of it with her flip-flop.

"You takin' down braids?"

"Yes. Could you move your foot please?"

She obliges and I snatch up the towel, throwing it back over my head.

"Can I ask *why*? They look real nice and brand-new."

I rewrap the towel, tucking it tightly behind my ear, then slowly kneel, with one hand holding the towel, to gather the mail spread in all directions in front of the door. "I'll be sure to tell them you stopped by."

"You know, I do hair."

I look up. "Seriously?"

"Mmm-hmm. I can help you. You look like you could use some help. Can I take a look?"

I hesitate.

"Child, I done already seen it."

I stuff the mail under my arm and stand, removing the towel to reveal my mess of hair.

"Don't mind if I touch it, do you?"

"Go ahead, I guess. Hopefully it won't cut you."

She forces her fingers through my natural hair where I've removed the extensions and my head moves from side to side with the motion of her hand. She pulls my head down for a closer examination. "What's wrong with you?"

"Huh?"

"What you got? Alopecia?"

My jaw drops. "You can tell?"

"Honey, I do *hair.* Now, why you taking brand-new braids out, anyway, when you got alopecia? Braids is the best thing for you."

"My...dad told me to."

"What's wrong with your daddy? He got a problem or something?"

"He doesn't allow extensions. Anthony Stone... I'm his daughter." I'm hoping she doesn't notice how not sure of myself I sounded when I said the words *daughter* and *dad.*

"Anthony Stone is your *father*? Well, damn. How many kids does this man got?"

"Pretty sure I'm the last of them."

She gives me a once-over as I rewrap my hair with the towel. "You sure are pretty like his other daughters. Man got good genes. Where you been all this time? How come I ain't never seen you around?"

"I'm from Chicago."

"Girl, stop. We're from Chicago."

"No way! What part?"

"Just outside. Born and raised mostly in Joliet. But went to high school in the city."

"Omigosh. We lived in Garfield."

"Garfield?" She smiles. "I guess being here is a big, big change. How you like it?"

"I dunno. I got here yesterday."

"Well, welcome. Why don't you come on over to our house. I'll fix your hair up real nice and neat."

"But I don't have any money."

"Child. Does it look like I need your little bit of money?"

I hesitate again and she rolls her eyes in a way so similar to my mom it makes me smile. Mom was a big eye roller.

"Way I see it, you got two choices. You can take all them braids out by yourself and try to make sense of that head of hair of yours. Or you can come and relax in my chair and let me do all the hard work. I'll be fine either way. Plus, that means I got the morning to relax and catch up on my DVR."

"Okay, okay. Let me…clean up my mess and leave a note."

"Now, that's more like it."

"You want something to drink?"

"Sure."

I stand behind Mrs. McKinney as she fiddles with a lock on a door inside their six-car garage. Back in Chicago I saw two-car garages, sometimes even three…but *six*? I check out a sick silver Mercedes S-class Coupe parked beside the black Hummer I saw last night. I know for a fact these cars are over a hundred thousand dollars. Mostly cuz of Keelah. She's really into cars and Mercedes is her favorite. There's also a vintage Porsche, a Tesla plugged into a weird outlet and a BMW. Keelah would go ballistic if she knew I was this close to all these amazing cars. Mrs. McKinney finally pushes the door open and we step into a separate room.

It's a hair salon. In their *garage.*

"Whoa. This is amazing." The floors are bright white tile and there's a salon chair, a washbowl and sink, wall-to-wall mirrors, a leather couch pressed up against the wall, a stainless-steel fridge and a mounted flat-screen TV.

"Thank you, sweetie. I'm supposed to be retired but I still do so much hair, the wife and I decided to have the garage remodeled. I got drinks in that fridge right there. Help yourself."

She flips on the lights and I move toward the fridge pushed up against the back wall. A grin spreads across my face as I pull open the door. It's pop! Rows and rows of it. Root beer, cream soda, Coke, even orange and red. I grab a can of cream soda, flip up the tab and down the whole thing within a few seconds.

"Slow down, now. You gonna make yourself sick."

"They only drink water over there," I say, out of breath. "And they put leaves in it to make it taste better."

"Leaves?" She shakes her head and I grab another cream soda. "Come on over and have a seat in my chair."

As I move toward the chair, the door to the shop opens and suddenly Marcus McKinney is standing across from me. I freeze, gripping the cold can so tightly I fear I might crush it and splatter pop everywhere. He's about the same height as me and his thick makeup is smeared so heavily the edges of his hoodie, pulled low over his head, are slightly stained with a light dusting of white. His emerald green eyes are piercing, two dramatic flashes of color against the white makeup on his skin. Last night, from a distance, in the dark, he seemed so scary. But up close…he's *terrifying.* He stands, hands deep into the pockets of his hoodie, staring at me like I'm the one who looks like the circus freak.

"This is my son, Marcus," Mrs. McKinney says with a smile, like she's introducing me to someone who doesn't look like they could haunt my dreams and rip out my beating heart. "Marcus is eighteen. He's a senior in high school. Marcus? Can you say hello to Tiffany? She's Dr. Stone's daughter. Just in from Chicago."

Marcus continues staring at me for what feels like the longest moment of my life before turning to his mom. He pulls a cell phone from his pocket with a gloved hand and holds it up for her to see. Mrs. McKinney grabs her own cell, resting on the counter beside her, and reads what's on the screen.

"I'm fine with that, Marcus. Take the Hummer, though. You not taking none of my babies out. The Hummer is your only option."

He shifts and our eyes meet for another long moment.

"Boy, stop starin'!" she says, annoyed. "You're scarin' the girl half to death. Now, 'bye. I got work to do." He sighs heavily but turns and quickly exits back through the door. Mrs. McKinney gestures me over. "C'mon and take a seat in my chair, Tiffany."

I do as she says, my heart rate slowing.

"You like National Geographic?"

"Sure."

She pushes a button on the remote and a giant grizzly bear is standing in shallow waters on the flat screen. "This is *World's Deadliest Animals*. Ever seen it?"

"I haven't, no. Don't get to watch much TV." I exhale, beginning to relax.

"You'll be hooked in a few minutes, trust me. This is my show."

She pulls a fine-tooth comb from a drawer under her station, unravels the towel around my head, sets it over my shoulders and begins to loosen my braids using the comb. I sip my cream soda, watching the bear on the TV bite the head off a poor, unsuspecting fish.

"So how is Anthony Stone your daddy? And where have you been all these years?"

"He and my mom… I guess they had a baby sixteen years ago. I guess that baby was me. Only, it's a long story." *That might end on the* Maury Povich *show.* "I really only met him yesterday. I'll be staying with him now. I guess. I'm starting at Curington tomorrow."

"Sounds dramatic." I watch large clumps of extension hair fall onto the floor. "Your mom must be something extra-special, though. I have a hard time believing Dr. Stone would ever touch a black woman. Men like him don't usually give us the time of day. Where is she, anyway? Back in Chicago?"

"She's…" I pause. At an ashram in India? Being helicoptered deep into the jungles of Africa to film a new season of *Survivor*? "She's dead." I exhale. There. That wasn't so bad. Only it *was* bad. Just saying the words makes my throat ache and my eyes water. And before I can do a thing to stop it, tears have exploded from my eyes. "Omigosh. I am so sorry."

"Oh, honey." She squeezes me tightly from behind and kisses me on top of my head. "*I'm* sorry. I know what it's like to lose someone you love."

"You do?" I use the bottom portion of my Grateful Dead tank to wipe my eyes.

"Mmm-hmm. My mama died when I was in college. And my son…he died, too."

"You have a son that died?"

"It was Marcus. Longest four minutes of my life. He came back to us. God must've decided heaven was too full that day."

"He *died*?" Another large bunch of extensions falls to the floor. Man, she works fast. I can only take out one braid at a time but she's getting them out in bunches of five and six.

"His heart stopped. HCM. Hypertrophic cardiomyopathy. You ever heard of that?"

The bear on the TV screen bites a fish in half and roars loudly. "No. I'm sorry. I haven't."

"I hadn't, either. Not till my Marcus was about five years old and doctors finally figured out it was the muscles in his heart thickening, causing him so many problems. It's been a long battle since then, but we manage. And he's here now. Praise God. I get to keep him a little longer."

A moment of silence passes between us. The bear has been replaced by a pack of lions munching on a bloody zebra. "My mom had Hodgkin's lymphoma," I admit. "It was stage four by the time they detected it."

"Life can be painful, huh?" She shakes her head. "Don't seem fair. Girl as young as you needs a mama."

"She tried chemo..." I pause and decide to veer the subject away from Mom, already feeling the lump rising in my throat again. "Is Marcus better now?"

"After his cardiac arrest, he got something called a prophylactic defibrillator implanted right here." She points to an area slightly above her chest. "You ever heard of a pacemaker?"

I nod.

"That's all it is. A pacemaker. Marcus needs it. He's a high risk for sudden death."

"Sudden death? You mean he could die *again*?"

"We're all gonna die, honey. Just Marcus has a risk of dying a little bit sooner than most."

She continues working on my hair and I marvel at how composed she is and how simply she states something so utterly sad and devastating.

"Is that why he—"

"Wears the makeup? Oh, that don't bother me. He could paint his face green for all I care. He's a good boy. Monique and I…we're lucky. He's a real good boy. He's got a book coming out next year."

"A book?"

"Wrote it himself. Mostly. He had help from a ghostwriter. He was all over the news after he died. All the publishers came a-knockin'."

"What's the book about?"

"It's about living…and dying. It's called *The Boy Who Lived Before*. You can read it when it comes out. It's really beautiful."

I imagine this is what aunts are like—warm and comforting and kind. I could stay in this chair for days, even though the TV is now displaying a giant black snake eating some kind of equally giant rodent. The male voice-over explains that the snake can only be found in Thailand, so I make a mental note to never, ever go to Thailand because I'm sure as soon as I landed that snake would be waiting for me at the airport.

"That was the last one," she declares, turning me around to face the mirror.

"I look awful."

"Tiffany, stop."

"But I do." The center part of my hair is where most of the breakage happened and it's supershort. The front is longer but *thin* and the back is all broken off and different lengths with bald spots here and there. "It looks like rats have been chewing on my hair. I'm gonna look terrible. I'm so ugly compared to him and his kids." I cover my face with my hands. "I hate my hair." I'm trying my hardest to hold back the tears. "I hate it. I hate it."

"You're too hard on yourself."

"But it's not fair." The tears finally spring free. "How come some people have good hair?"

"Stop that." Mrs. McKinney places her hands on her hips. "I don't allow those words in my home. There is not *good* hair and *bad* hair. Just the hair God gave you. You trust God doesn't make mistakes, right?"

I wipe my eyes. "Please don't hate me, Mrs. McKinney. But… I don't believe in God."

She sighs. "I don't hate you. I respect your beliefs. It takes a lot of faith to believe in a creator. Takes even more faith to not believe in one. So we both have faith and that's all right with me."

I wipe another flow of tears.

"Now about this hair." She kneels in front of me. "You been through something. Your hair's not bad. It's recovering from trauma. I can help it grow back strong and beautiful. You have beautiful hair. Stop that crying." She stands and grabs a handful of tissues from off the counter that I gratefully accept. "Here's what we're gonna do. Your hair has the least breakage in the front. So I'm gonna give you a good wash and deep, repairing condition. Then braid you up again in the back. We'll attach some extension tracks to the French braids and use your longer hair in the front to cover up the tracks."

"That sounds like a weave."

"Mmm-hmm. It is."

"But my... Anthony...he doesn't allow extensions."

"Child, when I get done with your hair *you* won't even be able to tell you got tracks."

"Wh-what if he somehow finds out?"

"The only other option is that we cut your hair so it's all even. It'll be too short to straighten and way too fragile to get a relaxer. So you'd be rockin' a one-inch 'fro. Is that what you want? It's up to you. A one-inch 'fro can be cute. You'll look like Michael Jackson when he was in the Jackson 5."

We exchange looks and I burst into laughter. "Really? The Jackson 5?"

"Honey, don't knock it till you try it. Natural is makin' a comeback." She turns serious. "Tiffany, I want you to feel *comfortable* with who you are. I want you to know you're beautiful. If it's fake hair that's gonna help you with that, then I got lots of it. Or try a natural 'fro. You're beautiful either way."

"But if I get fake hair, then Anthony—"

"Oh, poo. What your daddy don't know won't hurt him."

I nervously wring my hands together. "You sure he won't find out?"

"As long as he's not running his fingers through your hair. And when's the last time anybody ever did that to you?"

She's right. It's not like people go around touching other people's heads. "Okay. Let's do the weave. I trust you."

"Young lady, you are making all sorts of smart choices today."

★★★

"You ready to see?"

I nod. We've spent hours together in Mrs. McKinney's small salon. My head has been picked and prodded, twisted and turned so much it's throbbing like somebody beat me over the head with seventy-five tiny plastic baseball bats. And we've watched so many episodes of *World's Deadliest Animals* I'm strongly considering becoming a vegetarian. "I'm ready."

She spins the chair around and my jaw drops. "Whoa! It looks *so* real. Like it's growing straight out of my head!" The pretty black hair hangs just a bit past my shoulders.

"I told you. I'm a doctor just like your dad. A hair doctor."

I stand and lurch forward, embracing her, squeezing with all my strength. She laughs.

"You're welcome."

"I seriously don't know how to thank you." I pull away and move toward the mirror to take a closer look. My hair has *movement*. No more Donald Trump comb-over for me. I flip it over my shoulder and then flip it back and squeal with delight.

"Watch out now!" Mrs. McKinney says playfully. "Don't hurt 'em."

"It's amazing! You've saved my *life*. How can I ever thank you for this?"

She moves toward the fridge, grabs a Coke and takes a seat on the couch. "Well, since you bring it up. Perhaps we can talk payment now." She pops the tab and takes a long swig from the can.

"But… I thought you said I didn't have to pay."

"I said I didn't need your money. But there's gotta be a payment. Always gotta be payment."

Thump-thump, thump-thump: *This is where you offer a blood sacrifice in exchange for pretty hair! Run!*

"Don't look all scared like that, Tiffany. I need a favor. That's all."

"Um, okay?"

"I want you to talk to my Marcus."

"Oh? What about?"

"He's lonely at that school. He might not say so, but I can tell. A boy his age *needs* school friends. Especially of the opposite sex. People there are afraid of him—justifiably. I know he's different. I know he seems a little bit cold. But in truth, he's as harmless as a box of newborn kittens and as warm as a hug from Santa. I promise you he is." She downs the rest of the Coke and sets the empty can on the floor at her feet. "So, can you be his friend? If you do me this favor I'll keep your hair looking nice and pretty with weekly appointments and Daddy Dearest over there won't ever know you got a head full of extensions. Everybody wins." Her cell phone rings and she pulls it from her back pocket to answer. "Hey, baby." She pauses and nods. "I got her. Just finished up. She'll be out in a second." She stuffs the phone back in her pocket and gives me a smile. "Apparently, there is an Anthony Stone at our front door, looking for his daughter."

I glance at the time on my phone. "It's five thirty. I can't believe I've been here all day."

"You ready to test out your new hairdo on Daddy Dearest?"

"I'm nervous."

"Mark my words. He won't have a clue." She stands. "Now. Do we have ourselves a deal? You'll talk to Marcus?"

An image of Marcus flashes across my mind, his white face under the glow of the full moon. "I don't mind talking to him." And I don't. But to be his friend? How am I supposed to manage something like that? Just thinking about the boy with a high risk for sudden death sends a chill up my spine.

"Thank you, Tiffany. I knew there was something special about you the moment I laid eyes on you. I just knew." She beams. "And call me Jo. All my friends call me Jo."

Anthony stands, arms folded, brow furrowed, looking more than a bit angry in his dressy Sunday clothes: black pants, crisp white shirt, metallic-silver tie. But his blue eyes brighten as soon as I step out of the shadows of the garage and onto the pavement of Jo Stone's driveway.

"Look at my daughter."

I swallow. "You like it?"

"I *love* it. Can't even tell you have alopecia. See? You look so much more beautiful. Doesn't it feel good to be natural?"

Jo gives me an amused eye roll. "How you doing there, Anthony? Long time no see."

"Afternoon, Jo." Anthony puts his arm protectively around me and I tense a bit wondering if he's looking down at my head.

"Beautiful daughter you got there."

"Thank you. She is beautiful, isn't she?"

Jo smiles. "Inside and out."

"Jo helped me. She did my hair—" *Dad.* Nope. Still can't say it.

"Yes. I read your note," he replies with a bit of annoyance in his voice.

"Only a wash and condition and I pressed it out to make it straight. Tiffany's got nice hair, so my job was easy."

"What do I owe you?" Anthony reaches into his pocket and retrieves his wallet.

"No, no. No charge. It was my pleasure."

"Thank you. That was very nice of you." He stuffs his wallet back into the pocket of his dress pants.

"We're having a barbecue next Saturday. Got family comin' in. Y'all are welcome to stop by. We'll have lots of food. My wife on the grill. Be some good eats."

"We're taking the family to our Malibu rental on Saturday. The girls usually spend every other Saturday surfing and we take out the boat. Then we do church the next morning."

Surfing? I frown. No way I'm surfing. And a boat?

I imagine another newscaster. A man this time, standing in a downpour, rain pounding the sand, wind raging, blowing his bright yellow raincoat around as he struggles to remain planted near the beach waters, screaming over the howl of the storm. *"An entire family drowned this weekend when their boat sank deep into the Pacific Ocean."*

"Maybe next time, then?" Jo asks. "Monique and I would love to have you guys over."

"Yes. Perhaps." Anthony gently pushes me toward our house across the street. "Enjoy the rest of your day."

"You, too. 'Bye, Tiffany! Make sure you wear a scarf at night."

"I will. 'Bye, Jo!" I wave as she moves back into her garage and the door slides closed. I look up at Anthony. "How was church?"

"So good. Everyone is excited to meet you next week." He reaches into his back pocket and hands me a new phone.

"Oh. I forgot about getting the new phone I don't actually… need." I stuff the phone into the pocket of my shorts.

"You'll need it. Especially when we mail the old one to your grandma."

I sigh.

"Hey, I have some amazing news."

"Really? What is it?"

"I've been asked to teach a master class at the University of California San Francisco. It's a huge honor. I'd be crazy not to do it. I leave tomorrow morning at six and I'll be back Friday."

I'm stunned speechless. He's *leaving*?

"I know it's your first day of school tomorrow. But when I get back we'll have lots of time to spend together. And I already spoke with Rachel James. She's the girls' basketball coach at Curington. She's gonna let you practice with the team tomorrow after school. I told her all about you."

"Did you tell her I've never played basketball?"

He shrugs as if that very important detail isn't very important at all. "She's a coach. She teaches. You'll be fine. And, Tiffany?" We pause in the middle of the street. "I don't want you over at their house anymore."

"What? Why?"

"Because you're not allowed. In fact, I should mention I'm a bit upset that you went to their home and didn't have permission."

"They live across the street. I left a note."

"Is there a reason you didn't text me and wait for my reply?"

I run my fingers through my new hair. It falls over my shoulders. "You were at church. I didn't want to bother you. They're really nice people. What's the big deal?"

"The big deal? Tiffany, in the Stone home, children don't talk back to their parents."

"I'm not allowed to *talk*?"

"Not when it comes to rules. When Margaret and I give instruction, there is no argument. So *please* keep your distance from them and that son of theirs. Something's wrong with that kid. I don't want him anywhere near my family. Understood?"

"What if you told me to jump off a bridge?"

"Excuse me?"

"I have to agree to whatever you say. What if...you know... I don't agree?"

"Our rules are for your best interest. Bottom line. We would never tell you to jump off a bridge."

"Is it because she's gay?" I blurt without thinking, anger rising up in my chest. "Is that against your religion? Is that why you don't like them?"

"It has nothing to do with that."

"Then why?"

His cell rings and he answers it quickly. "Dr. Stone speaking." He pauses, listening. "Order a CBC and terbutaline for Helen. *Insist* Ana start the intravenous iron therapy. I can be there in fifteen minutes." He hangs up and smiles. "I've got an idea. How about you come with me to work? My office is across the street from the hospital. You can hang out."

I cringe at the thought of being near a hospital again. "I

need to start unpacking my boxes and look over my class schedule and all that boring stuff."

"Don't look so sad, Tiffany. I promise things aren't usually this busy. We'll have lots of time together."

"It's okay. No big deal," I mumble. Even though it's not okay and it is sort of a big deal. Because what Anthony Stone doesn't know is that it's very possible he and I *won't* have lots of time together.

It might even be just the seven days.

7

Stone House Rule Number 1: *Nothing negative or inappropriate is to be posted online. All social media accounts will be closely monitored.*

I refold the already crumpled and worn typed list of rules Anthony Stone slipped under my door before he left this morning and stuff it deep into the pocket of my pants, pulling on my seat belt for the fiftieth time, just to make sure it's secure. A list of typed *rules*. Who does that?

London's sitting in the front seat of the fancy Porsche SUV doing an incredible job of ignoring me. Not that I'm taking it personally; she's ignoring Heaven and Nevaeh, too, earbuds tucked tightly in her ears, reading a schoolbook. Pumpkin doesn't handle long car rides too well, so when Anthony's not home, which apparently is quite often, a driver drives everyone to school.

We're traveling up a long, winding road into the mountains. This particular driver, whose name is Darryl, seems to take his job way too seriously, which is fine by me. Hands constantly at ten and two, eyes always firmly planted on the road. Also, I think he likes sappy love songs because a radio station called the Waves has been playing the entire ride, a station where the DJs speak in whispery voices and only play heart-wrenching ballads. Mariah Carey's currently crooning out a tune about not wanting to cry, which, ironically, is sort of what I feel like doing. It's October and insanely hot. Everybody always talks about how amazing the weather is here. Maybe the people who talk about how awesome the weather is in Southern California have never *been* to Southern California.

"Curington was originally an estate owned by a Swedish billionaire," Darryl explains to me. He's a middle-aged man, dressed in all black with light brown hair that's starting to gray around the hairline. He pulls up behind a line of expensive cars at a check-in gate. "He had these grounds secretly built for his fiancée as a wedding present. It was to be their new home. The day he gifted her the property, she died."

My eyes bulge. "She…*died*?"

"Yup," Nevaeh says. "Dropped on-site. Like blam! Dead. They say if you listen carefully, you can hear her crying in some of the girls' bathrooms. Like Moaning Myrtle!"

Heaven yawns. "No, they don't. Don't listen to her, Tiffany. Nevaeh's trying to scare you."

Nevaeh shakes her head. "Do listen to me, Tiffany. If you hear a crying girl…run for your life."

Darryl chuckles and continues. "It was too painful for him to be anywhere near this development, so it was sold and eventually turned into a private school."

Fan-freaking-tastic. I'm going to a school that's probably haunted by the ghost of the original owner's dead fiancée.

I unzip my backpack and grab my small bottle of pills and, with my hands hidden inside the bag, quietly untwist the cap.

Stone House Rule Number 2: *In the Stone home, absolutely no drugs or alcohol of any kind are permitted.*

I discreetly stick the pill on the back of my tongue and swallow.

It was six weeks into Mom's chemo when I had my first appointment with a psychiatrist. Mom came with me, but waited in the reception area while I made the sojourn into Dr. Sylvain's cramped office all by myself. Dr. Sylvain wore a black yarmulke, had soft curly side locks tucked behind his ears and a short untrimmed beard. He calmly sipped coffee while we chatted, as if having a half-crazy teenager in his office wasn't going to keep him from enjoying his morning cup of caffeine.

"Tell me, Tif-phonie," he said at our first meeting, in his thick French accent, legs crossed casually. "What is going on?"

Right away I decided Dr. Sylvain was going to be a safe zone. Not because I trusted him, but because I needed to tell *someone* all the things I kept bottled up inside. Bottled up so tight it made my palms sweaty and my cheeks twitch just dying to get out.

"I feel like if I don't capitalize people's names they'll die. In text messages and emails and stuff. I have to capitalize their names. It's important. I feel like if I forget, they'll die."

He nodded and took another sip of his coffee. "Anything else?"

"If I'm too happy, I have to suffer sadness right after to keep the yin and yang of life balanced."

Sip. Sip. Slurp. "Go on."

"If I don't stare at the white divider lines on the street when we're driving, then we'll get into a car crash, and if I don't grip the side of the door we'll get into a car crash, too."

Another nod. Another sip. He adjusted his yarmulke and I continued.

"If I don't memorize lists something bad will happen. One bad thing for each item on the list. If I don't practice my guitar for at least one hour per day, God will take away my gift of playing as punishment. If I don't turn the lights off and on exactly eleven times right before bed, I'll have nightmares—Freddy Krueger–type nightmares where you can die in your sleep. If I don't turn off my cell phone at night, then someone will call me to tell me someone's died. If I'm up high… like at the mall on a top floor, I'll trip and fall through the glass railing."

He stood and moved toward his desk, said, "I see," and rummaged through a drawer. I decided he was probably looking for a pad and pen to take notes, but after a minute he found two tiny containers of cream, pulled off the thin plastic lids and poured them into his cup of coffee. He took another satisfied sip. "What happens if you should fall through the glass railing at the mall, Tif-phonie?"

"Oh… I'll die, I guess. Or be, like…permanently disfigured."

Mom joined us for the second half of the meeting, and by the time we finished our hour-long session and Dr. Sylvain his two cups of Keurig-brewed coffee, I'd been diagnosed with generalized anxiety disorder and obsessive-compulsive disorder. Though I thought being diagnosed with anything involved a blood test or a full body scan with multiple doctors at a computer looking at a digital image of your brain, pointing out the blue blob next to the yellow blob on the screen and saying that the blue blob should be yellow, too, and yep…that's why there's a problem.

"Selective serotonin reuptake inhibitor. SSRI," Dr. Sylvain explained.

"Come again?" Mom replied.

"Two per day. It is a low dose. One in the morning. One before bed." He scribbled something onto a small pad of paper, tore off a sheet and handed it to Mom.

"How long's she gotta take this?" Mom asked.

"With the help of a good family therapist, perhaps not too long. I would like to see you again, Tif-phonie. In six weeks? Yes? Good."

Mom grabbed her purse and stood.

"Are you mad at me?" I whispered as we left Dr. Sylvain's office, reading her body language: brow furrowed, jaw clenched, clutching her purse tightly.

Mom stopped in the hallway. "Not at you, Tiffany. Just… mad. You ever feel mad and not at anyone in particular?"

I nod. "On the daily."

Mom grabbed my hand. "We'll try this out, okay. If at any point these drugs make you feel worse, we stop. Agreed?"

"Agreed."

Dr. Sylvain must not have needed a brain scan to know how to help me, because within a month of taking my new medication, I stopped thinking every single thing was going to lead to my imminent death. And slowly…very slowly, I started to feel better.

The security guard at the gate waves us through and Darryl

continues up the road, now lined with beautiful palm trees. A moment later and we pull into Curington's parking lot at last.

"There's Krissy!" Nevaeh says excitedly. "D-Dawg, can you let us out here?"

"Absolutely," Darryl replies, and Heaven and Nevaeh jump out of the SUV.

"'Bye, Tiffany!" they both say in unison, and I watch their bobbing ponytails disappear into the sea of students in matching green polos and turd-brown khakis.

There is another line of fancy, expensive cars waiting to drop students off at the base of a wide set of stone stairs, while other cars are maneuvering into parking spaces. I take a moment to scope out this new school, this secret, magical kingdom tucked away in the mountains of Simi Valley. It's like we've driven to the edges of a national state park.

In addition to the main school building, there are smaller buildings scattered about the campus, too. The pristine stone structures are a stark contrast to the one run-down redbrick building surrounded by a chain-link fence that was my old public school. Everything here looks just as nice as the pictures from the brochures Anthony sent Mom and the website I've been trolling for the past few weeks. It sort of reminds me of a villa, standing alone in the Italian countryside. Cascading water flows to the right of the staircase into a beautiful water fountain and at the top of the stairs you can see scenic cobblestone paths leading from one building to the other with pretty benches strategically scattered about on the green patches of lawn and perfectly placed trees with a strange symmetry to them, as if they were all engineered in a tree factory. Lastly, a tall American flag waves high above on a silver flagpole. The perfect salutation! Like…welcome, welcome, one and all, to the greatest show on Earth—forty-thousand-dollars-a-year private school for your kids.

"We'll get out here." London yanks on her earbuds and tucks them into her backpack along with the schoolbook she's been reading the entire ride.

"You sure, miss? I can pull up. I don't mind waiting."

London pushes open her door and slides onto the pavement. "The line's too long."

Darryl scrambles out of his seat so that he can open my door. "Would you like me to walk you to the front, miss?"

"I'll walk her." London's eyes sparkle like blue diamonds in the bright morning sun. "She's with me. She'll be fine. Tiffany, are you ready?"

Before I have a chance to respond, she slams her door shut and moves through the traffic in the busy parking lot.

I grab my own backpack and quickly slide onto the pavement. "'Bye! Thank you for the ride, Darryl. You're an amazing driver. Not once did I think we were going to crash."

He smiles. "You're very welcome, miss."

I follow after London. "London, wait!"

She steps onto the sidewalk and I race to catch up to her, but within a few seconds, she's disappeared into the mass of students. I jog up the stairs, panic rising, hoping her long black hair and crimson-red backpack stands out in the crowd, but I can't seem to spot her anywhere.

She *left* me? What a *bitch*!

Stone House Rule Number 3: *Words in the Stone home should be kept clean and holy. Swear words are never allowed.*

I stop to gather my thoughts, which, at this point, are a

stream of curse words meant specifically for London, but it appears that the number of happy, chatting students and parents lingering about is growing by the second, and I need to be on a serious hunt for my first class—AP Geography—so I continue on alone.

Stone House Rule Number 4: *Until the age of eighteen, boys are only allowed as friends.*

I push through the double doors of the front entrance to behold even more magnificence. Curington clearly spares no expense. Dark wood floors, the walls covered in beautiful paintings and the superhigh, domed ceilings covered with hundreds of tiny green mosaic tiles so it looks like the view inside a kaleidoscope.

"Good morning."

I turn to see him. Marcus McKinney. The white-faced mystery boy with a high risk for instantaneous obliteration. He looks even scarier up close. There are bits of the makeup staining his Curington polo and his green eyes look creepy and catlike, making him look a little like one of the demons from *Evil Dead.* Without his signature hoodie, I see he's bald and the makeup is thickly coated everywhere: face, neck *and* head. In addition, he wears a white, long-sleeved T-shirt under his Curington polo with white gloves so that a small sliver of brown skin around his eyes is the only skin showing. *Super*creepy.

"Are you lost? Would you like help finding your first class?"

And he *speaks*! He's got a smooth, gentle voice. Deep and sweet, like he's a professional hypnotist. Like he should be saying, *You're getting sleepy, Tiffany Sly. Very, very sleeeeeeepy.*

"I, uh, thought you were half-mute," I blurt out awkwardly.

"Aren't we all?" he replies simply, tightening the straps on his backpack, the white makeup on his face almost glowing under the soft hallway lighting.

"Huh?"

"Considering we sleep eight hours per day, a person will sleep approximately two hundred thousand hours in a lifetime. That's essentially a third of your life. So really, we're not half-mute. We're all a *third* mute." I blink. His green, cat-like demon eyes blink back. "So? Would you like help finding your first class?"

It's not like anybody else is talking to me. I *could* actually use some help. Plus, don't I have to talk to him, anyway? "Sure. Yeah. Can you help me find my locker, too?"

"I could. But no one uses them."

"They don't?"

"There's only three minutes between classes."

"Three minutes?" I shift, the weight of my backpack already making my shoulders burn. "You mean, I have to carry these books in my bag all day long?"

"You *can* put them in your locker. But it'll probably make you late for class. There's a one-minute grace, but if you're late, they take points off your grade. You strike me as the kind of girl who cares about her grades."

"I am that type."

A group of students move past us; they stare at Marcus, eyes wide with horror. Then they stare at me like, *What the hell is wrong with you, girl?*

"What's your first class?"

"AP Human Geography."

"With Mr. Mills?"

"Yes! That's the one. You know it?"

"I know it well. That's my first class, too. Follow me."

What are the *odds*? I gratefully follow Marcus down the hallway; he turns up a flight of stairs to the second floor to another dimly lit, narrow hallway lined with more beautiful paintings and classrooms on both sides, but not a locker in sight.

"Where *are* all the lockers?"

"Second house. No lockers in the main house."

"House?"

"That's what the buildings are called here. Seven houses on the campus. All lockers are in House Two."

We walk down a new hallway with more dim, soft lighting. There are lots of students moving through the hallways, but I'm missing the roar of excitement that filled the halls at West. Here, everyone seems calm, subdued and, aside from horrified glances in the direction of Marcus as he moves past them, very much in their own world. There is a strange sensation rising up from the pit of my stomach. Not exactly like someone kicked me and I need to hurl, more like a knot has formed deep within my belly comprised completely of essential organs, and the only thing that will shake it free so that I don't die is to curl into a ball in the fetal position and cry. I sigh. Yes, a blanket, a bed, endless tears and the fetal position sounds like the only thing that could save me from the horror that is this situation. What if Anthony's not my dad? What if this isn't my school? What if I have to leave? What if Marcus McKinney drops dead before we make it to Geography?

We finally stop in front of a classroom and Marcus motions to the door. "AP Geography. Looks like we made it."

I breathe a sigh of relief. "Thanks for helping me. See you

around." I quickly move inside the class before Marcus has a chance to reply.

I take a seat near the back. Across the room, Marcus has taken a seat at a desk near the back, too. He turns and catches me staring at him and I look away.

The class is small; only about ten of the large desks in the room are occupied, which is probably the smallest class I've ever been in. Someone slides into the seat beside me.

"Oh, snap. Looks like we got a new girl."

I turn to see a boy prettier than most girls sitting beside me. He's got blond hair with extralong bangs that he keeps shaking out of his eyes. Paired with tan skin and electric-blue eyes, he looks like Brad Pitt and Superman had a baby.

He extends his hand. "I'm Aric with an *A*."

"Aric with an *A*?" I shake his hand.

"We got mad Erics at this school, but no Arics with an *A*. That's me."

He pulls out his cell phone and starts scrolling through Facebook without so much as a second glance at me. In fact, the class has filled up and pretty much every student is doing the same thing, sitting in their seats, pencil, pens and books ready, quietly fiddling with their phones.

The teacher rushes in and tosses his leather briefcase onto his desk. He's an amazing-looking guy, maybe thirty, in dress pants and a crisp white shirt, with a very thick head of dark, wavy hair. He checks the time on his watch just as a bell chimes sweetly.

"Phones away," he orders.

Right away, every student respectfully puts their phone in their bag or pocket and sits attentively.

"Grrrr! Good morning, Wildcats!" A girl's voice booms through the speakers as morning announcements begin.

The announcements aren't too annoying except for that "Grrrr! Good morning, Wildcats" thing. I find out there's a chess club today. No thanks. Blood drive next week. No way. School assembly in the first house on Friday. Could be fun. After-school music club…wait. My ears perk up.

"Don't forget music club has moved to the third house in the old auditorium. Every Thursday and Friday. Bring your instruments and rock out with Mrs. Brayden."

After-school music club sounds kinda cool. If only I didn't have to join the stupid basketball team.

The announcements end and Mr. Mills eyes me sitting in the back and smiles, brightening his face, making him appear even more attractive and making me more anxious and nervous than normal. Why is he a geography teacher? Shouldn't he be, like, a judge on *The Voice* or something?

"Class, we have a new student. Transferring from Chicago, right, Tiffany?"

In almost perfect unison the entire class turns to look at me and I begin sweating everywhere imaginable: armpits, hands, kneecaps, face. I give a nod and a polite wave, but they keep staring. *Stop staring at me, people!*

"Tiffany Sly." Mr. Mills displays another one of his killer, ten-thousand-watt smiles. "Stand up. Tell us about yourself. We're intrigued and want to know you."

I scoot my chair back—it moans as it slides across the wood floor—and stand slowly, wringing my hands together. "I'm Tiffany Sly and—"

"Louder! We can't hear you," a chubby boy with glasses from a desk in front calls out.

I clear my throat and try to speak louder. "Um, I'm Tiffany. I'm from Chicago. I'm a sophomore. I'm sixteen." I look at Mr. Mills. "Anything else?"

Mr. Mills sits on his desk, legs dangling casually, leaning back on his hands. "Why are you here?"

"Uh, to learn?"

The class laughs and I glance over at Marcus, who is writing on a sheet of paper, the only person not paying any attention to me whatsoever.

"No, no." Mr. Mills leans forward. "Why are you drinking the AP Geography Kool-Aid? I know it's good. But still. Tell us why *you're* here."

"Oh? I dunno. I like geography a lot."

More laughter from the class. Mr. Mills gives me a wink. "I like geography a lot, too. You can have a seat, Ms. Sly. You're a woman of few words and I can dig that."

I exhale, grateful those terrifying seconds have ended, and take my seat, wiping my hands on my pants to soak up all the perspiration.

"This course is designed for students who desire a rigorous, challenging and accelerated study of geography. To be here, you must have at least a 3.75 GPA, and/or have a personal recommendation from a previous geography teacher. To receive college credit, you must pass the AP test at the end of the year with at least a three out of five. Lastly, in order to reap the full benefits of this class…you must appreciate how awesome I am."

The class laughs again.

"So we welcome you, Tiffany Sly, knowing you have met those requirements, including recognizing my awesomeness, and we are thrilled to have you here with us. Now..." He removes a book from his briefcase and tosses it on his desk. "Please hand in your vocab worksheets from chapters seven and eight, as well as your latitude/longitude packets."

Everyone moves about, pulling papers from their backpacks and handing them to the front. Mr. Mills searches through a file cabinet and pulls out a thick packet, walking it to my desk and setting it down gently in front of me. "Syllabus, m'lady. Latitude/longitude packets can be found and printed from the website. The website address is listed on the syllabus."

"Should I do the vocab worksheets that were due today?"

"Nope." Mr. Mills moves back to the head of the class.

The rather round boy with glasses in front who shouted that he couldn't hear me raises his hand.

"Yes, Wyatt?"

"Mr. Mills, that's not fair." Wyatt turns and gives me the stink eye. "Vocab worksheets are, like, fifteen percent of our grade. The vocab from chapters seven and eight took forever. We all had to do them. Why doesn't she?"

"Tiffany is a transfer student, so whatever her grades were at her old school transfer in. Thus the word...*transfer*."

Wyatt raises his hand again.

"*Yes*, Wyatt?"

"That's crazy-not-fair. Besides, I bet her old school was easier. So now she has a high grade that she doesn't deserve. At least not here. She's gonna mess up the curve."

Stone House Rule Number 5: *We are the bright, shining lights in a world of sin and chaos. Let your light shine so that you might lead others to righteousness.*

"How about you mind your own business?" I blurt out.

Wyatt spins around. His fat face turns red with rage. "My grade *is* my business. Why don't you go back to Chicago?"

"Why don't *you* go straight to h—"

"Enough. Simmer. Down. Both of you." Mr. Mills walks toward Wyatt's desk. "Wyatt. One day when you're in your thirties like me, you'll look in the mirror and your hair will be thinning or perhaps gone completely. Then you'll remember your old geography teacher, Mr. Mills, and you'll declare: 'This is madness! Mr. Mills had a *glorious* head of hair at this age. Why don't I?' And it will be at that moment you'll realize that you are quite right—life isn't fair." The class laughs and he taps Wyatt on the shoulder. "Any more questions about Tiffany's homework? Or can I continue with today's lesson?"

Wyatt shrugs. "Whatever."

"I'll take that as a yes. Now..." Mr. Mills moves toward the blackboard and writes *absolute location vs. relative location.* "Since everyone but Tiffany did their homework over the weekend, can someone tell me the difference between these two?"

Every single person with the exception of Marcus and me raises their hand. Mr. Mills points to Aric-with-an-*A*.

Aric stands and shakes his bangs out of his eyes. "Absolute location describes the location of a place based on a fixed point on Earth while relative location refers to the position of a place or entity based on its relation to another point or place."

Mr. Mills's face contorts into an overexaggerated frown. "Wow. That was *frightening*. Can anyone say that without sounding like Wikipedia?"

Aric's face turns bright red and he sits. Hands rise again. Mr. Mills points to that chubby-checker Wyatt. He stands and tosses me a smug look, a look which makes his face look exactly like a pig with glasses. "In general—" he pauses for dramatic effect "—absolute location is a description of the exact site on an objective coordinate system, such as a grid or—"

"Stop. Coma. Death." Mr. Mills then does the unthinkable by pointing at *me*. "Tiffany?"

I look around in confusion. "Me?"

"Yes, you. Can you help us? Tell the class what Aric and Wyatt are trying to say, but say it *simply*."

"Um..."

"Please stand. When we speak, we stand. It opens up the diaphragm and it just feels good to stand, doesn't it?"

Once again, I slide my chair back and stand, rubbing my palms on my pants. "Relative location, um...no absolute location is like...like, uh...it basically uses coordinates, I think. But then, um, relative location...well... I don't know. I'm not making sense. I'm sorry." I quickly take my seat.

Mr. Mills sighs. "Tiffany. By this point you should know and be able to explain absolute and relative location. Perhaps it *would* do you some good to brush up on the vocab from previous chapters so you can be caught up."

"Told ya," Wyatt says under his breath.

Mr. Mills continues. "But thank you, Tiffany, for at least not sounding like *Webster's Dictionary*."

"Yeah, she sounded like, uh, um, er, ah..." Wyatt mocks me by biting his nails nervously and the class laughs.

"That's *enough*, Wyatt. Look, people," Mr. Mills explains.

"The point of vocab worksheets is not to memorize. To memorize is not to know. Does anyone know who said that?"

No one raises their hand.

Mr. Mills smiles. "Me. I said that. Stop memorizing stuff. 'Tell me and I forget. Teach me and I remember. Involve me and I learn.' Does anyone know who said that?"

A girl in front of me raises her hand. "You?"

"Wrong. Benjamin Franklin. You can always tell the difference between my quotes and Ben's quotes because his are way better."

Another girl with a short pixie cut sitting beside Wyatt raises her hand. "Is that going to be on the test? The Benjamin Franklin quote?"

"Seriously?" Mr. Mills shakes his head. "No. Ben Franklin quotes will not be on the test. Stay with me, people." Mr. Mills points to Marcus. "Mr. Marcus McKinney. Save us all. Absolute location versus relative location. Explain it to me like I'm five."

Marcus stands and every head turns to look at him. "I'm not sure a five-year-old would understand, either."

Mr. Mills nods. "Duly noted. So explain it to me like I'm six."

More laughter from the class.

"If you wanted to bury a treasure—" Marcus starts so softly I have to strain to hear "—and planned to retrieve it later, perhaps years later, you would need to document the exact spot on the Earth where you buried it—the absolute location. To notate it...you would use specific longitude/latitude coordinates. But since you're six, and probably don't understand location relative to the Earth's equator and prime meridian, then it would probably serve you best to remember where your treasure is buried using a relative location. A location in comparison to the location of something else. The treasure is buried beside the giant oak tree in the backyard."

Mr. Mills sighs dramatically. "And there you have it. Thank you, Marcus McKinney."

Marcus sits and our eyes meet again before I quickly look away.

Mr. Mills erases *relative* and *absolute location* and writes *GIS Mapping* across the blackboard. The class groans and I scribble *GIS* down on my notepad since I seem to be the only one who doesn't understand what the acronym stands for. "You and a partner are going—"

"A partner?" Wyatt interrupts. "There's nothing about a group project on the syllabus."

Mr. Mills sighs. "First of all, Wyatt, we raise our hands when we have a question."

Wyatt raises his hand.

"Yes, Wyatt?"

"How come there's nothing on the syllabus about a partner project?"

"The GIS mapping project *is* on your syllabus."

"Yeah, but it didn't say partner project."

"Which is why I'm telling you now." Mr. Mills continues. "You and a partner are going to find some significant, mappable data that relates to food, energy or water."

An Asian girl with long jet-black hair raises her hand. "Food, energy or water? Are those the only three options?"

"I'm open to other resources or related themes but they

must be approved by me. Now, the computer labs are equipped with the Arc-GIS software."

More groans from the class and I quickly scribble *Arc-GIS software*. What is that? And how come everyone but me seems to know? Is Wyatt right? In only a few minutes this class seems way more advanced than my previous AP Geography class.

"Stop with all the groaning," Mr. Mills says seriously. "There's a learning curve with the software, but lab techs are available every single day. No excuses. Repeat after me. I am smarter than the Arc-GIS software." The class repeats in unison and Mr. Mills nods. "Yes, you are. Partners of your choosing, but please choose wisely because this project is a huge percentage of your grade and I don't want people emailing me and whining that their partner didn't put forth the same effort. You both get the same grade no matter who works 'harder.' Pick someone you trust. As orderly as possible please, and sit beside them. This will be your assigned seating for the remainder of the semester."

Everyone excitedly stands, moving toward friends. I feel a tap on the shoulder.

"Wanna be my partner?" Aric-with-an-*A* says without any enthusiasm whatsoever. "At least we won't have to move."

"Sure. Do you know what *GIS* stands for?"

"Geographic information systems. GIS mapping is so easy. I can do it in my sleep."

"Class," Mr. Mills says.

I look up to see Marcus is standing beside Mr. Mills, his hands stuffed in his pockets, looking down at the floor.

"I forgot that Tiffany makes an odd number. One group will have three. Is there a group that would like to add Marcus?"

It's a very long, awkward silence as no hands rise and students exchange creeped-out and uncomfortable looks.

"Considering Marcus sets the curve in this class, I would think you'd be thrilled at the prospect of having him in your group." Mr. Mills crosses his arms, obviously irritated.

Still, no one makes a move to volunteer. I picture Jo's face and how relieved she looked when I promised her I'd talk to Marcus. Here's my chance to make good on the deal.

My hand shoots into the air. "He can be in our group."

"Great." Mr. Mills smiles at me. "*Thank* you, Tiffany and Aric."

"Are you bat-shit crazy?" Aric whispers, completely drained of color, but before I have a chance to respond, Marcus is standing over the two of us.

"May I pull up a chair?" Marcus asks, his voice almost a whisper.

"Sure," I reply, and Marcus moves across the room to grab an empty desk chair. I look over at Aric and shrug. "What?"

"Why did you *do* that?"

"He had to be in somebody's group."

"It's my senior year, man. That freak's not gonna ruin it."

"Nobody's ruining your senior year. It's a class project. Calm down."

Marcus returns with a chair and sets it across from Aric and me. He sits. "Hello," he says politely.

Aric pushes his chair back from the desk and stands. "I'm not doing this." Fuming, he moves to the head of the class and I watch as he and Mr. Mills have a hushed discussion. In fact, the entire class is completely focused on what's transpiring, whispering and looking back between Marcus and me, and Aric and Mr. Mills. A moment later, an extremely angry Aric returns.

"I can't switch groups." He slumps back into the chair beside me and I sit in horrified silence, not quite sure how to respond. "It's because no other groups volunteered to have three. So now I can't switch. *Fuck.*"

"You're being *rude,*" I declare.

"Whatever, man. *You're* rude," Aric replies, a scary edge to his voice.

Mr. Mills clears his throat. "I'm gifting you the next five minutes to discuss and plan. Tomorrow, I'll expect a five-hundred-word, typed proposal outlining your themes." Mr. Mills gives me a strange smile that I can't quite read.

Stone House Rule Number 6: *Everything that you do is a reflection of this family. Make sure your choices are made with wisdom and your actions carefully thought out, considering every possible outcome and how it could affect the members of this household.*

I take a deep, calming breath, trying my hardest to ignore my classmates' stares and whispers. I know Anthony won't be too thrilled with the idea of me spending time with Marcus McKinney, even though Aric-with-an-*A*—for *asshole*—will be there, too. *Stay away from that kid,* he warned me yesterday. *I don't want him anywhere near my family.*

Well…so much for that.

8

"So… GIS mapping." I swallow. "Sounds *fun*."

Aric folds his arms in annoyance, leaning back in his chair and staring up at the ceiling in a defiant, childlike gesture that reads, *Na-na na-na boo-boo, stick your head in doo-doo.*

"How about we start with introductions? Yeah? Okay, I'm Tiffany. I like the mall and my favorite food is spaghetti."

Marcus pulls at his gloves uneasily.

"Oooohkay. Don't everyone talk at once."

Two girls sitting in front of us are staring. One whispers in the other's ear; both girls smirk and giggle.

Aric raises his hand. "Mr. Mills?"

Mr. Mills looks up from the book he's reading at his desk. "Yep?"

"I ain't feelin' too good. Can I go see the nurse?"

Mr. Mills sighs. "You look healthy, vibrant and extremely tan."

"I think I might throw up. For real."

"Fine, Aric. Take the pass."

Aric bolts up, grabs his backpack and within a few seconds has disappeared out the door, leaving Marcus and me alone at the desk.

"Sorry about that," I mumble.

"I don't mind. It's tough to bother me."

"Really?" *What about the fact that you're a risk for sudden death?* I want to ask him about it. I look down at my notes instead. "So, we have to find some mappable information that relates to food, energy or water? Any ideas? I got nothin'."

"How about organic food providers. Whole Foods and Trader Joe's, for example. Did you have those in Chicago?"

"We have them…yeah."

"Well, we could overlay the organic food providers in the city by demographics."

"Demographics? Like what?"

"I was thinking race."

"You mean, see if organic food providers build their stores in mostly white neighborhoods? We don't need a GIS map to answer that."

"Or neighborhoods with a particular socioeconomic status. We can use census bureau stats about income. There could be a correlation. Would be fascinating to research."

I set down my pen, push past my anxiety and look him in the eye, like really look at him. His eyes are extremely green, demon-like sure, but kind. Like a nice demon. And his features are attractive—slanted eyes, full lips, angular cheeks. But there's something about his face I can't quite put my finger on. It hits me. Eyebrows! He doesn't have eyebrows? "You shave your eyebrows?"

"I have an extreme type of alopecia. I don't grow hair anywhere on my body."

"That's crazy. I have alopecia, too. I mean, I grow hair..." I notice his eyes glance up at my thick head of beautiful hair. "Your mom. She covered up all the bald spots. Made my hair unbe-weavable."

Mr. Mills clears his throat and stands. Time's up. "Let's talk about Google Earth, shall we?"

The bell chimes, signaling the end of class, and I close my book and notepad, stuffing them into my backpack. In addition to last weekend's homework, I have to write five hundred words outlining themes for the partner project *and* begin constructing a virtual tour on Google Earth for presentation on Friday. Plus, there's a vocab quiz tomorrow. I slide my backpack on, the weight feeling doubled since this morning.

"Don't worry about the outline," Marcus says as if reading my mind. "I can do it. Goodbye. It was very nice talking to you." I watch him head out of the classroom.

Mr. Mills waves me over. "Yes, sir?" I approach his desk as the class empties.

"Sir is my grandpa. Mr. Mills is bad enough. If I had it my way you guys would just call me Brian."

Brian Mills. I smile. What a nice name.

"Listen, I wanted to say thank you. That was a noble gesture, volunteering to have Marcus as a partner."

"Oh, yeah. No bigs."

I look down at Mr. Mills's left-hand ring finger, a bad habit of mine since Mom was always on the hunt for single men. Single men without prior felonies, as she used to put it. "Check his ring finger, Tiff," she'd whisper when a nice-looking guy was giving her the eye and I'd groan and oblige. Mr. Mills is not wearing a wedding ring. But, as I used to point out to Mom, that doesn't really give clear information.

"Also, Tiffany. If you should find yourself in need of some help, please come to my office hours. Wednesday and Friday till four thirty. I want you to succeed. That's why I'm here. Okay?"

He runs a hand through his mane of amazing hair and smiles at me. His eyes are the kind of eyes that seem void of color and every color all at once. My stomach churns as a surprising burst of butterflies spring free.

Thump-thump, thump-thump: *Could you* be *any weirder? He's your teacher! And he's* thirty.

"Thank you, sir… I mean, Mr. Mills. I'll catch up. I guess this class might be a little bit harder than my old one."

"I can tell you're a bright girl. You'll be fine. Where's your guide?"

"Guide?"

"It's your first day. You should've been assigned a guide and a pass to excuse your tardiness. Curington can be a bit of a maze if you don't know where you're going."

New students are filing into the class.

"Oh, right. My *guide.* We lost each other somehow."

He glances at his watch. "Better get moving. Time's ticking. What's next?"

"English."

"House Three. Find stairs and exit the building. It's the farthest house to the left. And touch base with Aric. Fill him in on what you and Marcus chose for the group project. And my office hours." He grins. "Don't forget, okay?"

I nod and exit the class, moving into the hallway, wondering if he invites everyone to his personal office hours with such a charming smile. Of course he does. Of course.

I'm late for English. Like ridiculously late, since apparently I don't know my left from right and thought House Five was House Three and I also thought Advanced Algebra was English. It wasn't until the teacher started writing equations on the board that I realized I was in the wrong place and excused myself. So embarrassing. I'm also late for my class after English. Geometry. And the class after that. Chemistry. Now it's lunchtime and I'm following behind a group of giggling girls who I know, by eavesdropping on their conversation, are going to lunch, so at least I won't be late for that. I review in my mind all the homework I have so far. There's a lot.

English: Read part two of *Nineteen Eighty-Four* by George Orwell. But since I haven't read part one, I might want to check that out, too. Basically…read the whole book.

Geometry: Simplifying radicals. A whopping thirty-seven equations.

Chemistry: Balancing equations and stoichiometry. Chapters four and five review questions. Twenty-five total.

Spanish: Five pages from the workbook. Verb conjugation and sentence structure.

The giggling girls exit House Five into the blindingly bright California sun and I shield my eyes, thinking back to my Spanish class. The teacher only spoke Spanish. I had no idea what she was even saying. I mean, sure I can tell the little boy not to stand under the table—*El nino pequeno! No se pare debajo de la mesa!* And I can conjugate hundreds of verbs. Name a verb. I can conjugate it. I'm running—*corro.* You're running—*corres.* She's running—*corre.* Everybody's freaking running—*corremos.* Still… I don't speak Spanish! The only reason I was able to get the homework assignment is because, thank goodness, Mrs. Richmond wrote it on the board in English.

The girls lead me to a courtyard. It's like a campus quad that sort of connects all the houses with lunch tables set up under the shade of tall sycamore trees. From the quad, I push through a set of double doors and move into the Curington lunchroom, which is something similar to a mall food court, only nicer. Lots of cool food stations and three checkout lanes. There's a burrito bar, a make-your-own-sandwich section, pizza and pasta bar, and a soup and salad bar. Also, there are fancy doorless refrigerators filled with yogurt and drinks and shelves stacked with fresh fruit and different varieties of chips. I move to grab a tray when someone yanks my arm.

"What is *wrong* with you?" It's London. Pretty face twisted into a nasty glare.

"Well, well, well. It's the world's *worst* first-day-of-school guide. I thought you got sucked into the Twilight Zone."

She grabs my hand and pulls me beside a counter with condiments and silverware. "I heard about Geography." She crosses her arms. "Please explain."

"GIS mapping? I still don't know what that is."

"This isn't funny, Tiffany. You picked Marcus McKinney as a *partner*? I'm so confused. Why would you do that? My dad's going to *flip*. We have specific rules not to talk to him."

"Why?"

"What do you mean, why?"

"I mean *why* can't we talk to him? He seems nice and normal. Aside from the whole white-face thing."

"He doesn't…match us and our belief system."

A girl squeals London's name. She spins around and waves happily at two approaching blondes.

"London Bear!" One of the girls grabs her and squeezes her in a tight hug.

I'm not sure why, I mean, both of London's superhappy friends are wearing the same outfit as me, but they look better in it than I do. It could be their perfectly manicured hands, their long, shiny blond hair or their glowing skin and bright eyes. But I think it's more than that. There's an aura about them, like life has been kind. Like the biggest pain they've ever experienced is when the ski lift breaks down on their annual trip to Aspen. Not like me. The biggest pain I've experienced is watching my mom die. Slowly.

"Tiffany," Mom said one day while I sat beside her bed at the hospice reading a schoolbook.

"Hmm?" I replied without looking up.

"I don't want you to be afraid to die."

I looked up then. She was a shell of her former self. Skin dark and lifeless. Head completely bald. Her body thin and frail. The whites of her eyes yellowing. Almost completely unrecognizable. I'm not sure if it's the cancer that destroys the person or the chemo and radiation. Perhaps it's our will to survive. The fight for life somehow makes life not even worth living.

"There's a peace in it," Mom whispered. "I can't explain it. Do you still believe in God, Tiff?"

"Why are you asking me that, Mom?" I closed my schoolbook and crawled into bed beside her. Peeling away the covers and the IVs and the wires until I was able to lay my head on her chest, listening to the faint sound of her weak heart and all the machines that were helping her hold on to her last shreds of life.

"Because I know you, Tiffany Sly. I can see the wheels turning in your head." She played with the braids on my head. "You think, if there's a God, why won't he save me?"

I didn't respond, but yes, that was it exactly.

"When I look back at my life, Tiffany, you know what I'm most proud of?"

"Me?"

Mom playfully pulled on one of my braids. "Jeez, conceited," she said so softly I had to strain to hear her. "For your information, I wasn't gonna say you."

I sat up then and looked into her eyes. Only a spark of life left there. "Mommy! It's not me?"

She shook her head. "Nope. You're at a close second, though."

I adjusted the nasal cannula that helped her breathe. Instead of bursting into tears and sobbing on her chest like I wanted to, I smiled and said, "Mommy, what are you most proud of that isn't me but should be?"

She smiled back. "My *faith*. Here I am, facing my *worst* fear, and my faith hasn't wavered. Not even a little bit. Everybody's gotta die, Tiffany. Just my turn, is all."

★★★

"OMG!" the friend hugging London squeals. "A new girl."

The other friend twists a slick-straight strand of blond hair around her finger. "Oh, my God, we're Rudeness with a capital *R*. I'm Isabel and this is Charlotte. But we call her Charlie Bear."

"Right. And we call Isabel Izzy Bear. And of course Londy Bear," Charlie explains excitedly. "We're the Three Bears. Get it?"

I don't. The Three Bears? This would've never been a successful trio at West. *The-Three-Girls-Who-Get-Beat-Up-After-School* would be more like it. "Tiffany Sly. Nice meeting you guys."

"You and London are the *exact* same height," Isabel exclaims.

I look over at London and realize for the first time…we *are* the *exact* same height. Coincidence?

"Is today your first day?" Charlie asks.

"Mmm-hmm."

Izzy wraps her arm around London so that now the three girls are standing in a line, arms linked around one another in adorable solidarity. "How do you know our bestie, Londy Bear?"

"She's my sister," I say, sounding way too unsure of myself.

Izzy Bear's jaw drops. "No way."

Charlie stares at me. "So weird. You guys don't look *anything* alike."

"We have different moms, obviously," London explains.

Izzy nods. "London, I swear sometimes I forget you're

even black. You're so light-skinned. You could totally pass for white."

"Why would she want to do that?" I ask, annoyed.

The color drains from Izzy's face. "I—I meant...like...she doesn't have to be one or the other. She doesn't have to be labeled as anything."

"Lucky her," I mumble sarcastically.

"Hey, you guys grab our table," London cuts in. "We don't want anybody taking our spot."

"We're so on it." Charlie grabs Izzy's hand. "Nice to meet you, Tiffany."

"Yeah, totes," Izzy says, and the girls move off.

London glares at me.

"What?"

"Izzy and Charlie are my two *best* friends. Don't be rude to them."

"Don't talk to Marcus McKinney. Don't be rude to your friends even though they say weird shit like, 'Omigosh, I totally forgot you were, like...black.'" I dramatically flip my hair over my shoulder. "Any other rules or would you prefer to type up a list and slip it under my door like *your* dad did."

"You're hopeless. I'll see you around, Tiffany." London quickly follows after her friends.

I'm sitting at a lunch bench with three young boys who are probably freshmen. I make this determination based on their high-pitched, cracking voices. They're also having a very animated discussion about a video game. I pull out my phone to text Keelah: School out yet?

Keelah texts back right away: Who is this?

Me: Tiffany. New phone number. Sorry.

Keelah: Tiff! I'm in my last period but it's Chemistry so whatever, I can text. How is it so far?

Me: Like another world.

Keelah: I'm jealous! What's a forty thousand dollar a year school like? Gold-plated toilets?

Me: Some silver.

Keelah: Ha! Making new friends? Don't replace me.

Me: I've met lots of cool people but no one as cool as you.

Keelah: Teach is giving me the stink eye. Not my fault this class blows. I'll call you later. Love you.

Me: Love you, too.

Technically, I didn't lie to Keelah. I mean, it *is* like another world. And I've met some cool people. Like Mr. Mills, for example. In two years I'll be eighteen and he'll be…thirty-two? I exhale. *Tiffany Mills* has a nice ring to it.

I take a bite of my sandwich. It's good. Turkey, lettuce and cheese. I have a bag of potato chips, too, and a bottle of grape juice. At the checkout, you swipe your school ID card to pay for your lunch. The cost is included with tuition but you can't go over the daily limit, which is ten dollars. I mean, you can, but you have to pay cash to cover the extra cost.

"Dude! You haven't been in the secret room on the ark?" one of the boys at my table squawks. "You gotta pause right after John jumps out of the Pelican in the beginning lands."

"I tried that!" another boy replies.

"Did you fly up the mountain and tap Y?"

I try to tune out the boys and take another bite of my sandwich when I notice Marcus push through the doors of the lunchroom and step outside. Students part to let him pass, scattering like roaches. We make eye contact and I give him a polite wave, feeling sorry for him. What would I do if people scrambled to get away when I walked by? Having taken my friendly wave as an invitation to come sit with me, he moves to my table.

"Hello. Do you mind if I sit here?" The startled freshmen boys look over in horror. He turns to them and waves politely. "Hello."

They quickly grab their trays of food and move to a nearby, free lunch bench.

Seemingly unaffected, he sits across from me and takes out a book from his backpack, sets it on the table beside his tray and begins eating his large vegetable salad. His white makeup looks less chalky and more smeared, like it's melting in the hot sun.

"You're missing a protein, Marcus."

"I had a protein smoothie for breakfast."

"Are you a vegetarian?"

"Vegan."

"Okay, riddle me this. I totally get the no-meat thing. But no eggs? What's wrong with eggs?"

"Did you know that on egg farms, even organic farms, when male chicks are born they toss them into meat grinders. They kill thousands and thousands of male chicks. They're considered useless. I can't support the unethical treatment of animals."

I see that some students have taken notice of Marcus and me. More whispers. More stares. I wonder how long it will take London to discover me cavorting with someone who doesn't *match* her *belief system*. Whatever that means. "What are you reading?"

He holds his book up for me to see. It's a white paperback with nothing on the cover but the words *The Boy Who Lived Before* in black print.

"Whoa. Is that your book? Your mom told me about it. I thought it didn't come out till next year?"

"It doesn't. This is an advanced reader's copy."

"Did it hurt?"

"I'm sorry?"

"To die. If you don't want to talk about it, that's cool. I don't even know why I asked you that. It sort of erupted out of me…like word vomit. Also, I don't know why I said that. I have foot-in-mouth disease, which is not the same as foot-*and*-mouth disease, which is red spots on your hands and feet and mouth. Like chicken pox. I had that once, too. Anyway, I say stupid things and then people realize I'm a big weirdo. It's my superpower."

"I'm sorry. What was your question again?"

"What *was* my question? Oh! Did it hurt to die?"

"No."

I take a swig from my grape juice and notice a few more stares from students. "Hey, can I ask you a personal question?"

He nods.

"Are you wearing contacts?"

"No."

"Someone in your mom's family have green eyes?"

"No."

"That's so bizarre. I never seen a brown-skinned black boy with green eyes."

"First time for everything, I suppose."

"Can I ask you another personal question?"

"You can ask me anything just so long as you stop asking if you can ask."

"Got it. Why do you wear that stuff on your face? It makes you look..." I want to say *crazy*. I decide on: "Not normal."

"I wear it because it makes me feel better."

"And the white gloves? Those make you feel better, too?"

"Yes, they do."

"It's all coming off a little Stephen King. I think if you toned down the Pennywise, people would be nicer to you."

"I see." He chews another forkful of salad and swallows courteously before speaking again. "In order for people to be nice to me, I have to look a certain way?"

"Not exactly. But a white-painted face is superodd."

"The antonym for *odd* would be *ordinary*, yes? So basically you're suggesting I be ordinary, so that I can have friends."

"Be *normal*."

"Interesting. May I ask you a personal question now?"

"Sure."

"Your mom's passed, yes?"

I take a bite of my sandwich, swallow and nod.

"Did she pass in a hospice?"

I nod again.

"Were you there?"

My chest tightens. The memories are fresh. It's not easy to talk about without bursting into tears. I was always there. But the night she died…I wasn't.

"I'm only asking because it's something I discuss in my book. Loved ones stay by their dying relative's side for days, weeks, months, and the moment they leave, even if it's to run quickly to the store…the loved one passes on."

"Is that true?"

He nods. "I believe it's a good sign. Confirmation that the soul desired to go and left in peace."

My eyes well with tears.

"I'm sorry," Marcus says even softer than his standard soft tone of voice. "I didn't mean to make you upset."

"I had this dream." I wipe the tears as they spring free. "Three weeks after my mom died. I dreamed she was walking down the corridors of a hospital and she looked beautiful and healthy again. She was walking and talking with one of her nurses and she said to him, 'Thank you for doing that. I had to go in peace.' And then I woke up from the dream." I blow my nose with a paper towel. "I feel like that dream makes sense now."

I was by Mom's side day and night when she moved into hospice care. The night she passed, a nurse came into her room and stayed awhile, listening to me play softly. When I finished Mom's favorite gospel song, he said, "Tiffany, your mom is stable. You and your grandmother should go home. Get some rest. Come back tomorrow." I was deliriously tired and probably smelled since I hadn't showered or even brushed my teeth in a couple of days, and the thought of a warm shower and a real meal sounded heavenly, so Grams and I went home. But when I stepped out of the shower, I heard Grams screaming. I wrapped a towel around me and raced out of the bathroom to see her fall to her knees, cell phone in hand.

Mom was gone.

Marcus hands me his book. "Here, take it. Keep it."

"Seriously? But it's your advanced reader's copy."

"It's cool. They sent me a whole box."

"Thanks." I take the book, placing it carefully inside my backpack. "Marcus, I have to confess something. Your mom, uh, she asked me to talk to you and be your friend and then she'd do my hair for free."

He nods, like the information doesn't bother or surprise him in the slightest.

"And again…word vomit. I don't know why I told you that. But what if I didn't tell you? Then we'd become friends and later on you'd find out and run away screaming and crying in the rain and I'd be like, 'Marcus, wait! You weren't my friend then, but you are now!' But of course you won't care and you'd never talk to me ever again."

"How come it's raining?"

"Huh?"

"In your fantasy. Why am I running away in the rain?"

"Oh." I shrug. "I like rain."

He nods and resumes eating.

"Anyway, I'm so sorry. I probably would've talked to you, anyway."

"It's fine. My moms, they mean well."

I take another swig of grape juice and see more students staring at us. In fact, we're attracting a *ton* of attention.

"They think we're dating," Marcus says.

"We're both black. Of *course* we're dating."

"The guys here will be sad to think you're taken."

"All these white boys? Pa-lease. White guys don't like black girls. Not black girls like me, anyway."

"What's a black girl like you?"

"Regular. I'm not light-skinned or mixed. I mean, maybe I…might be…a little…but it doesn't show. I don't have long, pretty hair or light eyes or look like Kim Kardashian."

"Interesting."

"What? You think I'm wrong?"

"Yes."

"We should GIS map it," I say.

"You're a very interesting girl. I don't typically talk to people here at Curington."

"How come?"

"I guess I don't have much to say, but I like you, Tiffany. Sort of the way you like a…cousin."

"You *cousin*-zoned me? Being in the friend zone is one thing, but the cousin zone?" I smile. "But you know something, Marcus McKinney? I like you, too. The way you like a…family pet."

"Pet-zoned?" He nods approvingly. "Should I bark in appreciation?"

"Marcus, you start barking, these people will *really* start running from you." I laugh. Man…it feels good to laugh.

9

I swing my arms behind my back to lift my backpack with my hands, my attempt to take the weight off my aching shoulders as I escape my final class, A Cappella. In A Cappella, we sing depressing songs in Latin, with no instruments, of course. The only way I got through it was to imagine every student dropping dead of boredom simultaneously while the teacher, Mrs. Brayden, continued conducting with her fancy conductor's wand, eyes closed in ecstasy like she was really feeling this sad, sad song that just killed everybody. An image that made me laugh out loud a couple of times and almost got me in trouble.

I move slowly down the hallway, not quite sure where to go since basketball practice doesn't start for another hour, but I know I need to find *someplace* to go…and preferably out of sight. *Everyone* is staring at me and whispering. And since this school is so damn quiet, I can easily hear what they're saying.

"Maybe it's Marcus's sister or something."

"I heard they were making out at lunch."

"Ewww, gross. How does he kiss with all that makeup on?"

"God, she's tall."

"She's like a basketball stud or something."

"I bet she's on scholarship. Basketball probably."

"He made her cry at lunch. She was sobbing. I feel so sorry for her."

"I'm pretty sure the school brought her in from inner-city Chicago to join the girls' basketball team."

Strangely enough, it's only the rumors that I'm here on a scholarship to play basketball that are infuriating me. Damn Anthony Stone for making their stupid stereotype play out in real life. Because I'm tall and I'm black, I have to play basketball? If I was tall and white, I wonder if they'd make the same assumptions. No, if I was tall and white, I'd be a supermodel. I check the time on my cell—2:45. The lunch quad area pops into my mind. That'll do fine.

Back in the quad, there are a few students milling about but I'm somewhat hidden, sitting on the ground, under the shade of one of the tall trees, away from the bug-eyed stares and loud, annoying whispers. There is a long, narrow flight of stone stairs that leads to another parking lot at the base of the hill. From my high vantage point, I see Aric-with-an-*A* jump into a white Toyota Tacoma truck. A few minutes pass and the truck doesn't move. How fortuitous, I think with a roll of my eyes. I need to talk to him about what Marcus and I chose for the mapping project. I decide now is as good a time as any. I push my backpack up against the tree and move slowly down the steep staircase, gripping the metal railing like my life depends upon it because I'm pretty sure it does. A moment later and I step off the final stair into the parking lot.

I approach the white truck, but don't see Aric in the driver's seat. Weird. I swear he got in the car a few minutes ago. I press my face against the back window and catch my breath. He's there, sitting in the back seat, pants down, moaning in pleasure, a girl's head in his lap. He looks over at me in shock. The girl looks up, too. I gasp and take a small step away from the car, London's panicked expression and disheveled appearance emblazoned across my mind as the back door to the truck is quickly pushed open and she jumps out.

"Tiffany, wait. I can explain."

I turn around and bolt up the stairs. I make it back to the tree and slump down, placing my head between my legs. London is dating Aric-with-an-*A*-for-asshole. What are the odds?

"Tiffany?"

I look up to see London standing over me, her long hair pulled off her face with an elastic headband.

"I can explain about that."

"I can't talk to Marcus because he doesn't match up with what you stand for. But you can *service* Aric on school property?"

"You make it sound dirty and gross. It's not like we're having sex or anything. It's foreplay. Like kissing. And I sort of clear my mind of all bad thoughts and it's like a massage or something. Nothing really sinful about it."

"Girl, you are a raging hypocrite."

"He's my boyfriend!"

"Oh, happy birthday. Did you magically turn eighteen today?"

"Don't tell my dad or my mom, okay? They wouldn't understand. Aric's not a Jehovah's Witness."

"What does that have to do with anything?"

"When we are old enough to date, we have to choose someone who practices our faith and is a baptized Witness."

"You're joking, right?"

"No. The Bible says you shouldn't attach yourself to a nonbeliever. But Aric likes my church and what it stands for. He's thinking of converting."

"Well, I'm not."

"You're not what?"

"I'm not thinking of converting. Based on what I'm seeing so far, I *don't* like your church and what it stands for."

"I won't tell my dad you said that."

"And I won't tell *your* dad you were working on converting Aric from the back seat of his truck."

She rolls her eyes. "So, we're good, then?"

"Good?"

"Listen, Tiffany. I'm sorry, okay? I know I've been acting like a B since you arrived."

"B?"

"Rhymes with *witch*?"

"Bitch?"

She nods.

"London, you just had a *penis* in your mouth but you can't say *bitch*?"

"Can't you take an apology? Jesus! I'm trying to say I'm sorry for being…mean or whatever. It's just that Dad announces he fathered a child with some random woman and we're—"

"Whoa!" I stand in fury. "Don't call my mom a random woman. I'm two months older than you, so *my* mom came first. What if your mom is the random?"

"Mom and Dad met in high school."

My eyes grow big and then narrow. "They did?"

"They were engaged their senior year of college."

"What?"

"You didn't know that?"

I feel heat rushing to my cheeks. *My* mom was the other woman?

London reaches into her back pocket. She hands me a business card. "I forgot to give you this. It's Darryl's cell phone number. He's here. Call him and he'll pull up to the front for you."

"Why is he here? We both have basketball practice."

"Coach had a family emergency. Practice resumes tomorrow."

"You're not coming home with me?"

"We're allowed to stay at school studying till four thirty. I'll come home later."

She turns and heads down the stairs. My phone buzzes and I snatch it from my pocket. It's Grams. I take a deep breath.

"London says Dad and Margaret were engaged in college. That means he cheated on her with Mom."

"Hello to you, too, Tiffany."

"Is that true?"

"Yes. It's true."

"Why didn't she tell me that?" A group of students move through the quad and take notice of me yelling into the phone. I don't care. Let them spread more rumors. Let me be the subject of more stupid Curington gossip.

Did you hear about Tiffany? they'll say. *She was crying in the quad because Marcus dumped her.*

"Tiffany, please calm down."

"No! Don't tell me to calm down!" I scream at the top of my lungs. "She owed me an explanation!" There is something interesting to note about reaching a state of hysterics. It's like your personality splits and hysterical-you takes your body hostage, while calm-and-rational-you stands off to the side, watching in dismay. "Did Mom know he was *engaged*? Mom was smart and…smart! She wouldn't be the other woman! She wouldn't!"

"Ask your father. It's his responsibility—"

"Was there another guy?"

"Excuse me?"

"Was Mom, like…dating another man *and* Anthony Stone?"

"Tiffany Sly, you watch your mouth, do you hear me? Do not disrespect the memory of your *mother*."

"So what if she was dating two men, Grams. It's not the end of the world."

"Imani would never have done that. Tiffany, what is wrong with you? Are you saying you don't believe Anthony to be your father?"

I take a deep breath and wipe my face as calm-and-rational-me seizes her opportunity to step back inside the body. What will Grams do—what will she say when she finds out the truth? Mom actually *was* dating *two* men at the same time.

"Your mother met Anthony Stone at an ER in the city. Apparently, they were short-staffed and he volunteered to finish out the last six months of his residency in Chicago."

"Is that when she broke her hand?" Mom always talked about breaking her hand when she was younger. How she thought she'd never play guitar again. And she might not have. But she retaught herself how to play left-handed.

"That is correct, Tiffany. Anthony was her doctor and they started spending time together after that."

"And then what happened?"

"What do you think happened? Your mom got pregnant."

"And she didn't tell him?"

"She told him."

"What?"

"He asked her to get an abortion."

The pain in my head intensifies, like it's seriously about to explode. I grab it with one hand, as if that can somehow stop the blast. "He *knew*? He knew about me? What a liar!"

"Tiffany, *listen*. He said he wasn't ready to be a dad and gave her the money for the procedure. Your mom couldn't go through with it, though." Grams pauses. "But before she had a chance to tell him the truth, his residency ended and he went back to California."

"Why didn't she call him and tell him she was still pregnant?"

"She did call him. But it was after you were born. She thought once he knew you were here, he'd have a change of heart."

"And he didn't?"

"Well…when she got back in contact with your dad, she found out he was married."

"To Margaret?"

"Mmm-hmm. Married with London on the way."

"Omigosh…"

"Your mom was devastated, of course."

"She *still* didn't tell him?"

"I never agreed with that decision but she was adamant. She didn't want to be the reason their marriage didn't work. Her choice was to raise you as a single parent and that was that. Now, Tiffany, you gotta understand something about age. We get older and we get wiser. You can't fault your mom for her choice and you can't fault your dad for his past. We make mistakes. We grow. We get better."

I wipe fresh tears. Something's not quite adding up. Grams has to be missing a key element to the story.

"Anthony wants a chance to right his wrongs, Tiffany. That's what matters. When he found out he...he wanted you."

"Yeah, right. That's why he's in San Francisco."

"Did he take the other kids with him to San Francisco?"

"No."

"What about his wife? She travel with him?"

"No."

"Sounds to me like he's not treating you any different than the rest of his family."

A moment of silence passes between us. "What if he changes his mind?"

"Tiffany, what are you talking about?"

"Like, what if you get a phone call in a few days and Anthony says he doesn't want me anymore. For...whatever reason."

Grams chuckles. "Tiffany? Child, please stop. You're being dramatic and you sound crazy."

"It could happen. I mean, anything is possible."

"You're his daughter."

Unless I'm not. I groan. "London says I'm putting a financial strain on them with me going to the private school, too. I dunno. Everything feels wrong."

"Oh, pooh. Do you know who Margaret is? She is the only child of Charles Vaughn."

"Charles Vaughn?" I pause. Why does that name sound familiar? Then it hits me. I even remember reading about him on the *Forbes* billionaire list. "The *furniture* guy?"

"Mmm-hmm. Founder of FWICK, Inc. Margaret is his sole heir."

"No *wonder* they seem so rich."

"Because they are. You think they got that fancy house and fancy schools for them kids on a doctor's salary?" Grams huffs. "Please."

"Unbelievable."

"Exactly. Don't feel bad about that private school."

I exhale, the tiniest amount of calm returning.

"Where are you?"

"I'm at school still."

"Take a moment. Get your bearings. It's been a lot for a few days. Go home and take a nap."

"I have, like, five hours' worth of homework."

"Take a short one, then."

Grams has a way about her. Coddling's not really her thing.

"I'll check on you later, Tiffany."

"Sorry I screamed at you, Grams."

"I probably deserved it."

"Love you."

"Love you more."

I hang up and look for the Facebook app on my new cell. Of course there isn't one. Good ol' Dr. Dad and his "no internet on the cell phone" rule. How stupid is that? I click on the Safari icon and connect to the web via the school Wi-Fi. No way he can monitor that. I quickly type *Xavior Xavion, Chicago, Facebook.* I wait for the screen to load, then click on the link to his page. The hair on my arms stands when I see his face again. Dark brown skin, warm brown eyes, almond-shaped like mine. He really does look a lot like me. I scroll through his photos. Looks like he's a car salesman. That would make Keelah very happy if my actual dad sold cars for a living. I keep swiping. Don't see any kids. No wife or girlfriend. Another swipe. Holy. Hell.

A photo of him playing an electric guitar.

My hands shake, palms sweating profusely causing the phone to almost slip from my grasp.

I swipe again.

Another photo of him playing yet *another* guitar—acoustic this time.

Thump-thump, thump-thump: *You're not with the right family.*

Thump-thump, thump-thump: This *is your real dad.*

I swipe back to the picture of him at the car dealership—Chevrolet. It looks like a big lot. Most likely the one by Midway Airport. I key in another search. *Xavior Xavion, Chevrolet dealer.* Right away, his business profile pops up with a link to the dealership phone line. I take a deep, calming breath and click the link to make the call.

"Auto Nation Chevrolet?" A perky woman's voice booms through my phone speakers.

"Oh, um, may I please be connected to Xavior Xavion?"

"Sure," she replies. "One moment."

Omigosh. *Omigosh.* I slump down under the shade of the tree and place my head between my legs, confident that this will be the moment my head actually explodes.

"Xavior speaking." A deep voice interrupts the hold music and my thoughts of internal combustion.

I'm frozen. Not sure what to do or say or even why I'm calling. Why *am* I calling?

"Hello?" he says. "This is Xavior."

"Hi. Um…" I pause. "It's Tiffany."

"Tiffany?" He says my name as if he's saying the name of the most important person in the whole world. "*Wow.* It's so amazing to hear from you. How did you find me here?"

"I Googled you."

"Ahh. Clever. Everything…okay?"

"Yes. No. I mean… I'm in California. Living with…my… you know."

"Your dad?"

"Yeah. That."

Silence. Deafening silence. Is he mad now?

"Hey, what's your favorite Beatles song?"

"Excuse me?" he replies.

"The Beatles. You like them, right?"

"Not really a big fan of the Beatles. I mean, they're okay."

"Okay?" I frown. "*Sgt. Pepper's Lonely Hearts Club Band* is like the best album ever made."

"I don't know that album."

"Omigosh, that's tragic. Go buy it."

"Okay, Tiffany. I'll do that today." He laughs. "Is that all? You only called to tell me to get *Sgt. Pepper's Lonely Hearts Club Band*?"

"And get *The Wall* by Pink Floyd. And *The Rise and Fall of Ziggy Stardust and the Spiders from Mars* by David Bowie. These are all concept albums. *Don't* get the CDs. Gotta listen to them on vinyl and just, like…escape for a few hours. Go to Disco Kings. They have the best records. They have everything. On Second and Lincoln?" There's silence on the other end of the line again. Did he hang up on me? Was I talking too much? *Am* I talking too much? "Xavior?"

"Sorry. I'm here. Writing. David Bowie. Second and Lincoln. Okay. Got it all. I'll go this evening." There's that deafening silence again. "Tiffany?" he finally says. "I thought you wanted me to go away forever?"

"I did. Are you going to?"

"I don't want to disrupt your life or your plans. It's just… I think you're *my* daughter. And I want to be your dad. I really do." He sighs. "My lawyer will be in contact. Have you spoken with your grandmother or—"

"I should go." And I should. Especially as I'm suddenly remembering this call was a really bad idea.

"Wait. Tiffany, can we talk again? I mean, after I listen to the music? Your number came up on caller ID. Would that be okay if I contact you?"

"Sure. I guess. Yeah. I think."

He laughs. "Okay. It was so nice to get your call. Made my day."

I hang up.

I made his day. He'd like to talk to me again. Says he *wants* to be my dad.

I lean my head back against the tree. What if he is my dad? Things might go back to normal. I'd return to Chicago. My old school. All my friends. I'd be with Grams again. Away from all this *sun*.

I close my eyes and feel tears sliding down my cheeks. No idea why the thought of Xavior and returning home makes my broken heart break just a little bit more.

10

Darryl and I ride home in bumper-to-bumper traffic. The slow pace allows me to somewhat relax for the first time all day. But as we approach Margaret and Anthony's giant mansion, I notice flashing police lights. There's a *squad* car in the driveway.

"The police are here?" I bolt up, grabbing my backpack and unhooking my seat belt. "Do you know what's going on?"

Darryl shakes his head in confusion. "No, miss. I—I don't."

I push open the car door. I can hear Pumpkin screaming—bloodcurdling, pained screams. Something's wrong. Oh, no, something's really wrong! The police officers seem to have just arrived. I race past them, unlock the front door, shove it open and throw my bag to the side.

"Margaret!" I yell.

Pumpkin's screams are amplified within the house. It sounds like she's hurt. I speed through the living room and down a hallway. "Margaret? Pumpkin?" I can *hear* the screams, but I can't quite make out which direction they're coming from. I race back into the living room, around a corner and through a small den, finally pushing through a door at the end of another long hallway. I find myself in what must be Margaret and Anthony's master suite. The room is enormous and Pumpkin is definitely in here. The cries appear to be coming from behind a closed door at the far end of the room. I pause. Dear God, what could be behind that door?

Thump-thump, thump-thump: *Margaret's unconscious, bloodied and bruised.*

Thump-thump, thump-thump: *And Pumpkin's tied to a chair.*

I push aside my fears and hurry across the bedroom, shoving the door open, and rush into an adjoining bathroom where I see Margaret. Not unconscious, bloodied and bruised like I imagined, but standing in an extralarge Jacuzzi bathtub, dressed in a bathing suit, holding Pumpkin's head under the running water. I gasp. She's trying to kill her!

"What's happening?" I scream. "What are you doing to her?"

Surprised, Margaret turns. Her eyes are red and swollen, her face tear-streaked. I take a step forward and see the open bottle of shampoo tipped over and spilling into the tub, Pumpkin's naked body flailing about in the water as she howls, kicking and thrashing about with water splashing everywhere.

Margaret gives me a polite tilt of the head. "I'm so sorry. I only wash it once every three days. This is normal. Not to worry. She's completely fine."

She's getting her *hair* washed. My knees buckle, still shaking from the sheer terror of what I thought was happening.

"You look spooked. Did we give you a scare?"

"Margaret..." I'm still trying to catch my breath.

"Don't worry. She's afraid of the water. She'll be fine as soon as I'm done."

"No—someone must've called the police. They're here. They're outside! The police are *here*."

She nods, not shocked or surprised in the least, and pulls the naked and crying child from the tub, quickly wrapping a towel around her body. She hands her to me.

"You want *me* to take her?"

"Please. Our neighbor Mrs. Lieberman must've called the police. Child Protective Services stopped coming. So, I suppose the police is her only option now. I'll go and talk to them and explain the situation."

I take Pumpkin into my arms; she howls even louder, thrashing about in a panic.

"*No!* Want *Mommy*! Don't want you. You get outta here!"

Her sopping wet hair drenches my Curington uniform and my sneakers slip on the wet marble floor. I catch myself before we both tumble over.

"Are you okay?" Margaret asks, grabbing a robe off a hook behind the bathroom door and sliding it on.

I nod, strengthening my grip on Pumpkin.

"Mommy will be back, Pumpkin."

I wince as Margaret slips through the bathroom door. My ears ring as Pumpkin takes her screams up an octave. She's writhing around in my arms, trying to free herself, so I move out of the bathroom and carefully set her down on the edge of Anthony and Margaret's bed. I get close to her face so that I look scary and intimidating, grab the towel wrapped around her body with one hand and pull her close, giving my most threatening whisper, imitating what my grams used to do when I was small.

"Pumpkin, if you do not stop that screaming…! Do you hear me? *Stop* it. Now!"

Her eyes get big and round like a cartoon character's. "I don't like you! You get outta here!" She backs away to a far corner of the bed, like I'm a superscary monster she's running from.

I don't care if she doesn't like me. She's not screaming anymore. Now I can hear myself *think*. I slump down onto the floor beside the bed. A few moments pass and thin, wet arms lie over my shoulders.

"You sad?"

Pumpkin's hanging over the edge of the bed. A sincere look of concern on her adorable face, her blue eyes wide with concern.

"No. I'm not sad."

"You fus-tated?"

"Frustrated? No. I'm okay."

Her sopping wet hair is dripping on me. I slip the towel from around her shoulders and wrap it around her head, squeezing out as much water as I can.

"Ow! That's hurt me!"

"Sorry, Pumpkin." I give one final squeeze and place the towel back around her body. She's cold now and shaking, so I sit her in my lap, placing my arms around her in an effort to warm her.

Margaret returns, two police officers trailing behind her.

Pumpkin climbs off my lap and rushes to her, the towel

falling to the floor, exposing her tiny, little naked body. Margaret scoops her up and covers her with her robe.

"Hey, kiddo," one of the officers says to Pumpkin. "How you feeling?"

"I very, very sad," Pumpkin replies seriously. "I so scary."

"Why are you so scary?" the officer asks with a warm smile.

"I get water in my ear. It's very owie."

The officer and his partner exchange bemused looks.

"I think we've seen enough," the other officer says. "We're sorry to have disturbed you." He looks at me and waves. "How are you today, miss?"

My only experience with cops is when the local Chicago police would follow us home from school, shouting through their car speakers for us to get out of the street and stay on the sidewalk. I give the man what I mean to be a smile but what probably looks more like the gaze of a mentally deranged person.

"It's totally understandable that she would have called you," Margaret explains in her eerie polite manner. "I'm positive she was only concerned for Pumpkin. But as you can see, she's fine."

"Absolutely, ma'am. Again, we're sorry to have disturbed you. You ladies have a wonderful day."

"Let me walk you out." Margaret turns to me. "Tiffany, can you take Pumpkin for me? Get her dressed? Her clothes are hanging in the bathroom."

I stand, moving to retrieve Pumpkin. Margaret exits with the police officers, leaving Pumpkin squirming and screaming once again in my arms.

★ ★ ★

"There." I kneel beside a large, cushy chair in the bedroom as I finish buttoning up Pumpkin's colorful dress. "You look very pretty."

"Don't like pretty. Don't like dress! I want princess dress!"

"I...I don't know where that is, Pumpkin. Maybe you can wear the princess dress later."

She balls her hand into a fist and hits me across my shoulder. "Ow!" Strangely enough, her hand feels like a tiny hammer. "That hurt!"

She does it again. Harder. Slamming down on my shoulder.

"Pumpkin, *stop* that!" I grab her wrist but she uses her free hand to slam down on my other shoulder, so I clutch both wrists tightly. "Pumpkin! You can't hit me."

She throws her body onto the floor. Cue another *epic* tantrum. Shrieks, shrills and screeches so loud my ears are ringing again. Thankfully, Margaret pushes through the door to rescue me from the attack of the two-year-old monster.

"Pumpkin!" she bellows. Pumpkin's kicking and pounding the floor with her fists like she's possessed by the devil.

"I want princess dress! Don't like Tiffany dress. I very, very not happy!"

Margaret kneels at her side and wraps her arms around the toddler, gripping her so that Pumpkin is unable to move. "I will not allow this behavior! Do you understand?"

Like a pint-size Houdini, Pumpkin frees herself from Margaret's grasp, hits her in the face as hard as she can and races out of the room.

Margaret sits on the edge of her bed, nursing the spot on her face that Pumpkin smacked. She looks up at me, eyes watering. "I'm sorry for Pumpkin's inappropriate behavior." Then she places her head in her hands and sobs.

"Omigosh. Margaret? Please don't cry."

"I apologize. I'm so overwhelmed." She tries to pull herself together, wiping her eyes with the corner of her robe. "Hair day is always like this. Well, maybe not *this* bad. The police have never come."

"Have you considered cutting her hair off?"

Margaret's crazy eyes get as big as saucers. "Oh, my goodness, Tiffany. Anthony would never allow that. Your father… he prefers the girls' hair long and natural."

"But this is a disaster. Make *him* wash it, then."

She gives me a polite tilt of the head. "Oh, it's fine. I don't mind. Really. It's just one of those days. I should get dinner started. The girls will be home soon." She stands, her personality flipping back to supersweet with that creepy, strange calm. "I promise this won't happen in three days when I have to wash it again. The next time will be better." She moves into the bathroom and I hear the door click shut.

She has to do this again in three days? I shake my head.

Dear Life, *please* help Margaret.

I move into the all-white kitchen. Margaret is dressed now, in long, flowy pants and an equally flowy button-up flower-print shirt. Her hair is wrapped in a neat bun as she stands at an island with a white marble top, chopping up something green. Pumpkin is strapped into a high chair watching her iPad peacefully, as if she didn't rain down a special kind of horror-movie-style terror on this house.

I've slipped out of my Curington uniform and am now

in a pair of jeans and a Bob Marley tank top. My new hair tied back with a black-and-white bandanna. One thing about weaves…they hurt and they *itch*. The coolness of the cotton bandanna feels nice and soothing on my head.

"Don't you look so adorable?" Margaret says as I enter. "You're so trendy, Tiff. I love your style."

Margaret seems as cool as a cucumber. Like *Terminator: Judgment Day* starring Pumpkin Stone didn't happen. Nope. She's just…chopping up a salad.

"Now I feel silly getting you those Anthropologie dresses. You're so not Anthropologie. You're more Urban Outfitters. Or Chaser. Or Free People. Oh! I would *love* Free People on you. Their clothes are so you. I hope you let me take you shopping. It's probably my favorite thing to do. How sad am I?"

I decide not to answer that. "What are you cooking?" I sit at a square kitchen table next to Pumpkin, who is so engaged in her iPad it's like I'm not even there. No idea what she's watching. A bunch of bees are doing the hokeypokey. And of course, now I see why Pumpkin's mound of curly hair is so massive. Margaret washes it and lets it air-dry. Doesn't even look like she took a comb to it. Yikes.

"Sautéed kale with a bit of garlic and chopped scallions," she starts. "Turkey loaf and sweet and purple potatoes. Oh, and apple spice bread for a sweet treat after."

"Wow. Do you always cook a lot?"

"I love cooking, yes, and Anthony likes for the family to have variety, so I try to come up with interesting dinners. We have the chef on Wednesdays and Fridays, so I do get a break. Plus, cooking makes for such a nice family bonding time. How was school?"

Margaret is probably the one paying for my school. How rude would that be to tell her I sort of hated it? "It was great."

She beams. "Isn't it a fantastic school? Your father and I *love* it." She pauses and gives me a polite tilt of the head. "Oh, Tiffany, you have no idea what it means to me that you like it there." She sighs. "That makes me really happy."

I nod, happy to make Margaret happy, wondering if it will make her equally happy when Maury Povich declares that Anthony Stone is *not* the father. "Hey, Margaret," I start apprehensively. "Don't you wanna go over to your neighbor's house and tell them exactly where to go?" *Like straight to hell?*

"It's Mrs. Lieberman. Jehovah God bless her. Her husband died last year. Her only child lives overseas. She's all alone in that big house. I don't fault her."

"Really? I'd want to strangle her for calling the cops on me." I put my hand over Pumpkin's iPad to block her view. She looks up and I give her a silly grin.

"Hey!" she says with a dramatic frown.

"Bees don't hokeypokey," I whisper. "They only do the chicken dance. Everybody knows that."

"Wanna play by myself." Pumpkin moves my hand away and returns to watching her show.

I turn to Margaret. "Don't hate me but I Googled autism and hair washing."

She turns to me. "Really?"

"Have you ever done that?"

"Googled autism and hair washing? I can't say that I have." She looks intrigued. "What did it say?"

"Just that lots of autistic kids don't like getting their hair washed because of sensory issues. But I didn't find out what that meant."

"There is *so* much unknown with autism. I'd give anything to understand."

I stand. "I should probably get started on my homework."

"The loft is all set up for you girls to study. London's finishing up her homework at school, so enjoy the privacy."

"Yeah. I saw her. She looked *very* hard at work."

"I don't know how she manages with basketball, volunteering with the church and maintaining some semblance of a social life, but she does it. We're *so* proud of her."

I resist the strong urge to roll my eyes.

"And again, Tiffany, I'm sorry if we startled you. That had to be scary."

"Margaret, you don't have to say sorry to me. *I'm* sorry. I used to say there are no bad kids, only bad parents. I used to judge parents *so* hard when I'd see kids going nuclear at stores and stuff."

"Trust me. We get the evil glares from people when we're out. They think Pumpkin's just out of control. They don't understand she's suffering...and we are, too. But we've made such strides with her. Taking out the gluten and chemicals like unnecessary preservatives from her diet created a big change in her behavior. She's like a different person."

I have a tough time imagining a worse version of Pumpkin. "Does Anthony go out of town a lot?"

"He has been putting in more hours than usual. He's thinking of taking on a partner for his private practice. So many babies. Babies are booming."

"What time does he usually get home from work?"

"Typically around six or seven."

"What time does Pumpkin go to bed?"

"Six thirty."

"Oh. That's gotta suck. I mean…sorry. That's unfortunate. You're with her all day by yourself?"

"Well, he can't help it. He's working. And of course we have the weekends."

I note the defensive tone of her voice. But still, she ends the sentence with a smile.

"No nanny?" I don't know much about nannies, but I always thought rich people had bunches of them.

"Oh, no. Anthony doesn't believe in nannies. Parents should raise their children. It's better that way. But we do have the behavior therapist. She comes every other day. And housekeeping comes Tuesdays, Thursdays and Saturday mornings. It's three women from Melly Maids. They adore Pumpkin and always help out, too."

"Well…hey, if I can ever help. I'm great with kids. At least, I think I am. I can babysit. I can research how to watch her. Take a class or something. Let me know."

"You have no idea how much it means to hear you say that. That you try to understand. You're a…a special girl. Thank you, Tiffany."

Up in the loft, seated at the nice white lacquer desk, in front of a giant picture window that overlooks the tennis court, I write out a plan for tackling my mound of schoolwork, giving each assignment the estimated time I think it'll take me to finish. By my calculations, with a half-hour break for dinner, my homework should be completed by 11:00 p.m.

My new phone chimes and I check to see a text has come through from a Chicago area code. 867-5309: Mind. Blown.

I text back: Who is this?

The response: Xavior X.

Me: How is this your number? You realize that number is a song by Tommy Tutone?

Xavior: :-) I have a friend who works for the phone company who worked it out. Can I call you?

He doesn't wait for my reply because within a second my phone is ringing. I hit the green answer-call button. "Xavior?"

"Tiffany Sly?"

I grin. "In the flesh."

"Okay, so I skipped out on work." He starts with his warm baritone voice. "Went straight to Disco Kings. I can't believe I said the Beatles were just okay! What is wrong with me?"

I lean back in my seat. "Dude. I forgive you for saying that."

"I feel like finding a magic mirror and traveling to wonderland."

"Omigosh, right? If only."

"Next up, David Bowie. I just had to call you and tell you how much I enjoyed it."

Is he for real? He actually left work for *me*? I decide to quiz him. "Favorite song on the album?"

"First song on side two. Something about that sitar."

He really *did* listen to it. Omigosh! "That's George Harrison! 'Within You Without You.' Best song ever, right?"

He laughs. "Maybe second best. Listen to 'Bold as Love'

by Jimi Hendrix. I think *that's* the most beautiful song I've ever heard."

"You're kidding? 'Bold as Love' *is* the most beautiful song. Omigosh. You're seriously awesome, Xavior."

"*You're* seriously awesome, Tiffany Sly and the Family Stone."

"My mom used to call me Sly and the Family Stone. I always thought it was because she knew I like psychedelic music."

"They are known for a sort of psychedelic, soul fusion."

I sigh. "Right. But now, of course, I see the correlation."

Xavior sighs, too. And suddenly a tension reaches through the phone line. "Listen, Tiffany. I know it would shake things up for you. But you are the coolest kid. I hope you turn out to be mine."

His last sentence sort of hangs in the air and a smile stretches across my face. I imagine walking through Chicago Park District with Xavior by my side. The sky would be gray. The air would be cool and crisp. Both of us would have identical acoustics slung over our shoulders. A kid from school would see us strolling by and call out, "Hey, Sly! Who's that guy you're with?"

Xavior and I would exchange knowing looks before I'd shout back to the kid, "Just my dad."

"Tiffany? You still there?"

"Oh, um, I should probably get back to my homework."

"I understand. I'm here for you, okay? Call me anytime. Goodbye, Tiffany Sly."

"Goodbye, Xavior Xavion."

I turn my phone off and log on to YouTube on my laptop.

As I begin the process of tackling my mound of homework, Sly and the Family Stone's "Hot Fun in the Summertime" gives me the sweetest psychedelic serenade.

11

I tighten the straps on my backpack and move through the narrow, oddly quiet hallways toward Geography, so grateful Heaven and Nevaeh were able to convince Darryl to stop at 7-Eleven. I wonder how Margaret would feel knowing her homemade, gluten-free breakfast muesli was washed down with Skittles, glazed donuts and iced coffee.

I step into my geography class. The desks in the back have been slightly rearranged to accommodate our group of three. It's now two desks pushed together to face one another. I head toward the back and slide into one of the chairs. Mr. Mills is at his desk reading. His hair looks wet from the shower and pushed away from his face, which makes it appear darker and wavier than yesterday. He glances up and our eyes meet. Butterflies burst free as he gives me a smile and a nod. I wave. *Uggh.* That was lame. I should've smiled and nodded coolly like he did. That would've been better.

"'Sup, Sly."

I look over to see Aric standing across from me, and withhold a guttural groan longing to burst free. Something about this guy—*uggh*. He gives his signature bang shake and his blond hair falls right back over his bright blue eyes. He plops his foot onto the chair beside me and reties the laces on his black Nike high-tops.

"Hi, Aric." I take my book and supplies from my backpack and set them on the desk.

"Hey, check it. I got a homey. I want us to double-date. You and him and London and me."

"I can't do that."

"Why?"

"Because one, I don't want to, and two, the house I live in has strict rules about dating."

"So lie. London does it."

"London's not allowed to lie."

He holds out his phone. A Facebook photo of him and his African American friend with short, cut hair, leaning up against Aric's white truck, is displayed on the cell. His friend is a dead ringer for a young Idris Elba. What is with this city? Is it a prerequisite to be really, really ridiculously good-looking in order to live here?

Marcus enters, white face and all. Odd how something as simple as white makeup can make a person look so terrifying. Or perhaps it's not the white makeup per se. Perhaps it's the nonconformity that makes Marcus appear so frightening. Like back home, one of the local homeless men in my neighborhood would sing at the top of his lungs and swing around utility poles. I totally wrote him off as crazy. Everybody did. But why *can't* we burst into song on the side of the street? What *is* that thing that makes us follow an unwritten order? And what *is* the thing that makes us label those who don't as…odd?

Marcus takes a seat across from us, unzips his backpack and hands us both individual, typed sheets of paper from a folder.

"The outline," he says softly.

"Thanks for doing it."

"Yeah, no doubt," Aric mumbles in agreement without looking up.

"You're both very welcome."

"Hey," I start as more students file into the class, "wanna sit with me at lunch again?"

"We have early out today."

"We do?"

"School in-service. I'm going home for lunch."

"Oh."

"But you could come with me."

"I wish. I'll have to stick around here. I have basketball practice."

"I can bring you back."

"Really?" I grin. "Cool. It's a date, then."

Aric grunts in annoyance. "What about our date? C'mon, Sly. He's a nice guy. He's funny. He smells good. He's attractive."

I roll my eyes. "Jeez. Maybe *you* should date him."

Marcus laughs.

"What the fuck you laughin' at, clown boy?" Aric snaps. "Fuckin' freak."

"Don't talk to him like that!" I growl. "I wouldn't go on a double date with you, Aric, if a man holding a gun to my head ordered me to. I'd close my eyes and welcome the darkness of death."

"Fine, then, stupid bitch."

I turn to Aric. The Chicago girl in me boiling to the surface. "Call me a bitch again."

Aric laughs. "*Ooh*, I'm so scared."

"Like a said. Call me a bitch again."

"I call 'em like I see 'em," Aric replies smugly. "Bitch."

I ball my right hand into a fist and, without so much as a second thought, connect it with his face.

Blood spurts. "Fuck!" Aric stands and covers his nose with his hands, which instantly become covered with thick, crimson-red blood. Mr. Mills stands quickly, grabs a box of tissues and rushes toward us.

"What just happened?" Mr. Mills holds a wad of tissues up to Aric's face. "Tilt your head back."

Aric follows his orders and tilts back his head. The class is completely filled. All eyes on us.

"Answer me, Aric!" Mr. Mills growls. "What just happened?"

"Nothing," Aric snaps back. "Can I go to the nurse?"

Mr. Mills glares at me. My hand is still balled into a fist but resting at my side. My breath is quick. My heart beating so fast I'm sure everyone can hear it.

"Who saw what happened here?" Mr. Mills asks. But no one makes a sound. He turns to Marcus. "Marcus? Tell me what happened?"

"Aric's nose started bleeding," Marcus replies.

"I can see *that*, Marcus. How did it *start*?"

"Mr. Mills." Aric's voice is mumbled, and since his face is

partially covered with a giant wad of bloody tissues, it sounds like he said "bister bills" instead of "Mr. Mills." "It started bleeding on its own. Now can I please go to the nurse? *Fuck*, man."

The bell rings, signaling the official start of the school day, and Mr. Mills anxiously runs his hand through his thick mane of damp hair. "Fine, Aric. Take the pass. Tiffany? May I see you in the hallway, please?"

A dozen pairs of eyes gaze at me in wonder as I follow behind Mr. Mills.

"You do understand we have a zero-tolerance policy for violence?" Mr. Mills speaks in a hushed tone as we stand alone in Curington's dimly lit hallway. "If at any point Aric decides to swallow his pride and admit you clobbered him in the face, you get *expelled*. You understand expulsion? It means you can't come back. Ever."

This is the stereotype. This is what they expect of me. How could I be so stupid? How could I have let anger allow me to do something so reckless? I want to apologize. Tell Mr. Mills I'm better than this. Beg his forgiveness. But instead, I fold my arms across my chest and shrug, like I couldn't care less.

"Oh, that's no big deal, huh, Tiffany?"

"I didn't say that!"

"You don't have to." He leans his weight on one foot, arms folded across his chest, and rolls his eyes in a typical Chicago-girl, dead-on imitation of me. "Your body language says it all. You're so cool, huh, Tiffany? Whatev, right? Shoot, Aric deserved it. Had it comin'?" He smacks his lips.

I look down at the floor. "I hope that's not supposed to be me."

"Tiffany, look at me."

I refuse.

"Tiffany *Sly*?"

I burst into tears. "I'm *so* sorry," I wail. "I've never hit anybody in my life. I swear I haven't."

"Shh. Don't cry, Tiffany." Mr. Mills pulls me in, hugging me. "Just don't screw up your life because you can't control your rage."

"I don't have a problem with rage. I just have a problem with…Aric. He's an asshole. He was making fun of Marcus. He called him a clown boy."

"Tiffany, you will meet so many assholes in your life. We don't punch them in the face for it. At least, not at school. And trust me when I say that Marcus does a fine job of taking care of *himself*. Shh. Please stop crying, Tiffany. I believe in you. Something deep in my soul says you're quite special. The next time you get an urge to punch a guy like Aric in the nose, take a deep breath, close your eyes and think of me standing in this hallway. Remember that I am going to pretend like I *didn't* see you punch him in the face." He lifts my chin so that I'm staring back into his magical eyes. "Even though I did."

"What?"

"I won't ever admit that again. Understand? I am giving you a chance. Can you remember that? Can you close your eyes and think of me, giving you this chance?"

I nod and wipe my runny nose.

Mr. Mills hugs me again and sighs. "Let's get back to class."

Marcus parks in the handicapped section of one of the lower-level parking lots, which is quite a long walk from

Spanish and down one of those crazy, steep staircases. Though when I hop into his Hummer, I find out there was an elevator.

"An elevator? That would've been a *lot* easier." I glance quickly at Marcus behind the wheel of this giant car. His gloved hands gripping the steering wheel tightly. His green eyes like two bright pieces of Jolly Rancher candies surrounded by thick smears of white makeup.

"You punched Aric in the face."

"Correction. I *tried* to punch him in the face. His nose got in the way."

"I heard it's broken. Everyone knows you punched him, but strangely, no one saw it."

"You saw it."

"I blinked and technically missed it. Aric could've easily got you kicked out of school, you know."

I click on my seat belt. "I know."

"That was pretty decent of him to save you an expulsion. Maybe he's not so bad, after all."

"Please. You think he did it for me? He did it to save his reputation."

Marcus shakes his head. "No. Aric is easily the most popular guy on campus. And he's dating your sister, who is easily the most popular girl. His reputation is pretty much solid. Even a punch from you couldn't mess that up."

I quickly change the subject, a little sick to my stomach that the new black girl from Chicago punched the most popular boy in the face. Way to go, Tiffany. Way to go. "So, I have to read *The Shadow of the Wind*. Like I don't have enough stuff to read."

"I've read that."

"Oh? But have you read it in *Spanish*? Es La Sombra del Viento*, muchacho*."

"Sorry, I don't speak Spanish."

"Me, neither!" He pulls out of the parking lot. "What's with this car? Are we, like, headed into battle?"

"I was rear-ended this summer. My Prius was totaled."

"Yikes. Were you okay?"

"A little whiplash and a dislocated shoulder but nothing serious. My moms panicked. They now feel this is the only 'safe' car until they decide what new car to purchase for me… if any at all."

We move down the mountain road. I stare anxiously out the window as we approach the guard gate. I grip the car door handle and inhale slowly. Hold it. Exhale.

Thump-thump, thump-thump: *You're* not *gonna die in this car…or maybe you* will.

"Would you like me to drive slower? I can." Marcus slows the car to a crawl and I exhale appreciatively.

"I get nervous in cars. Sorry."

"No need to apologize. I do understand."

"Thanks." I stare out the window at the blurred lines on the pavement. "The way you talk. It's so…"

"Proper?"

"I was gonna say…alien."

We move through the gate. "Years ago I learned this: 'If you propose to speak, ask yourself, is it true, is it necessary, is it kind.' That's not my quote, by the way. It's Buddha. Anyway, I began to think before I spoke and I suppose that turned into a new way of speaking. I promise it wasn't intentional. Does it bother you?"

"No way. I should probably think before *I* speak."

"And perhaps before you punch? Remind me never to call you a bitch."

"I would never hit you, Marcus." I groan. "I'm going to apologize to Aric. I hate stereotypes. I don't wanna be that girl. Hey, how come you didn't want to eat lunch at school?"

"I forgot one of my medications. Figured I should head home as early as possible."

"Gotcha." I lean back in the car seat, relaxing. "What's it like winning the lottery?"

"This is what people say about us, yes? That we won the lottery?"

"You mean, it's not true?"

Marcus turns off the mountain road and into fast-moving traffic on the street, though he continues slowly. "My mom and her business partner created a popular line of hair-care products made from natural ingredients. Ever heard of the Kinkiest Kurl Haircare?"

"No way!" I sit up. "I swear by that stuff! I use the hair cream and the oil, and the detangler is the truth. Omigosh. That's your mom's company?"

"Was. She sold it after I died. Went into early retirement. Though they hire her as a consultant before they release new products."

"Being hired by the company you used to own. So cool. What does one major in to do something like that?"

"Organic chemistry. She studied at Berkeley. In fact, my mom was pregnant when she started her freshman year there."

"With you?"

He nods.

"Wow. What did she do when you were born? Take you to class with her?"

"My grandma moved to California temporarily to help her."

"What about your dad? Sorry. If I'm asking too many questions just tell me to shut up."

"I've never met him. Mom met Monique, my other mom, when I was four. She was the company accountant. Still is to this day. At least one of them."

"So you guys winning the lottery? How did that rumor get started?"

"I'm not sure."

"Probably tough for people to believe a black family could have earned a substantial amount of money without lottery winnings. Or without sports or, like...being a drug lord or a rapper. Uggh! Doesn't that make you so mad?"

"It doesn't. The great Zen master Hyakujo Ekai said this: 'When you forget the good and the nongood, the worldly life and the religious life and all other dharmas, and permit no thoughts relating to them to arise and you abandon body and mind—then there is complete freedom. When the mind is like wood or stone there is nothing to be discriminated.'"

"Um, could you translate that?"

"There is no good and bad, right and wrong. It's all relative."

"No offense to the great Zen master. But the Earth is filled with bad people who do wrong stuff. That's a fact."

"Good and bad is relative, Tiffany. Not fact. For example, I don't think you breaking Aric's nose is such a bad thing. Someone was bound to punch him in the face sooner or later. Curington, however, would not agree. See? Good and bad is relative. If God created everything, then God is everything. And life on this plane is simply an experience where you're gifted an opportunity to make choices that define who you desire to be."

"I don't believe in that."

"In what?"

"God."

"Then this should make perfect sense to you. A thing is only bad or good because *we* declared it to be so. Not God. Just like Tuesday is only Tuesday because *we* named it that. Today is not really Tuesday."

"It's not?"

"No. It's simply movement within space."

"You just made my brain hurt."

"Let's talk about something else. Zen master Seng-Chao says, 'The ten thousand things and I are of one substance.'"

"*Oy.* Marcus, stop. You're like a riddle. Wrapped in an enigma. Painted white."

He laughs as we pull up to the gate at our housing community, lowers his window, waves a card over a sensor and the gate slowly opens.

I follow Marcus as he moves into his kitchen. "Lots of food here. Take whatever you want."

I head toward the fridge as Marcus reaches into a cabinet and removes a large prescription bottle among dozens of others. And I thought taking two pills a day was overwhelming.

"Wow. That's a *lot* of medicine. You have to take *all* those?"

"Yes." Marcus sticks the pill on the back of his tongue and swallows with a gulp of bottled water. "You get used to it."

Last time I was here, I only saw the tricked-out garage, so I take a moment to scope things out. It's cozy, similar in design to Anthony and Margaret's place, and seems to have all the fixings you'd expect of these monstrous mansions, including superhigh ceilings, a winding staircase and a large, ornate entryway chandelier. Though their home is way more modern. The kitchen especially. It's got black slate floors, black cabinetry, lit countertops and all these hanging light fixtures that look like works of modern art. Billie Holiday's soothing voice sings the haunting words to "Strange Fruit" through hidden speakers.

"This song is so beautiful." I pull open the fridge. A tray of giant blueberry muffins stands out to me. "Hey, can I have a muffin?"

"Whatever you want."

I grab one, close the fridge and take a seat on one of their bar stools at the kitchen island, inhaling the soothing sound of Billie Holiday's voice. "You know what this song is saying?"

"The strange fruit hanging from the tree? It's definitely not apples."

"Definitely not." I take a bite of the muffin. *Yum.* "Strange Fruit" ends and Nina Simone's baritone vocals echo through the speakers in her version of "I Loves You, Porgy." "Ahhh. Nina and Gershwin. Like peas and carrots. Like Halloween and candy corn."

"You know music."

"Is it obvious?"

"Not too many people can identify Nina Simone and Gershwin. Also, when I first saw you, you had a guitar on your back and a Guns N' Roses T-shirt on."

"GNR? Love them. They have that classic rock 'n' roll attitude, you know."

"What's the classic rock 'n' roll attitude?"

"'Fuck you! We do what we want.'"

"I think you have that attitude, too."

I laugh. "Touché. Maybe that's why I like them so much. Slash on guitar? Always with his hair in his face, top hat, cigarette poking out of his mouth. Tell me that's not the most timeless rock 'n' roll image. GNR *is* rock 'n' roll. I'm rock 'n' roll, too."

"Wow. A black girl who likes rock 'n' roll."

"And a black *boy* who paints his face white." I smirk. "First time for everything, I suppose."

"Touché. Take a look in our living room. I think you'll like what you see."

I set the half-eaten blueberry muffin on the counter and move around the kitchen corner into their living room with Marcus at my heels. The furniture is so eclectic. Giant bearskin rug, pink velvet couch, turquoise chair and an asymmetrical bookcase that looks whimsical, like it should be in Oz. Hung on the walls are six different electric guitars.

"Sick!" I move toward them and study the guitars. My eyes widen. "Marcus, these are *Fenders*. I didn't know you could play the guitar."

"I can't. They're my mom's. Mom #2, that is." He moves to lift one off the hook. Hands it to me.

"No way. For real?"

"Play me a song, Sam."

I scratch my head. "Huh?"

"*Casablanca*? Humphrey Bogart?"

I shrug and Marcus laughs. "We need a movie night." He pushes an antique amp that's set on a rolling stand toward me and connects it to the expensive electric guitar.

"What do you want me to play?"

"Surprise me."

So I do. Playing a rock rendition of *The Marriage of Figaro* that I learned from YouTube. Eyes closed, fingers moving with expert speed and precision. I open my eyes for a second, just to see how Marcus is feeling my musical stylings. He's leaned back on the pink couch, his expression pained, rubbing his chest. I stop cold.

"Marcus?" I unplug the guitar and carefully hang it back on the hook on the wall. I sit beside him. "You okay?"

"Please, don't worry, Tiffany. This is normal. Sorry if it makes you uncomfortable." He sits up and claps, bringing his gloved hands together gently in sincere appreciation. "That was amazing. My mom has never sounded *anything* like that."

I can see sweat forming on his brow. White beads of sweat. He dabs at his forehead with his gloved hand and the makeup smears a bit.

"You sure you're okay, Marcus?"

"I promise." He sits up. "You're very good."

"Thank you. I practice a lot."

"It shows. I have a feeling you're going to grow up and write music. Beautiful music that elevates the world."

A chill rushes up my spine. "How did you know I was a writer?"

"They still poisoning you with leaf water?"

I turn to see Jo. She's got her purse slung over her shoulder and dark sunglasses on top of her head. Wearing a pair of workout pants and a tank top.

"Hey, Jo!"

"Hey, yourself," she says with a smile. "Who taught you how to play the guitar like that?"

I grin. "My mom a little. Mostly self-taught."

"Girl, I thought Jimi Hendrix had risen from the dead. And your hair looks *good*."

I flip it over my shoulder. "Nobody can tell."

"Told ya." She looks over at Marcus. "You okay, sweetie?"

Marcus nods, but Jo makes a beeline for him. She sits on the coffee table across from the couch and yanks off one of his gloves. I'm able to see the brown skin on his hand for the first time.

"Mom, don't."

She ignores him, her two fingers pressed firmly against his wrist. "Heart rate's up, Marcus. Shit."

"I forgot one of my medications this morning."

"It's okay. Don't worry." I notice he's shaking slightly. "Deep breath in… Look at me." She looks into Marcus's bright green eyes and he inhales. "Exhale *slowly*." He exhales and she checks his heart rate again. Shakes her head. "Upstairs now, Marcus. You need rest."

"Mom. Tiffany has to be back at school and—"

"I'll give Tiffany a ride back."

Roaming the halls at school, I can do nothing but think of Marcus. My phone chimes. It's a text from Anthony: Hey, hun. Coach wants to see you before practice. You should go to the gym now. House Three.

I groan and text back: Okay. On my way.

I head for the exit. Basketball practice? *Uggh.*

"Good to meet you, Tiffany." Coach James shakes my hand as I stand on the basketball court across from her in a pair of black shorts and a black Nirvana T-shirt. I pulled my hair off my face with a gray cotton headband. "What are you…five-eleven?"

"Yeah."

She beams, looking me up and down. She's a large lady, dressed in a Reebok tracksuit. Maybe in her early forties. Six feet tall at least and big boned, as they say in Chicago, though here in Southern California, in the land where everyone is pretty and thin, they would probably call her slightly overweight. Her hair is cut short and in that sort of style that is no style at all. A short blob of dishwater-blond hair. I imagine she's the kind of lady that goes to see her beautician and says, "Just cut it."

"I'm not sure if my…Anthony told you. I don't actually play basketball."

"With that height? You'll learn. That's what coaches are for, right?"

I shrug and imagine the blue aliens from *Avatar.* They were tall. Didn't see any of them playing basketball.

"We'll run a few drills before the girls get here. Nothing fancy. See where we're at. Sound good?" She grabs a basketball from a large bin on wheels in the center of the court, positions herself and tosses the ball toward the hoop. It slides through the net silently.

"Grab that ball for me, Tiffany?" I walk toward it, watching as it bounces. She claps her hands. "Faster! Let's see how you run."

I run, catching up to the ball before it rolls past the bleachers. I stick it on my side and let my arm rest on top, already out of breath. Coach James extends her hands in what I'm imagining is the universal basketball symbol for *toss me that ball.* I use both of my hands, swing it under my legs and lob the ball toward her. It soars high into the air and within a second comes back down, about half a foot in front of me. I cover my face as it bounces once and thankfully rolls in the opposite direction. This is senseless! I could've been *maimed.* I hear a giggle and look up in the bleachers to see London and her bears watching with amused looks on their pretty faces. Oh, *no.* I don't want witnesses to this fiasco.

Coach claps again. "Tiffany, my four-year-old throws better than that." She grabs another basketball from the bin and tosses it at me. I catch it clumsily. "Did you see how I did that? I pushed it off my chest. Try it again."

I oblige; thankfully, it lands in her hands. Whew.

"Nice." She tosses it back to me, hard. I cough. "You all right, soldier?"

I nod, still coughing.

"Let's see how you dribble. Start out."

"Huh?"

"Out of bounds. Under the basket." She points to the basket and I move in that direction, resisting the urge to look at London and the bears. This has got to be prime entertainment for them. Coach James claps. "We're not strolling on the boardwalk, Tiffany. Move it!"

I run and make it under the basket, sweaty and breathing *hard*.

"Full length of the court and back." She blows a whistle hooked to a thin black cord that hangs around her neck.

I run as fast as I can while trying to keep the ball in constant motion. It's shockingly easy. The ball feels bouncy under my hands and I'm able to control it with little to no effort, but I hear the shrill pitch of Coach's whistle.

I stop and look up, taking in quick gulps of air, trying to catch my breath and slow my racing heart. I cannot *believe* people do this for fun. "What now?"

"What now?" She grabs a ball and moves toward me, dribbling with one hand. "Tiffany, I haven't seen double dribbling like that since second-grade recess."

"Oh? My bad."

"Your bad is right. And is there something interesting on this court that I'm unaware of?"

"What do you mean?"

She imitates me, dribbling the ball with two hands and staring at the floor. "This is not how we dribble, Tiffany. What if a killer made his or her way onto the court? You wouldn't know it, because you'd be too busy staring at the floor!" Once again, she demonstrates the proper way to bounce a stupid orange ball. One hand, eyes up.

"Got it." I yawn.

"Are you tired, Tiffany?" she asks incredulously as she glances at the time on her watch. "It's been a full *five* minutes, so I can certainly empathize. Try dribbling again."

She blows her whistle and I try again. This time running

and staring straight ahead. Within two seconds, I trip over my own feet and fall. Hard. *Shit!* The ball rolls away.

I look up. I could be wrong, but it looks like one of London's bears is recording me with her phone. Sweat is dripping into my eyeballs, partially blinding me, so perhaps she's only taking a selfie. Yeah, we'll go with that. I stand and turn back to Coach as another ball is hurled my way. "Jesus!" I move out of the way before it hits me in the head.

"Tiffany! Do you think we're playing dodgeball? Catch the freakin' thing." She tosses me another and I catch it awkwardly. It makes the tips of my fingers burn and I imagine breaking both of my hands and having to teach myself how to play the guitar with my feet.

"Let's try shooting." She grabs another ball and moves to the free throw line. "You'll want to get base set, shoulder width apart with your legs, like this."

I note her stance and nod, wondering what time it is and how much longer I have to endure this unreasonable torture. How much longer till Coach James says, *Tiffany, my dear, there are hopeless amateurs and then there's you. Get off my court and make sure I never see your face around here again. You hear me? Out!*

"Legs can be parallel," she continues, "or favor a bit with your left or right foot. Either-or. Whatever makes you comfortable and balanced. Balance is key. Got it?"

I think of Stevie Wonder. I bet he never played basketball. Nope. And look how his life turned out. Oscar. Golden Globe. Emmy. Grammies up the wazoo. Internationally known megastar. I bet he'd say, "Basketball schmasketball, Tiffany, ya dig?" and shake his head to the left and right before bustin' out an a cappella rendition of "My Cherie Amour."

"Are you with me?" Coach James asks.

I nod.

Pop-Tarts.

Gummy Bears.

Rainbows.

Pixy Stix.

"Good. Focus on your target. Reach for the rim and keep that ball on your fingertips. Aim and follow through." She shoots the ball and it swishes through the net and bounces away. "See?"

I do see. She lobbed a ball through a net. Hoo. Rah.

"Now it's your turn, Tiffany."

I take a ball out of the bin. Line up, legs apart…blah blah. One arm in the air…yada yada…dumb ball on my precious, music-making fingertips…and shoot.

The ball soars high and slowly lowers until it moves silently through the net. My jaw drops as the bounce of the ball echoes through the nearly empty gym.

"Will you look at that?" Coach James says, astonished. "You wanna try that again?"

I grab another ball and do the same thing. Once again, it moves silently through the net.

"Again," Coach says.

I do it again. And again. And again. No idea why, but the same thing keeps happening. I keep…making the basket. I remember what Anthony said at dinner. Basketball skills run in the Stone family. Genetic taste in music? Genetic basketball skills? What are the odds? I smile.

Coach James is almost salivating. "Let me get one of my

bears down here." She looks up into the bleachers. "Londy Bear! I need you."

London quickly moves down the bleachers, her long ponytail swaying from side to side. Oversize boobs bouncing underneath her green tank. Her long legs look muscular and supertoned in her shorts, making me realize my bean-pole legs could use some sort of emergency fitness. Stat.

"Tiffany, my varsity starting lineup is Goldilocks, the three bears and the big bad wolf. You're looking at one of my three bears."

Ohhhh. Now it makes more sense. Oh, thank goodness they weren't stupid enough to name themselves that.

"London Bear, I want to see if Tiffany can make these shots with some defense at her front. Nothin' too fancy. Just some standard, white-belt defense. Tiffany, I'm gonna pass you the ball. Your goal is to make the shot. You still with me?"

I'm eyeing London, who is crouched low, arms extended toward me, face intense. This looks serious. What's happening here?

Coach passes me the ball. I grab it with both hands and turn, but London's arms are waving and blocking my ability to take the shot. She easily slaps the ball out of my hands, retrieves it and runs under the basket, tossing the ball in effortlessly.

"All right, London Bear," Coach says. "Take it easy on her."

"I'll try, Coach," London replies.

We do the drill again. Coach James passes me the ball; I turn in to make the shot, and of course London's waving her hands and trying to get the ball from me, so I decide to lunge it at her foot.

"Hey!" she yells, moving her foot out of the way. The ball

bounces; I grab it and take the shot. It rolls around the rim before tipping over and moving through the net.

"Yes! Touchdown."

London scowls. "This isn't football."

"It was a joke, London Bridge. Get a sense of humor."

Coach nods in approval as she grabs her buzzing cell from the pocket of her warm-up pants. "James here." She holds the phone away from her ear. "London Bear, run the drill again." She tosses her another ball and steps a few feet away, turning her back to us to take her call.

London passes me the ball. Hard. I want to flinch but suck it up. Not going to let her think she could ever hurt me.

"Let's go, Tiffany," she says. "No more white-belt defense. Let's see how you do against real ball playing."

I grip the ball and extend with my left hand and London moves to the left, but with the ball extended left, I move right and she lunges out of my way, giving me plenty of time to set up the shot and make yet another basket. *Swoosh.*

"Home run!" I crack a smile. "I thought you said no more white-belt defense?" I bust out a break-dance move, then pretend to brush dust off my left and right shoulders. "Like takin' candy from a baby."

She wraps her ponytail around and around until it's a bun on the back of her head.

"Oh, is that your secret move?" I chide. "Now that your hair is in a bun your basketball superpowers spring forth?"

She grabs another ball from the bin and chucks it at me. I catch it; my fingers burn from the impact yet again.

"Did that hurt?" she asks. "Wouldn't want to hurt your

hands. Then you wouldn't be able to waste your life away trying to make it in the music business."

"How thoughtful of you. By the way, how's your boyfriend's face?"

She's back in position, crouched in front of me, arms extended. "You shouldn't have done that, Tiffany. He could ruin you."

"Oh, I'm shaking in my Air Force 1s." I decide to try the same move, entertained for the first time since this pointless basketball tryout began. Not having learned her lesson the first time, London lunges left and I dribble to the right when her leg extends. To dodge it, I spin around. Pain shoots up my ankle as it twists one way and I fall another. My shoulder slams down hard onto the court. The impact makes me see little white flickers of light around my eyes. This must be what people mean when they say they "saw stars." I scream in pain.

"What happened?" Coach shouts.

I'm writhing on the floor, groaning, clenching my teeth in agony. Coach rushes over and kneels at my side. She reaches out to touch my ankle, which sends excruciating pain through my whole body. I scream again.

"Tiffany, are you all right?" London kneels beside me.

Coach looks at London. "What just happened here?"

"She tripped."

"You lie!" Tears are welling up. Damn it. Stupid tears. "*You* tripped me. On purpose!"

"That's not true," London explains calmly. "Tiffany, I wouldn't do that."

Coach looks up at the bears in the stands. "Girls! Who saw what happened? Right now!"

Izzy moves down the bleachers with Charlie at her heels. Both blondes are dressed in matching green tanks and shorts, hair in high, bouncy ponytails.

"London's telling the truth," Izzy says. "She fell on her own."

"That's her friend!" I shout. "She's lying for her."

Coach looks to Charlie.

"I—I didn't see it." Charlie wrings her hands together nervously. "Sorry."

I cry out again, the pain intensifying.

"You girls get ready for practice. I'm gonna walk Tiffany to the nurse."

"So does that mean you didn't make the team?" Anthony's voice booms through my cell speakers. *Is he serious?* I lean my head back in the car. Darryl turns off the radio and places earbuds in his ears to give me privacy.

"My ankle's twisted. The nurse recommends I stay off it for six weeks. She loaned me crutches and wrapped it. I'm sorry I disappointed you."

"I'm not disappointed." He sighs, clearly disappointed. "Accidents happen. When you get all healed, I'll work with you privately and next year you can try out again. Coach said you showed real promise."

"You're going to make me do this *again*? Why? I hated it."

"House rules say you must play a sport. You have another one in mind?"

"Look, I don't have any sports in mind because I don't play sports. So why are you making me? Jeez."

"Tiffany, we really need to talk when I get back. The way

you speak to me is borderline disrespectful. I won't tolerate that sort of behavior."

"I'm just talking. Voicing my opinion. I didn't realize house rules banned me from saying how I feel."

"Listen, hun, I gotta run. I'll be home tomorrow. Keep it elevated. Ice packs are in the freezer. I'll call Margaret and let her know what happened. We'll talk about appropriate speech when I return."

Appropriate *speech*? "Sounds superexciting. Can't wait."

I hang up and text Keelah. I explain every detail of what happened, including the conversation with Anthony. After I click Send, I delete the message. Within a minute, my phone rings.

"Your phone gets confiscated at night?" Keelah asks, shocked. "Guess you better stop sexting with your imaginary boyfriends."

"Keelah? Seriously?"

"So he's extraprotective. Big what? Stacia's dad started making her wear a uniform to school."

"But we don't have to wear uniforms at West."

"I know. She looks positively insane. See? Your new dad's not so bad. And about your new sis. What if she really *wasn't* trying to trip you, though?"

"You think I'm making it all up?"

"No, no. I'm just sayin'. You're majorly clumsy and basketball illiterate."

"Omigosh! You're siding with her?"

"No. I'm siding with logic."

A text comes in. I check the screen and sigh. *Aric.* "I have to go. I'll call you back, Keelah."

"You mad at me?"

"Can I just call you back?"

"Tiff, wait. I'm on London's Facebook page and there's a YouTube video of you at basketball practice."

I sit up. "I'm sorry…*what*?"

"Tiffany, it's bad. You're falling all over the place and it's scored. There's that circus theme song playing as background music. It's already got three hundred and fifty shares."

"Keelah. You're *lying*!"

"And lots of comments."

"She posted a video of me?"

"It looks like somebody else did it. Isabel Alex? You know her?"

"Izzy Bear? How bad is the video, Keelah? How bad do I look?"

"Put it this way—at the end, you're screaming in pain, laid out on the court, and then it cuts to a monkey screaming in the jungle."

"Omigosh!" Another text comes in from Aric. "Fuck my life, Keelah. I really have to call you back."

I hang up and read the two texts from Aric: My parents want to press charges against you. Is there any way you can meet me at Menchie's Frozen Yogurt so we can talk. Privately.

Fuuuuuck! I respond: What's the address?

He texts back within seconds.

"Hey, Darryl?" I say. "Can we make a quick pit stop at Menchie's?"

12

Aric's sitting at a table. A white bandage covers his nose, the skin surrounding it all black-and-blue. I turn and see Darryl's eyes glued on me, watching me curiously. I wave happily so he thinks I only ran into a friend from school and slide into the chair across from Aric.

"My parents are going to call your dad when he gets back in town," Aric explains.

"Okay."

"You have to say you didn't hit me."

"Look. I'm a big girl. I can own up to what I did."

"No." He looks serious. "You can't. You don't know my parents. They hate black people. They'll sue your whole family. Do *not* admit you hit me."

"They hate *black* people? You're dating a black girl!"

"Right and you wanna know what my mom said when she found out? That I'd be better off gay. And my dad said if I married one of *them*, he'd disown me and cut me out of his will."

"Wow. Nice family."

"Look, Tiffany. Everyone basically knows it was you who broke my nose. And what everyone knows, my parents know, too. When they found out you're black, they flipped. They're already talking to the principal about getting you expelled. But as long as we keep our stories straight there is nothing they can do. You did *not* hit me."

Only I did. Becoming exactly what his parents expect of me. I lay my head into my hands. "Aric, your nose is broken. How'd you explain that?"

"I said I fell asleep and my face fell on the desk."

I look up. "What? You are the world's *worst* liar."

"And you're the world's worst person! You broke my fucking nose!"

"You were being so mean!"

"What? Are we in kindergarten?"

I shift in my seat and glance out the window. Darryl is still eyeing me suspiciously. "We should at least get yogurt. My driver's looking at me weird." I laugh like Aric said something funny, stand and gesture dramatically toward the yogurt stations. "Just play along."

Reluctantly Aric stands. We both grab cups and move toward the line of yogurt choices.

"I won't admit you did it. No one saw it. Just say you didn't do it, Tiffany."

I pull on the silver handle for harvest pumpkin. An orange ribbon of yogurt swirls into my cup. The smell is like sweet autumn and makes me long for Chicago. "Why are you trying to save my ass? I thought you'd *want* me to get expelled."

Aric pulls the handle for cookie dough. I watch as light brown yogurt swirls into his cup and contemplate adding a bit of cookie dough onto mine. Would pumpkin cookie dough be weird? "Trust me, I *do*," he growls. "But London made me promise to fix this."

"You're only doing this because *London* told you to?"

"Yeah. She tells me what to do and I do it. It's called being a boyfriend."

We both move toward the checkout counter.

"Oh, like she told you to go to her church and convert to her religion? Back in Chicago we have this thing. It's called 'be who you really are and see if people still love you.' You should try it."

"I'm standing here, saving your life, and you're trying to lecture me? You think because you're from Chicago you know everything? You think you're better than all of us because you grew up in the fucking 'hood?"

"The whole city of Chicago's not the 'hood, *asshole*."

He shakes his bangs out of his eyes. "Careful, rage machine. You gonna break my skull next?"

I want to scream and shout that I'm not violent. That he shouldn't judge me and the whole city of Chicago based on one dumb punch. But what right do I have? He's the one with the twisted face. So instead I say, "I'm sorry, Aric. I really am."

"Too bad 'sorry' can't fix *anything*. Stick to our story. Got it?" He places his cup of cookie dough yogurt on the counter and slides it next to mine. "Knock yourself out. I'm lactose intolerant." He exits the restaurant.

The loft and crutches don't exactly go well together, so I'm lying on my bed finishing up my homework when someone bangs on the door.

"Come in."

Nevaeh peeks in; her silver braces shine bright as she grins. "I heard you wiped out at basketball practice." She rushes inside and Margaret comes in behind her with an ice pack.

"Mom, I'll take it." Nevaeh takes the ice pack from Margaret and sits on the edge of my bed. "Tiffany. Dude. This is supposed to be elevated." She grabs one of my pillows and sticks it under my injured ankle, then gently places the ice on top. I wince.

Margaret folds her arms under her chest. "I hate that you're injured. You'll miss out on surfing and boogie boarding with the girls in Malibu this weekend."

"I know," I say, faking disappointment. "Being on a board in the middle of the ocean sounds like fun." *Like a fun way to die.*

London bursts through our bedroom door. Her eyes are red. Has she been crying?

"What's wrong, London?" Nevaeh asks.

"My contacts are bothering me." London quickly moves toward her dresser and begins rummaging through her drawers, back turned toward us. Then she slams the drawer shut and spins around. "Can you guys get out? I need to take a shower and get dressed."

"Jeez." Nevaeh frowns. "What's up your butt?"

Margaret clears her throat. "Nevaeh? Language."

"Mom, what's wrong with *butt*? Everybody has a butt. Pumpkin has to know that she has a butt."

Margaret grabs Nevaeh gently by the arm. "Dinner in half an hour, girls."

They exit. Shutting the door behind them.

"What did you say to Aric?"

"What do you mean?"

"Tiffany! What did you say to him? I know you guys met at Menchie's and now he's being crazy weird about my faith. He says he's never coming to my church and won't ever be a Jehovah's Witness."

I sit up and remove the ice pack from my ankle. "Wait... seriously?"

She grabs her hair and pulls at it, completely out of sorts and frantic, pacing around the room. "I can't be with someone who's not a Jehovah's Witness. Not like for real. I don't get it. He's been totally on board this whole time and now he's pulling a one-eighty. You said something to him. I know you did. He wasn't acting like himself at all. Do you like him or something? Are you *trying* to break us up? It's not my fault your ankle got busted at practice. You sucked."

"Actually, Coach said I showed promise. Until you tripped me."

"I didn't trip you!"

I swing my legs off the bed and stand on one leg, leaning against the dresser for support. "Right. I saw that circus video of me on Facebook."

"You saw that?" At this point, tears are streaming down her pretty brown cheeks. She wipes them away. "Tiffany, I swear I had nothing to do with that. Izzy posted it on my page. She showed me after practice and I made her delete it. I got really mad."

"You did?"

"Yes! I wouldn't do that to you. And Dad monitors my

Facebook page. My *pastor* is one of my Facebook friends. Why would I let something like that stay on my page?"

"I'm so sorry. I thought…I thought you had something to do with it."

"Well, I didn't."

"Okay."

"*Okay*. Now what about Aric? What did you say to him?"

"I mean, I might have mentioned something about being who you really are and people loving you for you, but it wasn't specifically meant—"

"I *knew* it! I've been sharing the good news of the Kingdom with Aric. That's our job as Witnesses. He was coming around to it and then you go and say something stupid like *that*?"

"Why is that stupid? It's true! You can't convert everybody. I'm not converting to your religion, either."

"So how is that going to work, Tiffany? We drop you off at another church or something?"

"No church for me."

"You have to go to church. It's house rules."

"London, I don't even believe in God."

She gasps. Covers her mouth with her hands. "You're an *atheist*?"

Shit. Why did I just say that? "Look, I don't like being labeled. I'm Tiffany Sly. That's it."

"If you don't believe in Jehovah, you're an atheist."

"Who is Jehovah again?"

"Infinite Creator. Almighty *God*."

"Oh. No. I don't believe in that sort of thing."

"Where do you think you go when you die?"

"Nowhere. You just die."

She gasps again. "Tiffany, this is really bad. Your eternal *soul* is at stake here."

"No, it's not. Look. You keep working on converting Aric. You will *never* convert me. I won't ever believe in God again. There is no such person. Or man. Or Jehovah sitting up in the sky, granting wishes and counting on us to not fail."

"I'm going to pray for you."

"Pray all you want. I've been there. Praying and praying and let me tell you something I know for sure. Prayer doesn't work. Because if it did, we wouldn't be having this conversation because my mom wouldn't be dead right now!"

"Everybody has to die, Tiffany. You can't pray away death."

"And you can't pray for my salvation. Do *not* pray for my salvation."

She shakes her head in dismay. "An atheist. Seriously, Tiffany? I feel so sorry for you." She turns and quietly exits out the bedroom door.

I slump down onto the bed, that strange sensation rising up again from the pit of my stomach—like a knot has formed deep within my belly and the only thing that will shake it free, so that I don't die, is to curl into a limb-shaped ball.

So that's exactly what I do—assuming the fetal position on the edge of my bed. I close my eyes as silent tears slide down my cheeks. An *atheist*. I've never heard anyone call me that before. Probably because I've never really told anyone, aside from Keelah. It sounds like a bad word. Like I should be offended that someone would dare call me that. But I suppose that is what I am now. I watched Mom die. I watched her shrivel up and die. She fought. She begged. She pleaded. Sure, she went in peace, but she did *not* want her life to end.

She got down on her knees and she prayed and I prayed, too. Grams prayed. All the people at church prayed.

She *still* died.

If there really is a God…fuck that guy.

13

The nurse gave me one of those you-can-be-late-to-every-class passes because of my ankle and new crutches. So for the past two days I've been able to take my time, evading stairs, using elevators and avoiding eye contact with pretty much everyone. But still, I can hear the whispers and the snide remarks. London might have made Izzy Bear take the video down, but so many people must've seen it.

God, did you see that video of her?

I can't believe the school gave her a basketball scholarship. What a joke.

Does that mean she loses it? She should.

It's not fair she got a scholarship, anyway. My parents work overtime to pay for my tuition.

It's affirmative action. That's what my sister says.

And she's sooo violent. She almost killed poor Aric.

Stay away from her. Totally crazy.

Being the new fake affirmative-action-receiving, imaginary-scholarship-losing, basketball-sucking psychopath is the least of my concerns. Because I'm seeing so much red my eyes are crossing. Red ink. Like a pox. Like Mercutio put a plague on all my homework.

Wrong.

Incorrecto.

Please redo and resubmit.

Check minus.

Tiffany, did you read this chapter?

Not so sure you're understanding.

Still, my favorite splotch of red comes from Mr. Brian Mills himself.

Tiffany, come to my office hours. Please. I look forward to it.

I knock timidly on the large oak door to Geography even though it's propped open. Mr. Mills is leaning back in a chair, chomping on a piece of gum, legs resting on his desk, fiddling with an iPad. He brightens when he sees me and sets the device down.

"Tiffany Sly! Yay. You're here. Come in. Come in."

I move into the classroom and take a seat at one of the desks in the front, laying my crutches carefully on the floor beside me. He opens a folder and pulls out a stack of papers. "You did good on the quiz, Tiff."

"Oh? I did?"

He sits beside me, scooting his chair close so we're almost touching. He smells like shampoo and cinnamon chewing gum. Oh, I feel sick from the butterflies. He places the quiz in front of me and I see a giant C+ in red ink across the top.

"Huh? I thought you said I did good?" I rest my head on my hand and take a deep breath to stop myself from crying.

"Maybe you should talk to your parents about a tutor.

That's what the other kids here do. Unless, of course, their parents are doing their homework."

I turn to face him and look deep into his magic eyes. They're hazel. Hazel with tiny flecks of green. But I swear this morning they were green with tiny flecks of hazel. "Parents doing homework?"

"I can always tell when parents are doing their kids' homework. And let me tell you...it's *often*."

"That's so unfair."

"It is what it is. Most of the parents who send their kids here have a specific plan. They'll do anything to make sure their children leave with a great GPA. Great GPA ensures great college. Great college ensures great job so they can make great money to pay for all the great therapy they'll need when they discover that the school of life is the only school where your parents can't do your homework."

"Jeez. Maybe I should get someone to do *my* homework."

"A tutor might be a better option." He hands me a sheet of paper. It's a flyer. "This tutoring company is expensive but they guarantee results." He lays his hand on my shoulder. "Can you see if your mom and dad can spring for a tutor?"

"My mom is dead. I live with my...dad and stepmom. For now at least."

His hand still rests on my shoulder. Are teachers allowed to *touch* students?

"I'm sorry, Tiffany. I didn't know that."

"Cancer. Diagnosed in March. Gone by September."

He sighs. "Again. I'm really sorry. That's so tough."

"Thank you." I take the quiz from his folder and stuff it in my backpack. "I can ask the parental figures if they can spring for a tutor. I'm sure they won't mind. Me not flunking out of Curington is a great cause." He squeezes my shoulder and our eyes lock for a moment. "Um, how'd I do on my Google Earth presentation?"

He cocks his head to the side and gives me an apologetic look.

"That bad, huh?"

"A little disjointed. There were no labels. It wasn't easy to follow. You seemed to be randomly finding points and—"

"Uggh. I get it. It sucked. I'm sucking at life right now."

"Don't be so hard on yourself. I want to give you some extra credit to make up for it."

"For real?"

"For *reals*, girlfriend."

I roll my eyes. "Sorry, I forgot where I was. Let me try that again." I put on my best Valley-girl imitation. "Oh, my gawd, like, totally, Mr. Mills? Like you swearzies?"

"I, like, totally swearzies." He laughs. "Research paper. You pick the topic."

"Something that has to do with geography?"

"Like, duh." He laughs again. "And you can connect anything to geography. Give me a subject. I bet I can connect it and come up with a research-paper topic. Make it a tough one."

"Um. My little sister is autistic."

"Autism and geography? That is a tough one. How old is she?"

"Almost three."

"Cute. Side note—I have a bag of lollipops in my desk drawer if you want to take one and give it to her."

"They'd have to be sugar free, gluten free and organic. My stepmom says when she took away all the fun from her food, her symptoms improved."

Mr. Mills's face brightens. "I got it."

"Yeah?"

"Tiffany, I want you to gather data on autism rates at the California county level. I also want you to gather data on autism rates in another urban region but with predominantly organic food consumption. Like an area of Costa Rica, for example. See if there's a correlation. Are autism rates higher in areas where organic food consumption rates are lower."

"Is there a GIS map involved in this research?"

"You know it! GIS maps changed the world, Tiffany Sly. Get on board." He squeezes my shoulder again. "I'll type up the details of the assignment and send it to your email. No firm deadline. As long as I have it sometime before holiday break. Where's your phone?" I pull my cell out of my backpack and hand it to Mr. Mills. "I'm adding my email address to your contacts. Message me so I'll have yours, too. If you have any questions at all, reach out. Anytime."

He hands the phone back.

"Got it. Thanks."

"And how are things progressing with Aric and Marcus? Any new felonies on your record?"

"Mr. *Mills.*"

"Kidding. Kidding."

"Aric won't really return my texts. We're all supposed to be meeting today. We'll see if he shows."

"He'll come around. You bruised more than his nose, you

know." Our eyes lock again. "I have a strange feeling about you, Tiffany Sly."

I swallow. "What do you mean?"

"I have a strange feeling that perhaps something's going on deep in that brain of yours. I feel this insane, jittery energy. You're here but you're not. Like your bags are in the closet but not unpacked. What gives? Wanna talk about it?"

"Are you my therapist now?"

"Didn't you know? Teachers aren't just teachers. We're therapists, fight breaker uppers, trash taker outers. We're also doormats for parents to walk all over and to scream obscenities at. We do a *lot*. Why do you think they pay us so much?"

I stare at the desk. He's right. I am here, but not. Bags are in the closet, definitely not unpacked. "If you had a secret and it didn't matter if you told the secret or not. Like…it's gonna be revealed, anyway. What would you do? Tell? Or wait for the truth to come out on its own?"

"Depends," he replies quickly. "If the secret was that the world was gonna explode, I'd definitely keep that to myself."

"My world is about to explode in a day. Maybe two. I dunno. I'm losing track of time." I take a deep breath and throw caution to the wind, telling Mr. Mills my entire two-dad dilemma. When I finish, he leans back in his chair and whistles.

"Bad, right?"

"Not necessarily. I have this weird life theory. Everything happens."

"For a reason?"

"Nope. It just happens."

"Nice theory, Mr. Mills," I say sarcastically. "Very helpful."

He laughs. "Let me finish. Everything happens. But it's

how we *react* to what's happening that shapes our experience. If my world was gonna explode in a few days...wanna know what I'd do?"

"What?"

"Just live." He smiles. "Don't forget. An explosion can create an entire universe."

"Do you think Mr. Mills could like me?" I say to Marcus as we exit the elevator and move toward his car in the lower-level parking lot.

"Sure. He likes everyone."

Groups of students move past us in their matching green polos and khakis; a few pause to stare at Marcus, pointing and whispering as he walks slow to accommodate me and my crutches. The bright Simi sun reflects off his white painted face and his gloved hands pull at the straps on his backpack. He's focused on the pavement, ignoring the stares as students pass by.

"No," I whisper. "I mean, like me like me."

His green eyes narrow as we walk. "Not like a cousin?"

I shake my head.

"Well, he is a man. And you are a very attractive girl."

I perk up. "So you think he could?"

"Of course."

I smile. "What if I kissed him? You think he'd kiss me back?"

"That depends."

"On what?"

"On whether or not he likes the idea of prison."

"Marcus, c'mon. You're the one who says there is no good or bad, right or wrong."

"Good and bad is relative. There is, however, what serves you well. Kissing a sixteen-year-old student would not serve him well. Unless, of course, he's itching to be incarcerated."

We make it to his car and my phone chimes. I grab the cell from my back pocket. "Got a text from Aric!"

"Really? He's meeting us?"

"He says he can't meet us and sends his apologies."

"He said that?"

"Actually, he said..." I read the text from my phone. "Yo. My bad. Got plans I can't switch up. Fill me in on the deets." I stuff the phone back in my pocket. "I have an idea."

Marcus pulls a green Curington sweatshirt out of his backpack. He carefully pulls it over his head.

"A sweatshirt, Marcus? It's, like, eighty degrees."

"My phone says eighty-five. What's your idea?"

"Let's ditch schoolwork. Drive me to our beach house. No one will be there yet. We'll have the place all to ourselves for a few hours. Margaret's heading to LAX with Pumpkin to pick up..." I trail off.

"Your dad?"

"Yeah. That guy. Come with me to Malibu. Watch me face my fear."

"What fear?"

"The ocean."

"You fear the ocean?"

"I fear drowning in a tsunami."

"That's oddly specific." He shrugs. "But sure. I can drive you to Malibu. Do you have the address and a key to get in?"

"I do! This is cool. I'm taking good advice. I'm living. The world's about to explode, anyway."

"Explode?"

"Don't worry. I've got time before the big bang."

I hand my crutches to Marcus and he places his gloved hand protectively on my back as I climb carefully into the vehicle.

14

Compared to Anthony and Margaret's house in Simi, the Malibu town house is downright tiny. Still twice as big as our apartment back in Chicago, though, and right beside an awesomely scary pier that reaches far out into the ocean, with restaurants and people fishing and walking. Marcus sets my backpack and crutches on one of the couches in the nautical-themed living room and moves toward the balcony doors. I hold back, hovering uncomfortably near the front door.

"You okay?" Marcus asks.

"Um..."

"Would it make you feel better if I downloaded a tsunami app?"

"They have those?"

He takes out his smartphone and starts fiddling with it. "Yes. If there is an earthquake off the coast of Los Angeles, a deafening alarm will now sound on my phone and I will throw you over my shoulder and race you up the hill to safety." He motions to the balcony. "Shall we?"

I hobble out onto the wood balcony painted white and inhale the fresh scent of turquoise ocean water as Marcus follows behind me. There is a steep staircase from the balcony that leads down to a private section of beach with stacked kayaks, surfboards and lots of kids' beach toys. Marcus leans over the balcony rail. A pack of seagulls circles the white waves before landing peacefully on the golden sands.

"In Chicago, we had a balcony attached to our apartment," I say, my back pressed up against the glass sliding door.

"Is that so?"

"Yep. If you were brave enough to squeeze out the window, you'd have a real nice view of a brick wall. Which sort of pales in comparison to this view."

"Not necessarily. What color was the brick wall?"

He turns to me, green eyes gazing out under the shadow of the hood pulled over his head. His makeup in clumps around his eyes as he squints to block out the bright rays of sun.

"I know you say it makes you feel better. But why? *Why* do you wear white makeup on your face?"

"I'm assuming you haven't read my book yet?"

"Oh. Um..."

"It's okay. I know you haven't read it, because in my book, I explain why I wear the makeup."

"So tell me."

"You don't want to wait and read it?"

"Full disclosure?"

"You're probably not going to read my book. I get it. Why?"

"A book about dying?" I shake my head. "Maybe it scares me a little? I dunno. Also—"

"You don't believe in life after death. I get that, too. Have you always felt the way you do?"

"No."

"But?"

"But then I grew up and stopped believing in Santa Claus and the Easter Bunny and, you know, God." I feel moisture emitting from my eyes. Crying *again*? Why am I *always* crying?

"What would you say if I told you I agree with you?"

I take a tiny step forward and sit on the edge of one of the balcony chairs. "You don't believe in God, either?"

"I do believe in God. Just not the way most people do. I can explain if you don't mind."

I eye him suspiciously. "You sure you're not trying to convert me, Marcus? Like a covert, sneak-attack conversion?"

"'Whether one believes in a religion or not, or whether one believes in a rebirth or not, there isn't anyone who doesn't appreciate kindness and compassion'...and a good conversation in Malibu on the beach." He smiles. "That last part was mine."

"And the first part? Lemme guess. Confucius? Buddha?"

"The Dalai Lama."

"All right, O wise, proper alien. I'm all ears."

Marcus leans against the rail to face me. "See, the God that I believe in is similar to energy: without form, indestructible, around all things and existing *as* all things. Let me simplify. May I use you as an example?"

I nod. "Sure."

"You are Tiffany Sly. But who is Tiffany Sly?"

"Just about the coolest girl ever in life. From Chicago."

"Modest. Let's make you more finite. Name something you like."

"I like rain."

"Why?"

"It rained a lot back home."

"What did you do when it rained?"

"We stayed inside if we could. Mom and I would make hot cocoa and cookies and watch the rain from the apartment windows. Curl up with a blanket and watch a movie. I dunno. Different things."

"Sounds like rain created feelings of family and togetherness for you. That's an experience. Experience is consciousness. The God that I believe in is infinite consciousness. *You*, Tiffany Sly, are a spark of consciousness."

"Not sure I'm following. Are you saying I'm a part of God?"

"I'm saying you *are* God. Just like energy is everything in different forms. God is everything in different forms. Therefore... you are God."

"*What?* No. If I was God, I would flick my Godly finger and make the world a better place."

"But it seems God became Tiffany Sly, not to wave a Godly finger and make the world a better place, but to bake cookies and watch the rain from a Chicago apartment window."

"Why would God want to bake cookies and watch rain?"

"In short? To experience it. God is always growing and expanding because God is always having new experiences. As Marcus McKinney, as Tiffany Sly and so on and so on."

"But, Marcus, some people are experiencing some pretty awful stuff. What do you have to say about that?"

"That there is no awful. That it's only awful because *we* said it was awful. And in that case...we should change it. Every one of us has the ability to wake up and realize we're God. Tell me—when did God ever come down beside you and physically do something for you?"

"Never."

"*You've* been creating all this time. In so many ways, you are the God you seek. And your power to create and manifest is much more amazing than you're currently aware of. Because remember, you are only a spark of consciousness known as Tiffany Sly and in this experience you don't realize your potential."

"But we all *die*. I mean, if what you're saying were true, we could just keep on living to have new experiences. There'd be no reason to die."

"The body *has* to die so that we can move on."

"To what?"

"What else? A new experience. Becoming brand-new is the only way to truly experience brand-new consciousness. Start from scratch. You really should read my book."

"Ahh, yes. *The Boy Who Lived Before.* The book that's gonna land you on the cover of *People* magazine doing this..." I strike a dramatic pose. "And make you as rich as your mom."

"No, it won't."

"Sure it will. Those 'to heaven and back' books always become bestsellers."

"After I died, so many publishers wanted my story. But only one was willing to acquiesce to my somewhat unorthodox demands. The ebook will be a free download."

"Free? Then how do they make money?"

"There'll be printed copies, too. But the digital edition will be available as a free download on the publisher's website for those who can't afford to buy it."

"You never fail to amaze me, Marcus McKinney slash God."

"Tiffany, I should go."

"Whoa. Wait—why? Did I offend you? I was only kidding calling you God. And I haven't even conquered my fear. I haven't made it onto the sand yet."

"London's here."

I turn and look through the balcony windows into the empty town house. "That's impossible. She's at basketball practice."

"She's here. She's been here the whole time, I believe. You should go check on her."

"What?" I stand and limp through the balcony doors. Sure enough, I can hear the distinct sound of someone throwing up coming from down the hall.

My brow furrows. I turn to Marcus as he steps inside.

He responds as if reading my mind. "I saw Aric's truck leaving as we were approaching. I figured she might be here. But I only just heard her. You should go check on her."

Before I have the chance to come up with a response or even say goodbye, Marcus has quickly moved across the living room floor and within a moment he's gone. The front door to the town house shuts after him.

I grab my crutches off the couch, move down the narrow hallway and push into another Pottery Barn bedroom that I assume all of us girls will share. There are two sets of white bunk beds but they're built into the wall, so there's lots of space in the bright, sunlit room. One of the beds is stripped of all bedding. A plush comforter and sheets are piled into a messy heap on the floor beside it. I hear a heave followed by a splash of what I imagine is puke hitting toilet water. *Gross.* The bathroom door is slightly ajar, so I move toward it, crutches in tow, pushing through to see London on her knees, holding her hair back with one hand as she vomits into a toilet.

"Omigosh. Are you okay?"

"Can you…please…get out?" she mutters between gags.

"No practice, I'm guessing?"

"I left after first period." She lets loose again. More vomit splashes into the toilet. I cover my nose and extend my foot forward to flush. If you're going to be knelt over a toilet, fresh toilet water is essential.

I turn to leave and notice a hint of gold foil in the garbage can ripped down the center. Mama didn't raise no fool. I recognize it immediately and spin back around. *"London?"*

She grabs the small trash can and pulls out the bag, tying it shut.

"Get *out*!"

I exit.

When London emerges from the bathroom, she finds me sitting on one of the bunk beds. Arms crossed. Waiting. Her forehead is covered in beads of sweat, face flushed.

"I know Aric was here," I say.

She bursts into tears.

"Did you guys have sex?"

"I didn't want to do it." She leans against the wall across

from me, still crying her eyes out like a little girl. "I'm so ashamed of myself."

"Why did you do it, if you didn't want to?"

"I convinced him again to come to church with us." She wipes her nose with the back of her hand. "But in order for him to go, he said I had to prove I could make some sacrifices for him, too. So I did it."

"He's awful!"

"It's your fault!" she cries. "You're the one who talked him out of joining our church in the first place."

"Oh. Seriously? You deciding to have sex with Aric is somehow my fault?"

She slumps down onto the floor and I wait for her to stop crying. No. It's worse than crying. It's like the "weeping and gnashing of teeth" they speak of in the Bible. Red faced, snotty, ugly wailing. Even a girl as pretty as London can't look good in this sort of state. When she finally calms, she yanks off her Curington polo and tosses it in a far corner of the room. "I hate that thing." She runs her fingers through her hair, damp from sweat.

"London, don't beat yourself up about this. You're not going to die and go to hell because you had sex."

"Jehovah's Witnesses don't believe in hell."

"Well...great. Then ask for forgiveness and all is well."

"You don't understand. There's more."

"Is there a place worse than hell? Do you guys get buried alive if you sin or something?"

"No, Tiffany. When Aric took the condom off it was split."

"The condom *broke*?"

"I'm going to the pharmacy to get the morning-after pill.

You can get it over the counter now. But I'm going to a drugstore far away. Maybe Los Angeles. So no one will recognize me or see me. People know us around here."

"And how are you getting there?"

"I'm taking an Uber."

"Why can't Darryl take you?"

"Darryl's a snitch. He'd let Mom and Dad know. They don't know I'm here."

"What about a friend? Izzy or Charlie could take you?"

"Charlie doesn't drive."

"Izzy?"

"We're not speaking. We got into a fight about that video of you. I thought it was rude and *racist.* A monkey at the end? I may never speak to her again."

"She's your best friend. Don't do that." I sigh. "But thanks for sticking up for me, though. I feel bad. I thought for sure you had something to do with that."

"I can see why you'd think that."

We sit in silence for a while. "Hey, what about Marcus? He can give you a ride and then I can go with you. He was just here. I bet he's not even that far away."

"Crazy-faced Marcus *McKinney*? Are you friends with him now or something?"

"Yes, he's my friend. And at least you know he's not gonna murder you. You don't know anything about some random Uber driver. With Marcus and me with you…you won't be alone. I'm texting him now."

I pull out my phone: SOS. Need a ride to LA. Can you bring your war-mobile back?

A moment later he texts back: I'm still out front. Haven't left yet.

He knew. Somehow he *knew* not to leave. I text back: Be out in a second.

"He says he hasn't left yet. C'mon. Let's go."

I can tell the idea of not being alone is appealing to her. Even if it means being with the sister she's not exactly fond of and crazy-faced Marcus McKinney.

"I wish I was like you."

"I'm sorry?"

"I mean, your mom died. And you seem so okay. You're strong. If Mom died, I'd be a mess."

"Oh. I *am* a mess."

"You seem fine."

"Can I confess? Promise not to judge me?"

She nods.

"This isn't my hair."

Her jaw drops. "No way."

"It's a weave. I have alopecia. It happened when my mom was going through chemo and radiation. My real hair is all jacked up now. Bald patches and…disaster-zone hair. So Marcus's mom gave me a weave."

"Shut *up*. Can I touch it?"

"Sure."

She stands and sits beside me on the bed, feeling the tracks on my head. "Whoa. That's amazing. It looks real."

"It doesn't feel real. It feels like an itchy, uncomfortable wig. Don't tell on me."

"Um, giant glass house right here. Not throwing stones. Your secret is totally safe with me."

"And yours is safe with me."

"Thank you, Tiffany."

"I also take medicine for anxiety and OCD."

"Why?"

"I have 'irrational fears.' Wanna know the first thing I thought when I saw the ocean?"

"What?"

"If a tsunami comes, we're all dead. In fact...I'm still thinking it."

"But if a tsunami came we *are* dead." She laughs. The laughter quickly melds into full-on sobs. I put my arm around her and she leans her head on my shoulder.

"Don't cry, London. It's okay."

"I love him. But I feel so *dirty* now. I'm a failure."

"Failures don't get straight As at the hardest school in the *universe*, volunteer with their church, play on basketball teams and look like Victoria's Secret supermodels. Sorry. Not buying failure. Thank you for playing. Please deposit twenty-five more cents."

"Tiffany, I have failed. Sex is supposed to be between two people who have taken a vow of marriage. I let my family down. My pastor. Jehovah. Everybody."

"London, there are billions and billions of people on this planet. Do you know how they all got here? Two people had sex. Sex is nothing new. The animals do it and they never get married. Can you imagine two lions signing paperwork before they did the deed? How weird would that be?"

She turns to me. Her eyes bright with curiosity. "Have you had sex before?"

"I have. Yeah."

"Really? You had a boyfriend back in Chicago?"

"No. He was my friend. At least, I thought he was my friend, the stupid jerk. I was feeling pretty tore up about Mom dying and he sort of took advantage of that. One of the worst days of my life."

"Today is *the* worst day of *my* life. I wish I could take it back. Undo what we did."

"The feeling goes away. Eventually you forgive yourself."

"How long did it take you?"

"When you see somebody you love more than anything lying in a casket and you know they are never coming back... most things seem sorta trivial after that."

"I'm so sorry your mom died, Tiffany. But you know I believe you could see her again. I believe there is life after this."

I nod. "Yeah. I know you do."

Marcus's giant black Hummer is parked on a side street. I'm still dressed in my Curington uniform but London's slipped into jeans, a black sweatshirt with a hood pulled over her head like Marcus and giant black sunglasses. Like she's about to go rob a bank or something.

I'm instantly comforted once we step into the quiet serenity of Marcus's car. As if he's our protector, here to make everything all right. London must not feel the same peace of mind because she clicks on her seat belt and slumps her head onto the car window, bawling her eyes out once again.

"Hi. Again," I say to Marcus.

Marcus gives me a polite nod. "Where to?"

I turn to London from the front seat. "Where should we go?"

"Let's try Santa Monica." She sniffs. "A random drugstore

in Santa Monica. In one of the gross areas. No one will know me there."

"Santa Monica it is," Marcus says without so much as a quizzical look as to what's happening and why we're headed to a "gross area" of Santa Monica.

Kudos to Marcus for knowing the gross areas of Santa Monica. For starters, it *stinks* here. Like rotten eggs and hot garbage. And the ocean water is a deep, muddy brown with tiny bits of colorful trash crashing in with the brown, foamy waves. There are homeless men and women asleep on benches or pushing around shopping carts stuffed with assortments of junk. And pigeons. Pigeons and their pigeon poop are pretty much everywhere. This place is disgusting! Santa Monica Beach gets lots of *incorrectos* and a giant red check minus in my book.

"I'll go in by myself," London mumbles.

"You sure, London?" I ask.

She doesn't respond. Only pushes open the door and exits the vehicle. Within a moment we see her crossing the street and entering the drugstore.

"How come you're not asking why we're here, Marcus?"

"Because it's none of my business."

"But don't you want to know?"

"Not particularly."

"But you *do* know why we're here? Don't you?"

"I suppose I do."

"You're psychic, huh?"

"Tiffany, it doesn't take psychic awareness to put two and two together. A trip to a random drugstore in Santa Monica with me as your chauffeur? Aric driving away as we were pulling up to the house. London's nonstop crying in the back seat."

"Uggh. Their condom broke."

He pulls at his white gloves and gazes out the front window. "Sorry to hear that."

"Do you think the morning-after pill is wrong? It's not like she's getting an abortion. She can't be pregnant in a couple of hours."

"You already know how I feel about right and wrong."

"Oh, don't remind me. Nothing's right. Nothing's wrong. We can all do whatever we want and act like lunatics. The great Zen master says so himself. But what about...I dunno... world hunger?"

"What about it?"

"That's obviously wrong and bad."

"If you think it's bad, do something about it."

"Like what? I don't have any money to end world hunger. I'm broke as a joke."

"Start a GoFundMe page."

"I can't. I have to read *The Shadow of the Wind* in Spanish."

"Ahh, yes, the hungry children of the world understand. It's a good book."

I see London step out of the drugstore, head hung low, clutching a small plastic bag and a bottle of water. She rushes across the street and within a moment is quickly climbing into the back seat of Marcus's Hummer.

I turn to her. "Everything okay?"

She slides off her sunglasses and nods. "Home. Back to the beach house. *Please.*"

★★★

The ride back is somber. Like we're at the head of a funeral procession. London hasn't stopped crying and all Marcus and I can do is be a captive audience to her misery. Traffic is moving fast, but Marcus drives a little below the speed limit; cars whiz past us in a blur of motion. A car length ahead of us, two semis speed along side by side on the freeway. I watch in irritation. When one speeds up the other truck drives faster.

"What are they, drag racing?"

"I'm sorry?" Marcus replies.

"Those trucks. They're not supposed to do that, are they? Drive side by side like that?"

Suddenly, one of the semis weaves into our lane. The large, rectangular trailer attached to the truck wobbles dangerously as the truck swerves. I scream.

"Marcus! Look out!"

Marcus slams on the brakes as the truck's trailer slowly begins to topple over onto its side. It's an explosion of debris; cars everywhere attempt to dodge out of the way as the truck makes impact with the pavement. I close my eyes as Marcus spins the steering wheel and the Hummer twists around until it tilts on two wheels, lifting off the ground.

I scream and everything turns to darkness. And in the darkness I hear a smooth, soft voice.

"Tiffany?" the voice murmurs. "Tiffany, sweetheart. Open your eyes."

15

"Tiffany, open your eyes," Mom demands.

So I do.

I'm standing with my back pressed up against the wall. Back in my old apartment in Chicago. Watching...*me*. *Younger*-me.

I cover my mouth in awe as I observe the scene. I *remember* this day.

Mom wipes her tears with a paper towel. Her bald head is covered with a pretty scarf and she wears pajamas. "Tiffany, are you just gonna sit there with your eyes closed?"

"If you're gonna cry, you should be in the designated cry room. Those are the rules," I state simply, arms folded, lips pursed in a tight scowl, eyes clenched shut.

"Can we suspend the rules for today, Tiff? Would that be okay?" Mom asks.

Younger-me opens her eyes slowly. They're red and swollen.

"I don't mind moving into the hospice. It's time."

"That means you're done fighting. People go to hospice

to die! We can keep trying." I look so desperate, so strangely young. But this was only a few months ago. I couldn't have aged all that much in a few months, could I have? Yet, for some reason, staring at young-me feels as if I'm staring at an entirely different person.

A little girl.

"Tiffany, the tumors have doubled in size and now there's one in my brain and two in my lungs. I can't do another round of chemo and radiation. I'm too weak. I'm dying."

"Mommy, *no*." I cover my mouth with my shaking hands. "Please don't give up. We can try other things. I—I read online there's this, um, this cancer center in South Africa. People get cured there. I read all about it."

"Tiffany, we don't have any money. Baby, I'm so tired…" She trails off.

I swallow the giant lump in my throat and I see young-me swallow the lump in hers.

"Grams is not equipped to finish raising you," Mom goes on.

"What do you mean she's not equipped to raise me? I'm already raised."

"Tiffany, please. Your grandma doesn't drive. She's got bad arthritis. She's seventy-eight years old. We talked long and hard about it, and both of us agree—the best option for her is to move into an assisted-living community."

"Assisted living? Oh, awesome. Sounds like a blast. Hope she has fun. And where do I go? An orphanage? I mean, what the hell is going on right now?"

"Tiffany, please watch your—" Mom trails off again, as if not only is she tired of living, she's tired of parenting and, in fact, couldn't care less that I just said *hell.* "It's already been decided. You're going to go and live with your father."

"The *sperm* donor? The file at the Chicago sperm bank? I'm gonna live in a folder?"

"There's something you need to know, Tiffany." Then Mom does the most bizarre thing. She looks at me. Not young-me. *Me.* Standing off to the side, watching. She smiles. "You need to know that everything is going to be okay. *Everything.*"

I open my eyes.

We're alive. The Hummer is facing dead-stopped traffic.

London wails in the back, screaming her head off as smoke fills the air outside. She pulls on the car door handle. "Let me out! Let me out!"

"You can't get out!" Marcus bellows with the first real emotion I've seen him display. "Stay in the car! You have to stay put."

I turn to catch a better look at the semitruck. It's on its side, smoke rising from the engine, trailer banged up and toppled over. We don't exactly seem to be a safe distance away from it, from what I can see.

"It's Jehovah God!" London's hysterical. "He's mad at me. He's punishing us!" She thrashes in the back seat in what I'd call beyond hysteria. Insane. London's gone insane.

Marcus calmly unhooks his seat belt and climbs into the back seat. He flings off his gloves and takes London's hands in his, massaging her hands slowly. Tears still stream down her face, but she begins to calm. Mesmerized by the calming effect Marcus is having on London, I, too, begin to calm, watching in fascination.

"I haven't been very nice to you." London wipes a fresh flood of tears. "How can I worship Jehovah God and not even be nice to my very own neighbor? Please forgive me, Marcus."

"No need to forgive," Marcus replies softly. "I was never hurt or angry."

A bang on the door startles us all. We turn to see a firefighter outside the car window.

"I need you to evacuate the vehicle!" he says seriously.

We push open our doors.

It's six o'clock when the truck is finally towed off the freeway and we're able to continue home. By the time we make it back to the beach house, the sun is beginning to set, transforming the sky into a blend of orange and purple streaks of color over the majestic Pacific. The beautiful serenity of Malibu seems an odd juxtaposition to the morose energy in the car.

"We have to call the hospital." London breaks the silence. "To make sure that truck driver is okay."

I nod, even though I saw him when the paramedics took him away. Barely moving, face streaked with blood, eyes clenched shut. Dead for sure.

"And we all agree," she adds. "We never tell our parents what happened."

"I won't say anything," I declare honestly.

Marcus nods as London leans forward and places her hand on his shoulder. "If it weren't for your excellent driving skills...who knows what would've happened to us. Thank you, Marcus McKinney."

"You're very welcome, London Stone."

The prodigal "dad" has returned. He's wearing a pair of brown cargo shorts with loafers, a brown T-shirt and a dark vest. He's also wearing a scowl. He looks thoroughly pissed when he, Margaret and Pumpkin push through the front door of the small beach house. Pumpkin's screaming her head off, which...seems like normal Pumpkin behavior at this point.

"I'm sick of it!" he bellows.

Margaret looks flustered in her pretty purple sundress and sandals, hair loose, grazing her shoulders, looking prettier than I've ever seen her look. She nods in agreement. "I understand, honey. I do."

"Our lives are being terrorized by a two-year-old!" I pull my legs under my chin and hope they don't notice me sitting on the lounge chair on the balcony, staring out at the black ocean waters under the light of the moon.

"She's a bully! A baby bully."

"She's *autistic*, Anthony. Sometimes it seems like you forget."

"On the spectrum. Not the same thing. And she still needs discipline. She gets a free pass to be terrible? An iPad out the window! A six-hundred-dollar iPad reduced to freaking freeway scraps!"

"What if we got more help?" Margaret asks, setting the screaming toddler down. "I checked with a few nanny agencies and they have autism specialists. Some are live-in."

"A live-in nanny? Are you kidding me? She needs a spanking, not a live-in nanny."

"You get spanking!" Pumpkin screams. "Bad behavior!" She stands and makes a lunge for Margaret, tiny hands balled into fists, but Anthony's too quick for her. He snatches her up by one of her arms.

"You're getting a spanking, Pumpkin! Upstairs. Now!"

"Nooooo!" she howls as he drags her upstairs kicking and screaming. I hear a door slam and more screams followed by silence.

Oh, shoot. Did he kill her?

Margaret begins pulling food from the fridge and Anthony returns. "Is she okay?" she asks with an annoyance to her voice I've not heard before.

"She's lying down on our bed. I whipped her butt."

"She lacks reasoning to understand why she's being spanked."

"She calmed down, didn't she?"

"But she thinks you spanked her because you were mad. 'Daddy's mad, so he spanked me.' She doesn't think, 'I threw the iPad out the window, *therefore* I got a spanking, *therefore* I should not do something like that again.'"

"What should I have done, then?"

"The class I took says it's better to let them calm down, *then* discipline. Perhaps it would serve you well to take a class, too."

"I refuse to let a bunch of wannabe-experts tell me how to raise my kid. And what's wrong with London? I got a voice mail from the school that says she came home sick after first period."

"Oh? I didn't know she left. I assumed she was at the scrimmage game with Heaven and Nevaeh."

I quickly stand and hobble inside from off the balcony. "It's food poisoning. Hi. Sorry. I was asleep on the balcony when I heard you guys talking about London. I got it, too. Lots of us were throwing up at school today."

"Hey, Tiffany, hun," Anthony says.

"Hey..." Dad. *Just say it, you fool!*

"I should call the school and complain." He's angry again.

"No, no. It wasn't the school. It was...Izzy. She brought sushi from home and we all ate it and...yeah. We got sick."

He frowns. "What kind was it?"

Crap. I've never had sushi before. "It was raw."

"That goes without saying, Tiff. What kind of fish was it?"

"Duh. Right." I slap my hand across my forehead. "It was...gray."

"Was it eel?" Margaret asks.

"Yep. Eel." *Ewww.* Raw eel? People eat that? Supergross.

He moves toward me, touches my forehead and looks in my eyes. "You don't feel warm. Any blurry vision?"

I shake my head.

"How's your stool?"

"It's...normal...now. It was diarrhea-ish."

"Diarrhea-ish? What is that?"

"You know...like...an explosion of...poop."

He grabs my arms, massaging them. "Any tingling? Numbness?"

"Nope. I feel good."

He squeezes my cheek and bops my nose. "Lots of water today. I don't want my daughters taken out by bad fish."

"Got it."

Margaret steps forward. "Tiffany?"

"Yes?"

"You'll never guess what I did today."

"Drove to LAX?"

She smiles. "I washed Pumpkin's hair. And guess what? Not one scream."

"No *way.*"

"I did some research based on what you said and discovered it's the water in her ears that changes the way she hears. Total sensory, like you read online. That's what makes her so scared. So I used a plastic cup. Let her sit up the whole time and poured the water over her hair that way. Her ears never got wet. She didn't scream. Not once."

"So cool, Margaret."

"Pumpkin screams when you wash her hair?" Anthony asks in a clueless fog.

"Not anymore," Margaret replies. "And there's a class at the regional center, Tiffany. December 12. I signed us both up. You still want to learn, right?"

"Absolutely, Margaret. I can't wait."

"I was thinking you and I could go and have breakfast together," Anthony adds like a rapid-fire afterthought. "Tomorrow? There's this awesome spot right on the water."

"Like a floating restaurant?"

"Not literally floating. Right on the edge. And I think it should just be you and me. Give us a chance to get to know one another."

I swallow. The thought of time alone with Anthony Stone is making my cheeks twitch and my palms sweaty. "Uh. Okay."

"And do me a favor, Tiffany? Next time one of London's legally blonde friends offers you rotten eel, say no thanks."

"Yes. Good idea."

"I'm going to check on her."

I send London a quick text: You ate rotten eel.

She texts back: Got it. Thank you, Tiffany.

16

Saturday morning I wake to a wretched knot in my belly, desiring nothing more than to curl my long limbs into my favorite position and stay that way all morning into the afternoon and evening. But the fetal position will have to wait. I have to take a shower...get ready for a private breakfast with Anthony. *Uggh.*

Heaven and Nevaeh are still wrapped up in blankets. Their cacophony of synchronized snores makes me grateful I'm sharing a room back home with London instead of them. I'd never get any sound sleep with these two growling bears. I sit up and swing my legs out of bed, immediately noticing my ankle has returned to its normal size. Cool. I stand, pulling the drawstring on my flannel pajama pants, pleased to discover no need to wince in pain. Even cooler. Maybe I can ditch the crutches if I'm careful. I look up to peek in on London. She's awake in the top bunk, staring up at the ceiling.

"Hey," I whisper.

She turns to me. Eyes red like she had an early-morning crying sesh. “I didn’t take the pill.”

“Say *what*? Girl, why not?”

“Because,” she whispers, “I heard the message from Jehovah loud and clear. It would be the wrong thing to do. I don’t want to make any more mistakes. I have to make this right.”

“By having a baby?” I shake my head. “London, be reasonable.”

“If that’s what Jehovah wants, that’s what will be. I’m ready to accept responsibility for my actions.”

I stand beside the bed, baffled by the hold her religion seems to have over her mind. “So are you going to tell…your dad? Does Jehovah want him to know you had sex with Aric?”

She climbs out of bed in nothing but an oversize T-shirt, flashing me her bright pink underwear. She grabs me by the hand and pulls me into the adjoining bathroom, shutting the door quietly and turning on the overhead fan and light.

“Why would I tell him anything?”

“I dunno. I thought you’d lost *all* sense of logic and reason.”

“I wouldn’t tell him. Like, he has room to talk about morals and right and wrong? He sucks so bad sometimes.” She turns toward the bathroom sink and grabs a hair tie from off the counter, pulling her hair into a ponytail on the top of her head. Underneath the early-morning Malibu sun rays that peek through the bathroom windows, London’s hair looks like spun silk, hanging down her back in soft waves. I’d *kill* for that hair. “How can you even stand him, Tiffany?”

“I barely know him.”

“Wanna know how he told me about you?”

“How?”

"A note. He typed up a note and slipped it under my door."

"I'm familiar with his typed notes."

"Mom cried for weeks after she found out about you."

"That sucks."

"Yup." She grabs her toothbrush and squeezes a glob of toothpaste onto the brush. "She would run bathwater so we wouldn't hear her, but I heard her. Everybody heard her." She brushes her teeth and rinses her mouth out with the running sink water. "And…" She places her toothbrush back in the holder; the scent of mint fills the small space. "I know for a fact he's pressuring her to have another kid."

"What!"

"Yep. I heard them arguing about it months ago."

"Maybe they can have yours."

"Tiffany! Don't *say* that."

"I'm keeping it real. Girl, you got twenty-four hours to take that pill. Don't take it and you and Aric could end up having a very pretty, screaming baby with long blond bangs that it'll have to keep shaking out of its eyes."

"Tiffany? Stop it. You're scaring me."

"Take the pill."

"What about Jehovah? The car accident? That was a sign."

"A sign that bad drivers cause car accidents."

"But I read about the pill. It makes you really sick. It's not good for you."

"I read about babies. They make you sicker. They're not good for you, either."

She reaches under the bathroom cabinet and pulls out a box of Kleenex. She digs underneath the tissues and retrieves the

Plan B box from the pharmacy, removes the pill from its foil containment and tosses it into the trash can.

"London!" I cry. "Why did you do that?"

"I know you're an atheist, Tiffany, and I don't even wanna talk about how scary that is, but when Jehovah God speaks to *me* like He spoke yesterday, I listen. You should, too. He was speaking to you, too."

I snatch the box from her hands, kneel over the trash can and fish out the pill.

"Tiffany, what are you doing?"

"You've got twenty-four hours from the time the condom broke. There's still time. You can change your mind. I'm hiding this in case you do." I turn to exit the bathroom and London grabs my hand.

"Tiffany, wait."

I turn back. "What?"

"When Marcus held my hands… I can't explain it. It's going to sound crazy. But I felt this strange sensation."

I raise an eyebrow, intrigued. "What do you mean?"

"Like an energy. Like I was absorbing it from his skin or something. I felt so at peace. I've never felt like that before. Have you ever *touched* him?"

"Can't say that I have. No."

"There's something weird about him, Tiffany."

"Oh, not this again."

"Not weird because he wears all that crap on his face. What if he's an angel or something? Maybe that's why he paints his face white. I'm telling you. Touch him. You'll feel it, too."

"Well…I did feel something *kind* of weird. Right after the crash. It was like I passed out and I was back home and my mom was telling me for the first time that I was coming to live here."

"Really? Do you think you were dreaming?"

"Maybe. But it felt so real. You know, I think I agree with you. About Marcus, I mean. There is something about him. Something special. Something magical."

It's a beautiful, sunny Saturday morning as Anthony and I hop into his fancy Audi, though what type of Audi I can't be sure. I'd need Keelah to tell me and I'm too uncomfortable to ask. We're still in that awkward phase. I can tell he feels the awkwardness, too, because he's been clearing his throat and pulling at the short strands of wavy hair on his head every fifteen seconds or so.

"This is nice, huh?" The garage door slides open and we pull into light traffic on Pacific Coast Highway.

"Sure. Yeah." I adjust the buttons on my white blouse even though they don't need adjusting. Why did I wear this stupid shirt? London loaned it to me. When I emerged from the bathroom in a Rolling Stones T-shirt, she reminded me that wearing a shirt with a picture of a giant pair of red lips with a tongue hanging out wasn't gonna fly. So now I'm stuck suffocating in this itchy thing.

"Tiffany, who's Xavior?"

"What?" I turn to him. My heart pounding so hard and fast I have to place my hand on my chest to dull the sharp pain it's causing.

He reaches into the pocket of his khaki-colored chino shorts and hands me back my cell. "He texted you a few times last night. Like around midnight."

"Oh." I grip the cell and swallow nervously. "He's…my friend. From Chicago."

"Remind him midnight texts are too late."

I exhale silently. "I'll do that. Sorry."

"Boy's got good taste in music, though. Apparently, he's a big fan of *Sgt. Pepper's*. One of my favorites, too."

"Really?" I ignore the fact that Anthony admitted to reading my texts and invaded my privacy since, to be fair, I was warned that he'd be doing that. "I love that album so much. I feel like concept albums are like—"

Anthony's cell rings, cutting me off. He quickly answers it and a female voice booms through his car speakers.

"Dr. Stone?"

"Yeah. What's up?" he asks somewhat impatiently.

"Shona just paged the emergency line. She's about twenty minutes apart now."

Anthony groans. "You headed to the hospital?"

"I am," the female voice replies.

"Call me when she's at ten? I'll start heading that way in a few." He ends the call.

"Should we skip breakfast?" I ask.

"You don't mind, do you? I'm really sorry, Tiffany."

I shrug.

"We can take a little drive along the coast for a minute or two. That sound good?"

"Sure," I say, faking enthusiasm.

"I have a surprise. I was gonna wait and tell you with all the girls, but now you'll be the first to know."

"Are you going back to San Francisco to teach another class?"

"No. We are all going to play hooky from church and go to Vegas tomorrow."

"Oh? Why?"

"Because of you. A little something to let you know how happy I am that you're here. I'm taking the entire family to see a matinee performance of *Cirque du Soleil: The Beatles Love*. Margaret's parents are loaning us their private jet."

Private *jet*?

"We'll fly out tomorrow morning, see the show and be home before bedtime."

I look out the window.

"What's wrong, Tiffany? You don't seem excited."

"I don't want to go."

"Why wouldn't you want to go to Vegas to see Cirque du Soleil? It's the Beatles. All the music we both love."

"I'm terrified to fly again, okay? I don't like flying. And in a private jet? That sounds as scary as I don't know what. Aren't those the planes that *always* crash?"

"Ohhh." He seems relieved. Like being afraid to fly is nothing. "I understand. Flying can be scary. But I'll be with you this time. It'll be the whole family."

"Planes crash."

"Thousands of planes land, too. Every single day. In fact, cars are less safe than airplanes."

"Yeah. Don't remind me."

"Jehovah God will protect us."

"Right." *Unless we die.*

"What church did you go to back home?"

"Can't remember." I smooth out the pleats on my yellow

skirt. Another loan from London. Pleats on a yellow skirt. What is this...*Clueless*?

"I know in the Christian faith you believe that Jesus Christ is God."

Uggh! Why won't he stop talking about God!

"That's not what we believe. But I don't want you to think I'm trying to convert you. I only want you to be exposed to what we believe. See how it feels. Understand?"

I roll my eyes and turn to stare out the window again. "Pretty day, huh? Malibu's nice."

"I personally think you'll love our church. It's such a wonderful—"

"*Omigosh.* Sorry. Can we talk about something else? Anything else?"

"You'd rather attend a Christian church? We can arrange that. The most important thing is that you stay connected to Jehovah God."

"What if I don't want to attend *any* church?" I blurt in exasperation. "Is that an option?"

"That won't work. We serve Jehovah God in our home. I thought you understood that?"

"I do."

He quickly switches lanes and I grab on to the side of my door, panic rising from deep within. He drives fast. Holy hell!

"You believe in God, don't you, Tiffany?"

Are we seriously *still* talking about God?

I twist a strand of my long extensions around my fingers and stare at the white lines on the pavement, then check the speedometer. Seventy-five mph on this two-lane Malibu road? "Can you slow down? I get scared in cars."

"I'm driving the speed limit."

"The speed limit is seventy-five?"

He slows. "Fine. That better?"

I exhale. No sense dying today.

"What does Jehovah God mean to you, Tiffany? I'd love to hear about your personal relationship with Him."

Him? I can't help but wonder why everybody refers to this God character as a he. If God were a man, he'd have, like, an epically giant penis just swinging around the universe. He'd knock the planet right off its axis and we'd all float into deep space.

"Please be honest with me, Tiffany."

"I don't believe in God, okay?"

He rubs his chin. He rubs his forehead and his head. He groans. Finally, he slows the car before pulling off onto the side of the road and clicks off the engine. "You understand that this won't do?"

Omigosh, what was I thinking? Why on *earth* did I just tell him that?

"In our house we serve Jehovah God. When you grow up and become an adult, you do what you want in your own home. But you're in our home. You must honor and obey and believe. Pumpkin, Heaven and Nevaeh will be looking up to you for guidance. London, too."

"So what do you want me to do? Pretend?"

"We'll get you into a Bible study and some counseling sessions with our youth pastor."

"You can't be for real with this."

"See, there you go again with the disrespectful tone."

"I literally just said, 'You can't be for real with this.' What's so disrespectful about that?"

"It's your tone, Tiffany. How would you speak to...Abraham Lincoln?"

"I wouldn't. He's dead."

"I know he's dead, Tiffany. I only mean how would you address him. Would you say, 'You can't be for real with this, Abraham Lincoln'?"

I scratch my trembling cheek. "If he tried to send me to counseling sessions with his youth pastor. Yes, I would."

Anthony shakes his head. Like I'm a hopeless cause. "Look, all the girls are in Bible study. Everyone on this planet should be in a Bible study class."

"There are people on this planet who don't even have access to clean water. And you think they should be in *Bible* study? They can't even read!"

Anthony rubs his head again in that fashion adults do when they look utterly stressed and unhappy, sitting over a pile of bills or on hold with the Wi-Fi customer service rep. "What would it take for you to believe? What could Jehovah God do to show you He's real?"

"I don't know."

Anthony starts up the car. "Think about it, Tiffany. Think about what it would take for you to believe. Because I want to start praying that God reveal Himself to you. Can we at least begin there?"

I stare out the window.

"You're my daughter, Tiffany. I care about my children. I love every one of you guys. And I care about your eternity. Is a sign from God too much to ask?"

I imagine asking this God person to make it rain Skittles and to DJ a leprechaun dance party on a cloud made of cotton candy. But instead, I come up with something even more ridiculous. I turn and watch Anthony as he clears his throat and pulls at his hair. "I want my mom back."

"I know you do, Tiffany. I'm so sorry she's gone."

"No. That's the sign I want from God. Mom back."

"Tiffany? Be reasonable. God doesn't bring people back from the dead."

"Why not? Jesus did it when His friend died."

"Resurrection comes later. God's not going to bring back your mom. That's not a fair request."

"If there's a God, then *He*'s not fair. I think my request is justified. I deserve her back. That's what I want."

"All right, Tiffany. You don't want to at least try—I understand. You'll still join a church Bible study. And we can talk about counseling sessions with the youth pastor next Sunday."

"What makes him qualified? Did he go to youth pastor university or something?"

"Tiffany, please."

"I'm not talking to your youth pastor!"

"Then it'll be an hour of silence with him once a week."

"Whatever." I fold my arms under my chest. Maybe it'll be a good thing if Anthony Stone's not my real dad. When Maury Povich opens up that manila envelope and says, "Anthony Stone, you are *not* the father!" Anthony and I will both be happy and relieved and this nightmare will be over.

"Let's head back, yeah?"

I nod, turning so he can't see me wipe tears from my face. I check last night's message from Xavior. It says: Tiffany Sly! I can NOT get tired of this album. Still listening and it's 2:00 a.m.! Sgt. Pepper's for life! lol xo.

We pull back into traffic, Anthony makes a U-turn at a traffic light and we head back toward the beach house, riding in a strange, sad silence.

I return Xavior's text: Sgt. Pepper's for life! xo.

17

I stare out into the water from the bedroom window watching the family Stone. Heaven and Nevaeh are on boogie boards and seem to be having tons of fun. Margaret is chasing after Pumpkin, who looks like the Michelin Man geared up with floaties on her arms, legs and chest. All she needs is a floatie over her head and she'd be a human floatie. London is lying in a conservative one-piece bathing suit on a brightly colored towel, soaking up the sun's rays, while Margaret frantically tries to keep Pumpkin away from the ocean, even though, with all those floaties on, she certainly seems ready to brave the water.

I smile. Though it's not one of those smiles that reaches your eyes. I suppose it's a sad smile. They're like a scene out of a Hallmark movie. They are the perfect family, and I, the perfect outsider. The one thing that isn't quite like the others, perched high above, staring through a glass window. I don't belong here. I don't.

I retrieve Little Buddy from under the bed and strum the

strings to tune him. Before I know it, an hour has passed with me strumming on my guitar and my fingers are beginning to feel numb. Perhaps I can get some homework done. Not that it matters, really. I don't imagine I'll be here much longer.

I slide Little Buddy back under the bed and grab my backpack, unzip the front section, retrieve my pills and toss one into my mouth. As I stuff the bottle back into my bag, I notice the Plan B box and pick it up. I forgot I hid it in my backpack. I check the time—only 11:00 a.m. Good. London's still got time.

"Tiffany?"

Anthony's at the door.

"I've been calling your name for like a minute. You didn't hear me?"

"No." I sit up. "You're back already?"

"False alarm. Contractions stopped." He surveys my mess of books and school papers on the bed, his gaze finally resting on what's in my hand. "What is that?"

"Huh?" Oh. No. I'm *holding* the Plan B box in my hands! "Um."

He moves into the room and quickly snatches the box away from me. "Is this yours?"

I'm not quite sure what to say. Not quite sure what to do.

"Tiffany, did you hear me? Is this yours?"

"It's not hers. It's mine."

London's at the door, wrapped in a towel.

"Yours?" he replies incredulously. London nods and Anthony sits down on the bed beside me, resting his hands on his knees. "I see. When? When did you get it?"

"Yesterday. Marcus McKinney took Tiffany and me to Santa Monica. To a drugstore. I got it then."

"London, go and get your mother."

London exits the room; within a moment she returns with a sun-kissed Margaret, who holds Pumpkin on her hip. "What's going on?"

"Have Heaven and Nevaeh take Pumpkin outside to build a sandcastle," Anthony says sternly.

More than a little flustered, Margaret quickly moves down the hallway. It's only a short moment before I hear the sound of Pumpkin crying outside with Heaven and Nevaeh trying to comfort her. A minute later, Margaret returns.

"Close the door," he orders, and Margaret obliges.

"What's going on?" She's thrown a pretty red sundress over her swimsuit and her hair is piled into a bun on the top of her head.

"Can I please be excused?" I ask.

"No, Tiffany. You stay."

"This is not Tiffany's fault, though," London explains with perfect calm as she sits beside me. "She only came to Santa Monica with me to help. She was just being supportive."

Anthony's pacing back and forth in the small room. "Tiffany is old enough to know right from wrong."

"Will someone please tell me what's going on?" Margaret asks impatiently. Anthony tosses her the Plan B box and she gasps. "Plan B? For who?"

"For London," he replies stiffly.

London wrings her hands together and stares at the floor. Her eyes begin to well with tears.

"London?" Margaret's voice is shaking. "You broke your purity vow?"

London nods, tears spilling down her cheeks. "And…the condom…broke."

"What do we do, Anthony?" Margaret cries. "London, did you already take the morning-after pill?"

"I didn't take it. I changed my mind and decided I'm ready to accept the consequences of my actions."

Margaret wails. "London, *why*? How could you have been so careless? How could you have gone against our faith and what we believe?"

"I'm sorry, Mom." London sobs.

Margaret's crying so hard. London's crying, too, and Anthony is still pacing. And then there's me, sitting in the middle of it all, wishing I could pull a lever where a trapdoor would open and swallow me up and spit me back out in Chicago.

"How long have you been having sex, London?" Anthony asks.

"Yesterday was my first time."

He turns to Margaret. "London should see Dr. Avery."

"As early as possible. Can we get her an appointment for Monday? She'll need STD testing, too, Anthony."

"Jesus Christ, London. Who is the boy?" Anthony asks.

"Aric Cook," she replies so softly I almost don't hear her.

Anthony turns to Margaret. "Didn't we just get a phone call from the Cooks? Is that why they were calling? About this?"

I grimace. Better save that conversation for a later date. Now is *not* the time.

"Aric Cook is my boyfriend," London explains.

"London, please. You don't have a boyfriend and never

did." Anthony finally stops pacing. "Did Aric meet you in Santa Monica at the drugstore where you got this godforsaken medicine?"

London shakes her head.

"Is he here now? Supporting you, as you could very well soon be pregnant with his child? Where is Aric Cook?"

London shrugs, looking as if it just hit her that she has no idea where the hell Aric is.

"Exactly," Anthony declares. "We have house rules for a reason. He is not old enough to understand what it means to be in a committed relationship and neither are you. He is simply a boy at your school who used you for sex. That is it."

London leans forward and sobs into her hands. Margaret rushes to her and comfortingly rubs her back.

"Margaret, I want you to braid London's hair. She's about to make a donation."

London looks up. *"What?"*

"Locks for Love. Since you easily give up things that are precious and valuable without thinking how it will affect others, I don't imagine you'll have a problem with it."

Holy *shitballs*! I did *not* see that one comin'.

"Mommy!" London cries. "You can't let him do this!"

Margaret shakes her head. Tears stream down her cheeks, flushed red.

"Say something!" London wails. "Protect me from him!"

Only Margaret says nothing and London continues sobbing so hard I fear she might have a triple stroke and die.

Anthony turns to me. "Where is your guitar?"

"Why? I'm not in this."

"I'm going to put your guitar in storage for one month.

Thank Jehovah London had sense enough not to take the pill, but you are an accomplice to reprehensible behavior."

"You're such a fucking hypocrite!"

He takes a step toward me. "You curse at me? In my home, acting like a common 'hood rat?"

"Oh, you *would* know about the 'hood, wouldn't you? Cuz you're really from Englewood. That's as 'hood as it gets."

"What are you talking about?"

"I'm talking about you. Pretending you're something special. Living in Simi Valley. Eating keen-wah? I see right through you!"

"Tiffany, I'm sick of your disrespect," he bellows. "Sick of it! You do not speak to your father this way."

"Father? Is that supposed to be a joke? You think I don't know?" Tears spring forth as the weight of everything that's transpired begins to erupt out of me like hot, burning lava. "You think I don't know you wanted me gone?" I can hardly breathe, hardly catch my breath. "You're as bad as Aric. You're worse! Now you want to cut off London's hair to make her suffer. How did *you* suffer for your reprehensible, heinous act? How much money did you give my mom for the abortion she never got?"

Anthony turns as white as a ghost. "Do not pretend you know the truth about what really happened between your mother and me."

"But I *do* know," I cry. "You ran. You're a runner. Your life's ambition is to be better. A cut above everybody else. But guess what? You rep Englewood *perfectly*. Absent black father. Deadbeat dad. A fucking *stereotype*."

He slaps me across the face with the back of his hand.

Hard. It stings, so I cover it with my hand in an attempt to dull the pain.

"Anthony!" Margaret cries. "What's the matter with you? You can't hit her!"

"I'm…I'm so sorry. I swear, I have never hit one of my children this way before. Tiffany, I apologize."

"Fuck you," I declare. "I'm going home."

"Please, Grams. *Please* let me come home."

"And stay where?"

"With Keelah?"

"Tiffany, how is that gonna work? Keelah and them live in section eight housing. Her mom is struggling with all those kids and her daddy ain't worth but about two cents. You can't stay there!"

"It's not fair! I hate it here. I wanna come back to Chicago."

And suddenly my world exploding sounds like the best idea ever. If Anthony Stone is not my real father…I get to go *home.*

"Tiffany, you need to go and apologize. You can't say 'fuck you' to your dad. What is the matter with you?"

"He hit me!" I start to cry again.

"I know. But sometimes our emotions get the best of us and we do things that we don't mean. Things that don't necessarily represent who we really are."

Of course she's right. And now who's the hypocrite? Didn't I just break Aric's nose and ask for *his* forgiveness? I didn't mean to hit him, either.

"Besides," Grams goes on. "If Anthony hits you again I'm gonna fly out there and kill him. I will wrap my hands around his throat and squeeze until all the life drains from his body.

And then I'll happily go to prison and live out the rest of my days in peace. Anthony is aware. I already talked to him."

"You did?"

"He called me right before you did and confessed everything."

"He sucks. He's the worst dad ever."

"You don't mean that."

"I do!" I really let loose, wailing into the phone. "I hate him!" The door to the garage creaks open and I stand, hands balled into fists, ready not to apologize, but to scream and yell some more, but it's only London standing at the doorway. She steps into the quiet garage space. Her hair still hangs in long waves down her back; her eyes are almost swollen shut from crying. "Grams, I'll call you back." I quickly hang up. "Why do you still have hair?"

"Dad changed his mind. Apologized for losing his temper."

"I should've let you throw the box away. I'm sorry."

"Not your fault." She fidgets. "Tiff. There's something else."

"What now?"

"Dad went through your schoolbag. He found your anxiety pills. He took them."

"What!" I storm past London, back into the house, not even caring that my ankle has begun to throb again. I bear the full pain, moving swiftly down the hallway toward Anthony and Margaret's bedroom. I pound on the door. A second later his deep voice replies.

"Come in."

I burst into the room. Anthony is sitting on the bed beside Margaret. They both look up, startled to see me standing there in a rage. "I need my medication back!"

"I'll let you two chat alone." Margaret excuses herself. The bedroom door shuts behind her.

"Look, you can have my guitar, okay? But you can't have my medication. I need it. I was diagnosed."

"Diagnosed with what?" he asks pointedly.

"OCD and anxiety."

"You understand I'm a doctor, right?"

"You're not a psychiatrist! It's *my* medication. I take two a day. Morning and night. It helps me. I know your rules say no drugs or whatever, but I need them. I do."

"I don't necessarily subscribe to all this psychiatric labeling. A few days without them. Let's see what happens."

"Oh, my fucking gosh!"

He stands, enraged. "What do I have to do to get through to you, Tiffany? What will it take for you to stop this insolent behavior and inappropriate speech?"

"I have some seriously bad news for you. This *is* my real behavior. This *is* how I speak. It's who I am. Maybe if you'd been around for the past sixteen years instead of the past six minutes, you'd recognize that."

"Then I have some equally bad news for you. This is who I am, too."

I scoff. "Highly doubtful."

"Enlighten me, Tiffany. Why is who I am doubtful to you?"

"Because," I state seriously, "I may not know *you*, but I know my mom. She would never have fallen in love with a guy like you."

Anthony winces. He looks genuinely wounded and I regret that those words came out of my mouth.

"Tiffany Sly. It is a parent's job to guide. Children need to be raised with authority—"

"See, there's your problem." I throw my hands up in the air. "You're trying to raise me."

"Because that's my job."

"Really? I thought your job was to get to know me."

He sits back on the edge of the bed. "I think we could use some space. I'm going to sit by the water. Cool down."

Good idea. "Can I take a walk on the pier?"

"Take Heaven and Nevaeh with you."

"I wanna be alone. So I can calm down. I don't wanna fight with you anymore." Only I *do* want to fight.

I imagine being suited up in the boxing ring. Anthony and I coming from our respective corners. The referee making us touch gloves before the bell rings signaling the beginning of the round. But it wouldn't be a regular boxing match. I would only throw things at him—spaghetti, mushy soup in giant bread bowls, rotten tomatoes—and the crowd would laugh. At the end, when he was dripping wet from old, rotten food, I'd be given the world title. The Throw Things at Your Dad champion of the world.

"Then just take Nevaeh. Thirty minutes, Tiffany. I'm setting a timer on my phone."

"You're setting a *timer*? What am I, four?"

"Be back in thirty minutes or I come and get you two."

"Fine. Whatever you say, *Anthony*."

18

I pull the straps on my backpack and move slowly across the pier sans crutches, biting my lip with each step I take as Nevaeh talks faster than I can listen. Faster than the Flash can *run*. Pain shoots around my ankle and up my leg. *Uggh*. I want nothing more than to take a seat on one of the few wooden benches lining the pier, give myself a break from the discomfort, but I forge ahead, my eyes burning as fresh tears spring forth. I wipe them away before Nevaeh can see. Not that she would notice. She's too busy in deep conversation with herself.

"So what do you think, Tiff?"

"About what?"

"About what Zac said."

"Oh, right. Um, I agree."

"You think I look like a Fraggle?"

"What? No. I mean…I don't agree. Sorry."

"Exactly, right! I mean, who does he think he is? Zac Ziegler is such a turd and I do not look like a Fraggle. What's a Fraggle?"

"Do you have your phone?" She shakes her head and her curly ponytail sways back and forth. I hand her mine. "Google it."

"How? There's not internet on our phones."

"I'm logged in to the pier's free Wi-Fi."

Her eyes stretch wide. "Dad would get so supermad if he knew you did that. He says absolutely no internet on the phones. Ever."

"He told me I get internet because I'm new here and I need a while to adjust."

"Really? Cool." She takes my phone and fiddles with it as happy and relaxed-looking passersby stroll past us on the pier. A mother and teenage daughter walk arm in arm within earshot.

"Let's go see the dinosaur movie," the mother pleads.

The teenage daughter snorts. "Mom. Dinosaurs are so over."

The mom laughs. "Exactly. That's why I want to see it."

The two move past me and I stare longingly after them.

"I hate Zac Ziegler!" Nevaeh exclaims. "Fraggles are hideous *puppets*? He called me a puppet!"

"They're kind of cute. I think he was giving you a compliment."

"Whatever. They're stuffed like puppets. They're orange and yellow like Sesame Street *puppets*."

Up ahead, a man is passing out flyers. I lower my eyes as we approach him. There were always these types of men on the streets of downtown Chicago. Passing out leaflets advertising shows or selling products. Mom always advised me not to make eye contact and not to take whatever they were passing out.

"Excuse me, young ladies?" the man says kindly.

I look into his eyes. Crap. I shouldn't have looked at him. He's an Asian man, much shorter than me, wearing board shorts, sandals and a loose-fitting T-shirt. He holds up the flyer.

"Thanks!" Nevaeh says happily as she takes the flyer. I give her a disturbed look. "What?"

"You can't talk to strangers and take things from them. That's not safe."

"Tiff, chill. This is Malibu. Even the homeless are safe here. See, look?"

I scan the bright yellow half sheet of paper. All it says is *11:11 Awakening*. I take it from Nevaeh and flip it over, assuming I'll see an address and time for a local play or comedy show, but the flip side is blank.

11:11 Awakening? "What does this mean?"

"I'll Bing it! Because everybody always says Google it and I'm all...Google ain't the only search engine, you know."

I stuff the paper into my back pocket, waiting while Nevaeh does her internet research.

"Weirdness," she says as she reads. "It's the symbol for the awakening of the mind. Some people think this is all a hologram and we're all dead asleep. Like in a dream. And 11:11 is the symbol for waking up."

"Hologram? What do you mean?"

"Like *The Matrix*! Like planet Earth and everything we see is like a hologram or like a dream or something."

"And what happens when you wake up?"

She shrugs, clearly over it. "Mom says Zac only teases me because he likes me. But I'm all…there is no way he likes me because I'm pretty sure Zac Ziegler only likes himself. Like he wants to grow up and marry himself. Like he wants to have a baby with himself."

Nevaeh drones on and on and I return to my thoughts of rage. I should've never taken my braids out. Never should have allowed Anthony Stone to think he can control me for even one second. Him and his *religion*. You gotta love Jehovah God, Tiffany, but don't talk to our supernice neighbors. A burst of happiness explodes in my heart. Didn't Jo say they were having a family barbecue today?

"Hey, Nevaeh?"

She pauses in her chatter with a perturbed look on her face, braces shining in the Malibu sun. "Huh?"

"Can I have my phone back?"

"Oh, sure."

She hands it back. I could ask Marcus to come and pick me up! I shoot him a quick text, imagining the look on Anthony's face when his timer goes off and I'm not back yet. I'll tell Nevaeh to tell him I extended my walk indefinitely so I could practice appropriate speech.

"Hey, Nevaeh…head back to the house without me, okay?"

"Why? I'm having fun." She links her arm through mine.

I sigh. Nevaeh really *is* like a Fraggle. Sweet, colorful, adorable and awesomely nutty. If I do end up leaving here, I wish I could keep her as a sister. "I'm actually going to Marcus's house. They're having a barbecue and I got permission to go."

"Really? You think Dad would let me go, too? Please, Tiffany. Can I come with you?"

There is no way I can take Nevaeh. Right? Anthony's head would *implode.* I grin at the thought. It would sort of serve him right to have an imploded head. Besides, it's not really a big deal. We'll go. Have a great time. He'll see that the McKinneys aren't so bad. Sure, he'll be a little pissed off. Okay, a lot pissed off. But Nevaeh will do something Fraggle-y. Like tell him a ten-minute story about a rock she found and I'll get a quick lecture about how this isn't the "'hood" and in Malibu teenagers don't sneak off and kidnap their little sisters. All will be well. "Let me call him and ask." I fake call Anthony and pause for a few seconds, like I'm waiting while his phone is ringing. "Hey! It's Tiffany and Nevaeh."

"Hi, Daddy!" Nevaeh calls out.

"He says hi," I say with a smile. "Hey, I know you said I could call Darryl and ride back home to the McKinneys' barbecue. Can Nevaeh come, too?" I pause. "Of course. We won't be long at all. I'll take good care of her." I pause again. "Awesome. Thanks! Love you, too!" I fake end the call. "He says it's cool."

"Yes!" She raises her arms in the victory symbol just as a text comes in from Marcus.

It says: Not feeling so hot today. Mom #2 has me on lockdown. Can the driver bring you?

Darryl the snitch? No way I can actually call *him.* Suddenly I recall Juan the driver telling me to call him if I ever needed a ride. Triple five, *eleven, eleven*!

I see a hot-dog vendor a few paces away and pull a five-dollar bill out of the front pocket of London's *Clueless* skirt and hand it to Nevaeh. "Buy me a hot dog?"

She frowns. "We're not allowed to eat food from the pier vendors."

"Goodness. What *are* you guys allowed to do? Just buy me a bottle of water."

"Sure." She takes the money and skips off.

I quickly dial Juan.

"This is Juan speaking."

"Juan. Hi! It's Tiffany Sly?"

"The giant? Moving to Simi Valley? What's up, kiddo?"

"Any chance you can pick me and my sister up in Malibu and take us back to Simi?"

"You're in luck. Just dropped off a client in Culver City. I'm about ten minutes away from Malibu. What part?"

I give him the address. "But pick us up…" I look around and notice a seafood restaurant. "At this little seafood restaurant across the street. Pick us up there."

"Gotcha. Be there in, like, fifteen."

I power down my cell. "Ready, Nevaeh?"

She hands me a cold bottle of water. "Superready."

The ride with Juan is much better than our first. He drives well below the speed limit the entire time and Nevaeh's chattering keeps me distracted and amused. When Juan finally pulls up to our cul-de-sac, I realize I pretty much know Nevaeh's entire life story. Including something that she *doesn't* know. I now know that Nevaeh has an intense, mondo, major crush on Zac Ziegler. Though she would probably never admit to it and I certainly don't want to be the one to break the news to her.

"Thanks again, Juan," I say, pushing open the door. "Charge the same card from last time. Add a twenty percent tip."

"No doubt, little homey! Hey, I'm always around."

Nevaeh and I move across the street toward Marcus's house. The door swings open as we approach and a cute teenage African American boy tosses up the peace sign with his two fingers. He's wearing black glasses, striped shorts, a black T-shirt and mismatched socks pulled up midcalf. "Hey, yo." He looks back and forth between me and Nevaeh curiously.

"Hi. Is Jo or Monique or Marcus here?"

"Aunt Jo? She's upstairs. Auntie Monique's in the backyard cookin'. Marcus? He's in his room praying to the Zen God or something. You guys wanna come in?"

"If you don't mind."

"I don't."

We both step inside.

"Tiffany?" Jo descends their giant staircase looking vibrant and happy. As usual, her short hair is styled perfectly and she wears a Berkeley sweatshirt with jean shorts and flip-flops. "I thought you guys were in Malibu this weekend?"

"We are. But, um, Dad said we could come to your barbecue."

"Really now?" She doesn't exactly look convinced.

"Yeah. He wanted to come, too…but, uh, sends his regards."

"I don't know why I'm so surprised. I always say I believe in miracles." She makes it down the stairs and embraces me warmly, then looks at Nevaeh. "Don't tell me." She scratches her head. "Heaven?"

Nevaeh grins, almost as if this is her favorite game. "Nope. It's me. *Nevaeh.*"

Jo snaps her fingers. "I can *never* tell you two apart."

The boy who let us in clears his throat.

"Oh, this is my nephew, Kevyn."

"Kevyn with a *y*, not an *i*."

"Hi, Kevyn-with-a-*y*. I'm Tiffany."

"And I'm Nevaeh. It's Heaven spelled backward, which I personally think is so dumb. I mean, why would anybody spell words backward, you know? My twin sister's name is Heaven. Get it? Heaven and Nevaeh? Why couldn't our parents have named us, like, Jenny and Penny or something? So lame, right?"

Kevyn's eyes widen. "Whoa."

"I like your name, Nevaeh. It's pretty," Jo says with a chuckle. "We got one of those giant bounce-house, obstacle-course-race things for the party and apparently it's my turn to make a fool outta myself."

"Omigosh, are you serious?" Nevaeh jumps excitedly. "I, like, love those things."

"You wanna come outside with me and meet the rest of the family?" Jo asks warmly, looking so thrilled to have Nevaeh and me here.

Nevaeh gives me an excited look. "Can we, Tiff?"

"Of course," I reply happily. "I'm gonna go say hi to Marcus real quick. I'll meet you out there."

"Upstairs, down the hall and to the left is where his room is. Tell him I said to grab your box out of the hall closet." Jo places her arm protectively around Nevaeh's shoulders. "Express mail accidentally delivered something here for you. Tiffany Sly Care of Anthony Stone from Juanita Sly."

"Really? That's my grams. Thanks, Jo. I'll ask Marcus to get it for me."

Jo, Nevaeh and Kevyn-with-a-*y* head toward the back of the house. I head upstairs.

★★★

"Knock, knock." Marcus's door is open. He's sitting on the bed with a pair of headphones stretched over his hooded sweatshirt. He slides them off his head when he sees me.

"Hello," he says in his sweet, soft manner, not seeming the least bit surprised that I'm standing at his bedroom door.

"Hey. You feeling okay?"

"Better. I tried calling you, but your phone was going to voice mail."

"Oh, yeah. I turned it off."

"Why?"

"GPS tracking. Long story." I move into the room. "Your mom said a package was delivered here for me?"

"Oh, yes." He stands. "One moment. I'll be right back."

He moves past me and I glance over at his desk, where small tubes of white makeup and dirty makeup sponges clutter the space. There are also books splayed out.

The Death of Ivan Illich.

War and Peace.

Anna Karenina.

Jeez. I thought I was doing big things by reading *The Shadow of the Wind* in Spanish. Within a moment Marcus returns with a medium-size express mailing box. He sets it on the bed.

"Hey, Marcus. What's with all the Tolstoy?"

He sits at his desk chair and spins it around to face me. "I'm doing a comparative analysis on themes in the works of Tolstoy before and after his religious conversion for my advanced writing class."

"I didn't even know he had a religious conversion." I move

toward the box, recognizing my grandma's handwriting. "You mind if I open this real quick?"

"Not at all."

I tear off the tape that seals the cardboard box and peel the flaps back to look inside. A handwritten letter is on top of a bunch of packing peanuts. I pick up the letter.

Dear Tiffany,
Some things don't belong in storage. I hoped they could find a place with you.
Love,
Grams

I dig through the packing peanuts and retrieve one of many items—Mom's high school yearbook.

"What is it?" Marcus asks.

I hold it up for Marcus to see.

Jo peeks through the door. "Kevyn told all the cousins there is a beautiful black girl here and so I've been sent to retrieve you. And Nevaeh is running through that obstacle course like an Olympic superhero. I'm tellin' you that girl got some serious speed." She eyes the yearbook. "Where on earth did you find that old thing? Haven't seen that in *years*. I thought I lost it when we moved."

"Oh, no. This is my mom's. My grams sent it to me."

Jo steps into the room and examines the cover. "J. B. Young. Class of 1996? Stop it now. Tiffany, this is not your mom's."

"I swear it is."

"Well, I'll be." Jo takes the book from my hand and carefully pries it open, gently flipping through the pages of the book. A moment passes. "Look." She lays the book on the bed and Marcus and I look over her shoulder at the page.

"What are we looking at?" I ask.

She points to a photo of a nice-looking Caucasian boy with strangely familiar bright green eyes. "Steven Harrison. God rest his soul."

I study the picture. "You knew him?"

Jo nods. "Knew him quite well."

"And he died?" I ask.

"About a month before Marcus was born. He was only eighteen." Jo gets a faraway look in her eyes.

"Was he a good friend of yours?"

"That's my dad," Marcus says.

I turn to him. He's sitting back at his desk chair. "Your *dad*? But I asked you if anybody in your family had green eyes and you said no."

"You asked if anybody in my mom's family had green eyes."

"Omigosh, Marcus. You're incorrigible!"

"He is incorrigible, ain't he?" Jo laughs.

I lean back on my hands. "Marcus, your dad and my mom went to the same school?"

"Who knows, Tiffany," Jo adds. "They might've even known one another."

"What high school did you go to, Jo?"

"A private girls' school in the city. Closed down a few years ago." She's still flipping through the yearbook, giddy as a high school teen as she turns the delicate pages. "You mind if I take this downstairs to show Monique? She will get a kick out of it. I promise to be real careful."

"Of course, Jo."

She hugs the yearbook to her chest and exits the room.

"Small world," Marcus says.

"No. The world's huge. There's, like...four hundred billion people on this planet."

"That number seems inflated."

"How could we both lose our parents, who incidentally went to the same high school, *and* end up living across the street from one another in an entirely different state from where we were conceived? It's bananas."

"Stranger things have occurred."

"And you're white!"

He shrugs. "Half-white."

"What are the *odds*?" I dig into the box and pull out a stuffed ladybug. "Lucky!" I show it to Marcus. "This is Lucky."

"You don't see too many ladybugs around these parts."

I place Lucky over my face. "Nice to meet you, Marcus McKinney," I say in a high-pitched cartoon voice. "I'm a ladybug. And you a white boy!"

Marcus laughs and I toss Lucky on the bed.

"What else is in that box, Tiffany?"

I dig around. "Let's see here. Pictures, cinnamon incense, some books. Oh..." I pull out an iPad. "This is my *mom's*. Omigosh. Grams gave me Mom's iPad."

"Tiffany, I find it tough to believe your dad would let you come here in a car, with Nevaeh, from Malibu. They've never darkened our doorstep and they live across the street."

"Yeah. People change. That man is full of surprises."

"Tiffany?" Marcus's bright green eyes gaze at me. He pulls the hood off his head. His white-painted face and head have a subtle luminescence under the recessed lighting in his bedroom. "Your dad doesn't know you're here, does he?"

"Nope."

"He's going to come here and get you two. He's going to be extremely angry."

"He's not coming here. He doesn't know where I am."

"*Tiffany.* This is a great example of doing something that *doesn't* serve you well. Coming here against the orders of your dad?"

"Dad? Please. His name is Anthony. And who cares about his orders. I feel happy for the first time today. That's serving me well just fine. I'm living. Just like Mr. Mills told me to do."

"Mr. Mills? *Tiffany.* You have to call your dad. Tell him where you are. He might call the police."

I close my eyes. "Marcus, he's not my dad, okay? Stop calling him that." Within a moment, my eyes begin to squeeze out more tears. Marcus quickly reaches over to his desk and hands me a box of tissues. I grab a bunch and blow my nose.

"What's wrong, Tiffany?"

I let it all out, telling Marcus everything I know and all about my encounters with Xavior Xavion. Marcus listens intently, hanging on to my every word.

"Wow," Marcus says when I finally finish. "This is like…"

"An episode of *Maury Povich*?"

"I was gonna say a soap opera."

I lower my head into my hands. "I feel like a homeless orphan. I'm Oliver Twist."

"Oliver Twist is a mid-nineteenth-century creation sprung from the mind of Charles Dickens. You're not Oliver Twist."

"Fine, Mr. Smarty Pants who knows everything about

everything. I'm not Oliver Twist. I'm the sad spark of consciousness known as Tiffany Sly. The 'god' who apparently came here to experience utter misery."

"That's dramatic." He moves from his desk chair and sits beside me. "Do you think Anthony is your father? Or do you think Xavior is your father?"

"What difference does it matter what I think?"

"Because it matters. So tell me."

"Well... Xavior looks just like me. He plays the guitar. He reminds me of me. He's nice like me. He wants me. Anthony... he just sucks."

"You still haven't answered my question. Who do you *think* is your father? Tell me what your gut says. How do you feel?"

"How do I feel?" I set Mom's iPad down beside me and grab my stomach. "I feel all this tightness in my stomach and my chest is heavy. Like someone is pushing down on me with all their strength and... I dunno. You know that feeling you get when someone you like doesn't like you back. Like heartache?"

"I know heartache."

"I feel like that. I feel heartache. Like my boyfriend broke up with me."

"Or your mom died?"

"Yeah." I sigh. "And the sad part of it all...the thing I really just can't...explain... I don't *want* Xavior to be my dad. Why wouldn't I want him to be my dad, Marcus? He's so nice. I think he'd make a much better dad than Anthony."

"Close your eyes, Tiffany." Marcus takes off his gloves and stuffs them into the pocket of his hooded sweatshirt.

"Why?"

"Humor me?"

I close my eyes. He takes my hands in his. They feel warm. Extremely warm. A strong feeling of peace begins to move through me. Like a slow-moving body of water flowing up my body from the tips of my toes, reaching all the way to my chest and inching out to my arms and hands. My body is tingling with this sensation of relaxation, harmony and love. "How are you doing this?" I whisper. "You have magic hands or something?"

"You ever turned the crank on a jack-in-the-box, Tiffany?" Marcus asks rather than answer my question.

"Sure. Yeah."

"You're turning and turning and the song is playing and you close your eyes and turn your head because you know the thing inside the box is about to jump out and scare you. But it's never all that scary, right? It's a toy. It's not like something could come out of that box and truly harm you." He squeezes my hand. "That's how you feel most of the time. Like you're waiting on something to jump out and scare you."

"I'm a real-life jack-in-the-box?"

"You're turning the crank. Waiting on the scare of your life. A giant tsunami. A horrific plane crash. You're waiting for everything to get all shook up again. If Xavior is your real father…things will definitely get shook up again." He stands, still holding my hands, and pulls me up off the bed. "May I show you something?"

"Of course," I whisper.

"But first you have to do me a favor."

"Okay."

"You have to promise you'll do me this favor."

"I promise."

"Good. I want you to turn your phone on."

"But, Marcus—"

"Tiffany. A promise is a promise. A deal is a deal."

"Fine." I reach into my back pocket and grab my phone. I press hard on the top button and the phone lights up, springing back to life. Within a moment, dozens of missed text messages come through from Anthony.

Where are you guys?

Tiffany, please call us.

Are you and Nevaeh okay?

Please come home.

Tiffany, please. I'm so sorry. We all love you. We're all so worried.

You're not in trouble, okay? This is my fault. I take full responsibility. Please come home.

"I want you to text your dad."

I groan.

"Tiffany, you need to do this right now."

I click on Anthony's last text to reply but can only stare at the screen. "What should I say?"

"How about this. 'I am at the McKinneys' house. I am with Marcus. Nevaeh is here, too. She's safe and having fun. I am sorry.'"

“No! I’m not sorry.”

“Regardless of all that’s happened, he’s most likely worried sick about you. Margaret, too. Say you’re sorry. I know deep down you really are.”

“Fine.” I compose the text and click Send. “There. I did it.”

“Perfect. Now that he knows where you are, we don’t have much time before he arrives.”

“Maybe he’ll let us stay.”

“Not a chance. So come with me, Tiffany Sly.”

19

We stop in front of a door at the end of a long hallway.

"Would you mind taking off your shoes?" he asks.

I lean against the wall, remove my shoes and place them on an area rug in front of the door. Marcus turns the knob and we both step through to the other side.

"*Wow.* What is this?"

It's a large room with snow-white, plush carpet and an epically massive movie screen, stretching the entire length of one of the walls.

"This is my meditation room."

I gaze up at the superhigh ceiling. "It's kinda like a movie theater. But without the seats. Man, look at that screen! It's ginormous."

"It's a two-hundred-and-one-inch Stewart Cinecurve film screen. We had a specialist from London fly in to install it and rig the wiring. It's got an Atlas sound system so we get THX-certified sound."

"Like your own IMAX theater. So rock star."

"Would you like to see how it works?"

"Omigosh, yes."

Marcus taps a panel on the white wall and a door pops open. He removes a remote and presses a few buttons. The lights dim. "You can have a seat if you'd like."

The screen flickers to life. I sit and cross my legs. My long fingers dig into the soft fibers of the carpet.

"Where would you like to go, Tiffany?"

"What do you mean?"

"Pick a place. Hawaii... Alaska... Australia. I don't have a program for everywhere, but I do have quite a few locations on file. Where have you always wanted to go?"

"How about Ireland?"

"Luck of the Irish. I have a file for Ireland."

Within a moment, the two-hundred-and-one-inch film screen displays rolling hills of green, as if we are high above the mountains, soarin' over Ireland!

"Marcus! This is the coolest thing *ever.*"

Soft violin music streams from the sound system as Ireland is shown in all its Irish glory. Sea mist rolls onto the rugged coastline as we circle the skies. The brightness of multicolored kayaks and canoes breaks through the gray fog as we move over waterways and lakes. The scenery is breathtaking. A landscape photographer's dream for sure. Waves crash in off the Atlantic, colliding in foamy bursts of water. And there's a stunning lighthouse, its beacon hazy in the fog.

"I'm in Ireland! Marcus, I'm in Ireland!"

The mist begins to clear and the sun breaks through the fog as we continue our flight over an ancient, medieval castle surrounded by hundreds of wildflowers. I inhale, almost as if I could smell the flowers from here.

"I would never leave this room," I whisper. "I swear I would never."

"Do you meditate, Tiffany?"

"I'm not sure what meditation is, to be honest."

"Meditation is a tool you can use to open up the mind. To 'wake up,' so to speak."

I think of the flyer from the guy in Malibu—*11:11 Awakening.* "Do you think we're all asleep? Like this is a hologram and we need to wake up?"

"To me that sounds a bit magical. It's not magic. It's science. Everyone has a brain. The brain is capable of all it's capable of. To me, waking up means attempting to tap into the full potential of your brain. That's what Jesus did. Buddha, too."

"Is that why you're psychic? You've tapped into the full potential of your brain?"

"I'm not psychic." Marcus pulls his hood back over his head. "But it is how I learned to manipulate energy. We're energy magnets. Energy cannot remain stagnant. And like attracts like. So, since you are energy, you are constantly drawing in more energy."

I uncross my legs and lean back on my hands. "Wow. I never thought about it like that, but you're right."

"And for me, drawing in energy, good or bad, can affect my heart rhythms. The makeup is like a shield. It helps me block energy. Completely psychosomatic. But it helps."

"So *that's* why you wear it. I get it. I totally get that."

"Energy still manages to come through. I guide it away from my heart and to my hands."

"How? How can you do that?"

"I imagine energy as something with form. Like a blue river rushing through my body. And then I imagine my heart and I place a bubble of protection around it while the river of energy flows to my hands. I literally think about that all day long."

"It works?"

He nods. "It's why when I touch you, you feel energy surge through your body. Even at my last doctor's appointment my doctor noticed that while my body temp was normal—98.6—my hands were hot. So he made me hold a thermometer—105 degrees."

"That's so cool. You should be on a morning talk show. For real."

"I'm not a trailblazer or anything. Many yogis and monks have mastered energy manipulation in such a way they can *transmute* energy and *heal* sicknesses."

"And they discovered how to do this through meditation?"

"I believe so. Yes. Would you like to try?"

"What do I do?"

"Okay. There is no right way to meditate. But I'll show you the way I do it. You can either lie down or sit. I usually get lots of pillows to make myself extra comfortable. The point is to be relaxed so you're able to clear the mind. In meditation, thinking does not serve you well."

"Never heard that one before."

"Would you like some pillows?"

"Sure."

He taps another panel on the wall and a door opens, revealing a closet of blankets and large, plush pillows. He hands me two. I set one of the pillows on the floor, lay my head back on it and stretch out my legs over the other.

On the screen, the flight over Ireland has taken us to a sandy beach where a stunning rainbow arches across the sky, its magical ribbons of color shimmering against the horizon.

"Now close your eyes."

I close my eyes.

"And try not to think of anything. Your thoughts are what make you Tiffany Sly. We know all about Tiffany Sly. In meditation, we want to tap into who we are *beyond* Tiffany Sly. So we remove the thoughts of Tiffany Sly and think of nothing. Then your soul can communicate with your brain. And you will start to get sparks of inspiration. Draw closer to the true God in you and in everyone and everything around you. Perhaps even remember. Buddha remembered. Who is to say we can't remember, too?"

"You mean past lives?"

"Yes. Now, I'm going to turn the projector off and only play soft music. Keep your eyes closed. Try to push out any and all thoughts."

Got it. Eyes closed—check. Mind free of thought—hmm.

I wonder why Ireland doesn't have more black people? Black people would love Ireland.

I can't believe Marcus is half-white. What are the odds?

Oh, shoot. I'm thinking. Go away, thoughts!

Okay. Clear the mind. Let's try again. Clear the… Oh, my leg is itching! Shoot.

I reach down and scratch my right leg.

Okay. Back to clearing the mind. Uggh. I have to pee.

Hold it, Tiffany. And shut up, will you? Stop thinking about stuff!

Okay. Think of darkness.

I imagine a big blob of dark.

But wait…isn't imagining a blob of dark thinking? I'm thinking of darkness and therefore I am thinking.

Thump-thump, thump-thump: *You're the world's worst meditator!*

Oy! And now my leg is itching. Again.

I reach down to scratch it and open one eye. Marcus is sitting beside me with his legs crossed, eyes closed, hands on his knees, not moving a muscle.

Uggh! He's probably learning how to harness the wind and achieve human flight. No fair! I want to have a clear mind so I can be powerful and tap into my true potential. Like what if I could shoot lasers out of my eyes!

I decide to sit up like Marcus. Perhaps the key to this thing is not lying down. I cross my legs and lay my hands on my knees.

Shoot. My hand is itching. How weird!

I use one hand to scratch the other. I clear my throat.

Now my head itches! My head is always itching. I'm never getting another weave. I'm so uncomfortable.

I tap my head and take a deep breath.

Okay. No more itches. No more scratches.

I think of a black blob again and imagine it oozing down the wall and plopping onto the floor. Gross.

I suck at this! Oh, no! There's that feeling again in the pit of my stomach. The knot is forming. What if Xavior's my dad? Will I move to his house? Does he have a house?

Gummy Bears.

Ice cream sundaes.

Snow days.

Warm hugs.

Happy thoughts aren't working! Uh-oh. I'm itching all over. What do I have, chicken pox or something?

Thump-thump, thump-thump: *Meditation will* end *you!*

I stand.

Marcus looks up at me, his white face piercing through the darkness in the room. "Everything okay?"

"I'm getting anxiety. I have to stop. I need my medication." I shake out my legs and arms.

"We can stop." Marcus stands. "Quieting the mind—it's tough. It was your first time. It takes people years and years to master meditation. Others might see results right away. Everyone is different."

"How long did it take you?" I place my finger on my neck to check my pulse. My cheeks are trembling.

"Years. But a master, I am not." He grabs our pillows from off the floor. "We'll try this again. Maybe once a week or something like that. Even five minutes a day is useful. May even help with your anxiety. Will you let me help you?"

"Of course, Marcus."

He turns the lights back up. "There are so many things I would like to teach you. Things that could help you when you're ready to stop taking your medication. Space clearing, unplugging from group consciousness, calling back your energy—"

"Whoa. For now, let's stick with getting me to stop scratching during meditation."

We move toward the door. I tug on Marcus's hoodie as he grabs the doorknob. "Hey, wait."

He turns. "Yes?"

"If I have to leave here I will miss you so much." I lurch

forward and hug him, not even caring that his white makeup is probably all over my face and London's *Clueless* outfit. A little white makeup never hurt nobody.

"Thank you for being my friend, Tiffany," he whispers.

"Thank you for being mine."

"On your mark...get set...*go*!" Nevaeh starts the timer.

Jo and Monique take off through the bounce-house obstacle course in the epically large backyard; at least twenty of Marcus's relatives cheer them on as they move through small spaces, climb inflatable ladders, swing on ropes and dodge plastic tubing. Monique is petite, brown-skinned, with hair in French braids pulled into a tight bun at the back of her head.

The two finally fall down a pair of high slides and race the rest of the way. Jo crosses the finish line first with Monique crashing into her at the end. The two fall over into a heap of laughter and limbs. Jo wraps one arm around Monique and raises the other in victory.

Nevaeh clicks the button on the timer. "One minute... twenty-two seconds! That's the new record! No way!"

"I won!" Jo cries.

I notice Marcus and Kevyn having a deep discussion. Kevyn looks over at me and winks flirtatiously. Marcus looks over at me and shakes his head and mouths the word *No.*

I laugh.

Another group of Marcus's older cousins excitedly play some kind of card game at a table. Adults mingle in the pool. I lean back on the lawn chair next to Nevaeh, soaking it all in. Maybe the sun is not so bad. *Sorry I've been so hard on you, sun*, I think. Shielding my eyes as I gaze up at it.

Thump-thump, thump-thump: *Are you crazy? People go blind from looking directly at the sun!*

A girl comes out onto the patio. She's probably my age. Hair shaved on one side. Dressed in a one-piece bathing suit. "Auntie Jo!" she says. "A man named Stone is at the front door."

Jo beams. "Really?" She glances at me and Nevaeh on the lawn chair. "Maybe he had a change of heart, too. I'm so happy he's here."

Before I have a chance to tell her I wasn't actually allowed to come here, she moves through the patio doors. *Shoot!* I jump up and follow close behind, dragging Nevaeh with me.

Anthony is standing in the kitchen, arms folded across his chest, looking worn out and exhausted. "Tiffany and Nevaeh, get in the car. Now."

Like a trained monkey, Nevaeh moves quickly across the kitchen floor, past her dad, and disappears around the corner. A second passes and I hear the front door close.

"Whoa. What's going on?" Jo asks, and I see Marcus step through the patio doors. "We took good care of them. The party's just getting started. Why they gotta leave?"

"Tiffany and Nevaeh did not have permission to be here," Anthony explains. "I am taking them back home."

"Tiffany? Is that true?" Jo asks. "You told me your dad said it was okay."

"I really wanted to come, so I lied. I'm sorry."

Monique steps inside. "Everything okay here?"

"No," Anthony bellows. "Everything is not okay. Tiffany came here without getting permission from me. You both should have contacted me to see if it was all right. That was negligent on your part."

"That's a big word for a Saturday afternoon, Anthony." Monique moves to stand beside Jo. "Let's not make this a bigger deal than it is. Nobody got hurt. The girls were with family here."

"You are not their family," he snaps. "And your lifestyle could have a negative..." Anthony stops cold, shifts uncomfortably.

Jo crosses her arms across her chest. "Don't stop. Cat's outta the bag. Might as well let it all out. *That's* what this is all about, huh, Dr. Stone? Our *lifestyle*? We don't pass all your religious requirements? I'm 'bad' because the person I choose to love and spend my life with doesn't have a penis? Where's the logic in that?"

Anthony gasps. "Jo, please watch your language around children."

Jo huffs. "Anthony Stone. *Penis* is not a bad word. And this is my house. I'll say whatever I want. Penis. There. Said it again."

"Jehovah *God*," Anthony exclaims. "I really think it would be best if you kept your distance from my girls. And your son, too. I don't want him associating with my daughters."

Jo steps forward, seething. "We have put up with your self-righteous, holier-than-thou bullshit for years now and we've tried our hardest to show you the love of God even though, in return, you've shown us nothing but contempt. And what have we ever done to you except be kind neighbors? You wanna look at my son and treat him like he's some kind of leper? Order your girls not to speak to him? And then you get all dressed up on Sunday mornings and take your family to church like a damn hypocrite. Let me tell you one thing." She puts her hand on her hip and points her finger directly at Anthony. "One day, we are all going to stand before God and be held accountable for our actions. I feel good about who I am and what I've done while I've been living. Jesus knows I have. Can you say the same? I am proud as hell to be Jo McKinney. And my wife and I have raised our son to be an upstanding young man who excels at pretty much everything he does in spite of the hand that he's been dealt. I am a grown-ass woman and he's a grown-ass man and I refuse to stand here and let you, of all people, a man who I believe hasn't raised a damn cat, tell me what to do with my son! Tiffany is welcome over here anytime, you understand me? Anytime. Now, you get the hell out of my house. How's that for watching my language?"

She turns and storms through the patio doors with Monique at her heels. Marcus and I exchange sad looks before he turns and exits, as well, leaving Anthony and me alone in the kitchen.

"Anthony," I start. "I'm sorry."

"Let's go. Now."

"I have to grab my things upstairs."

"Make it quick."

We ride to Malibu in the most uncomfortable silence since the creation of uncomfortable silences. I grip the car seat and stare out the window at the lines on the freeway, Anthony grips the steering wheel and stares straight ahead, and Nevaeh just seems utterly confused as to what's going on and is dead silent. Probably a first for her.

When we finally pull up to the Malibu town house, the garage door slides open and we all breathe a sigh of relief. Time out. Now we get to go back to our corners. Rest and recuperate for the next round of Sly versus Stone.

"Nevaeh. Bath and bed."

"Yes, sir." She quickly exits the car.

"Tiffany, I don't have words for what you did. You had Margaret in *hysterics*. You're grounded. I have your guitar in our room and it'll stay with me for the next month. No phone, either. Hand it over."

I give it to him. "Do you know why the McKinneys have family barbecues all the time?"

He doesn't respond. Only continues gripping the steering wheel and staring straight ahead.

"Marcus has a heart condition. Hypertrophic cardiomyopathy. He's already died once. He could die again…this time for good. They do it to celebrate his life. Because they don't know when it'll happen. His death."

He leans his head back against the car seat and rubs his temples. I wait for a few moments but he has no reply. Not even a *Gee whiz, I'm so sorry to hear that.*

"You're such a trip."

"Excuse me?" he replies.

"You just are. The way you talk to Margaret. The way you parent Pumpkin. All the weird rules."

"Are we about to start arguing again?"

"Definitely not." I push open the car door.

"Tiffany," Anthony says.

I pause.

"I like foreign films. They focus more on plot rather than all the fancy stuff like American films."

"Huh?"

He wrings his hands together like a nervous tween. "You said we were supposed to be getting to know one another. You said you couldn't imagine your mom loving a guy like me. So

I thought you should know I like foreign films. Imani did, too. We used to find random ones at the library and watch them together. I loved how she could see the beauty in life even when it looked so ugly. She had this amazing capacity to love."

Thump-thump, thump-thump: *He's* talking *to you. Like… really* talking.

I clear my throat and say timidly, "Um, which one is your favorite? Foreign films, I mean."

"I feel like picking a favorite is insulting all the others. So many of them are amazing. I don't know. Probably *Cinema Paradiso.*"

"I've never seen that one. Why is it your favorite?"

"Watch it. You will have a straight view into my soul."

I'm not sure why, but his words make my eyes well with tears. I twist my body around so he can't see. I suppose Anthony took the body movement to mean I was done talking and heading into the house because he quickly says, "Plans haven't changed, Tiffany. We leave for the airport at 7:00 a.m. tomorrow. You understand, right?"

I deflate. How could he force another flight on me when he knows how I feel? And here I thought we were getting to know one another. "Whatever you say."

I exit the car and slam the door shut. Soaring through the air in another tin can with wings? If they weren't already dead I could freakin' kill the Wright brothers.

20

"Breathe, Tiffany. Breathe." Nevaeh laughs.

"I'm not breathing?"

"Not enough. You're gonna die if you don't breathe."

The plane rumbles and I grab on to her leg. "I'm scared."

"It's turbulence." Nevaeh takes a giant bite from a granola bar and chews loudly, talking with her mouth full. "A little turbulence is superduper normal."

"Totes," Heaven adds from the tan leather seat across from us. "Besides, if the plane crashes, we'd pass out before we made impact with the ground."

"Good point, sis," Nevaeh replies. "And then *ka-boom*. It would all be over."

"Seriously, you guys?" I say.

"Nevaeh?" Heaven scolds. "Stop. You're scaring Tiffany."

"You're the one who said we'd pass out before we made impact with the ground." Nevaeh takes another giant bite of her granola bar.

"I know, but you said ka-boom." Heaven grimaces. "It was the ka-boom that scared her."

"Wanna get off plane. Go outside!" Pumpkin's squirming to get away from Margaret and thrashing around. In fact, Pumpkin's contributing to a good percentage of my anxiety. She's been an absolute *terror* for the past half hour.

"Pumpkin, sit *down*," Margaret says with calm authority, and Pumpkin starts to wail. Her big blue eyes pour out crocodile tears as she yanks at her massive mound of curly hair.

Anthony reaches into Margaret's purse and grabs a binky. He gives it to Pumpkin, who gleefully pops it into her mouth and sits quietly for the first time since the flight began.

Margaret frowns. "A pacifier? You say only at night."

Anthony holds his hands out for Pumpkin. She squeals with delight, slides off Margaret's lap and jumps into Anthony's arms. Margaret looks more than a little stunned.

"What are we supposed to do, right?" Anthony wraps his arms around Pumpkin and kisses her on the cheek. "We're thirty thousand feet in the air. She needs to stay seated? She gets a binky."

Anthony and I look at each other across the aisle of the small private jet. His eyebrows are raised. Eyes hopeful. I could be mistaken, but it's almost as if he's looking...for my approval?

"Unless," he goes on, "you think it's a bad idea? We can put the binky away. It's your call."

Margaret grabs a novel from the bag seated beside her. "She's quiet. I'm happy."

The plane rumbles again and my seat shakes. "Omigosh. Is this normal?"

Nevaeh wraps her arm around my shoulders. "Tiff, it's normal. Hey, let's play a game."

"Okay."

"This game is called…'tell me something I don't know about you.' You go first."

"My, uh, middle name is Major."

"Really? That's so cool!" Nevaeh squeals. "Hey, Dad, did you know Tiffany's middle name is Major?"

"No," Anthony replies. "I did not know that."

"I totally get what your mom did there with the Minor and Major and I love it," Nevaeh exclaims.

"What do you mean?" I reply.

"Did you not know?" Heaven cuts in. "Dad's middle name is Minor."

I could be imagining it, but Anthony's eyes look red. Is he about to cry?

Nevaeh takes the final bite of her granola bar and crumbles the wrapper in her hand. "You're the Major chord. Dad's the Minor. Holy cow, so clever! Hey, Mom and Dad, how come you guys didn't give me a clever middle name to go with Dad's name. Like Treble Clef or something?"

Heaven snorts. "Nevaeh Treble Clef Stone? That's the dumbest name ever."

The plane shakes again and I squeeze Nevaeh's leg. I feel her wince a bit, but she doesn't say anything.

"Okay, my turn," Nevaeh exclaims. "I love the rain."

I turn to her. "Really?"

She nods. "Oh, yeah. I love it. It makes me happy for some reason. And the sun kind of makes me sad. But I don't know why."

"You know, there's a name for that," Anthony interrupts.

"I think they call it weird," Heaven replies.

"They call it seasonal depression." He bounces Pumpkin

on his knee. "But for most people it's opposite. The rain and colder months make them unhappy. That's cool to know, Nevaeh. I'm the same way. Maybe we can take a vacation to the tropics in the rainy season."

"I like rain, too," I add.

"You do?" Nevaeh beams. "Of course you do! We're *sisters*. I bet we have tons of other things in common, too. I can't wait to find out." She lays her head on my shoulder. Her curly ponytail brushes against me, tickling my face. I lean my head on top of hers.

Sisters. It does have a nice ring to it.

Speaking of sisters, London is sitting by herself, staring out the window. She hasn't said a word all morning and she's wearing a terrifying-looking black dress that reaches all the way to the floor, as if she's in mourning or something.

"Hey, why is London Bridge falling down?" Nevaeh whispers. "She looks a mess."

"PMS probably," Heaven replies, and Nevaeh nods.

At this point, PMS would be all kinds of awesome for London.

Dear Life, please, please, *please* send some good, old-fashioned PMS to London.

I feel a tap on my shoulder and turn to see the male flight attendant kneeling beside us. "We're approaching. You guys need to put on your seat belts."

"Will you look at that?" Nevaeh says. "Tiffany, you survived!"

I click on my seat belt. "Tell me that when we've landed."

The Mirage hotel in Las Vegas is pretty rock star. Our ginormous suite is overlooking the Vegas Strip with bright rays of morning sun bouncing off all the colorful hotels, restaurants and shops. Heaven and Nevaeh are happily chasing Pumpkin around the room. London is hunched over, staring at a magazine, a look of pure misery plastered on her pretty face. Anthony and Margaret seem like they're pretending to be happy, but I sense the sadness and tension between them. It's my fault. I've ruined their happy home. I'm the one that's got them looking like the forlorn-faced farmers in Grant Wood's *American Gothic* painting. But then again, London deserves some of the blame for their misery. A broken purity vow would bring sadness to any parent's eyes.

And Pumpkin's a *handful.* She's an adorable nightmare. Definitely her fault, too.

And Nevaeh talks…a lot.

I grab my stomach. There's a new sensation there. Like I'm coming down with something. The flu or the black plague or *cholera.* I wish I had my pills. I'm behind three pills. By tonight it'll be *four.* Anthony's gotta come to his senses…if he has any. I don't want to rock the boat any more than it's already rocked, but this is not okay. Still… I can wait till we get home to make him give them back to me. That is, if we survive the flight back. Another freakin' *flight.*

Thump-thump, thump-thump: *You've survived two flights.*

Thump-thump, thump-thump: *Ain't no way you surviving three!*

I scratch my head. *Uggh.* This weave *itches*! I hate weaves. I want my braids back.

I can't help but wonder what the natural disaster is here in Vegas. In Chicago, it was crazy, wild thunder and lightning storms, and tornadoes. In Southern Cal, of course, it's earthquakes. But what does Vegas have? Instant death from extreme heat?

I move into the bathroom and shut the door behind me. There's a bathtub in here. I remember the moment I thought Margaret was drowning Pumpkin. That was so awful! What would it be like to drown? You'd inhale water and then what? You'd just black out? Or would you suffocate? Drowning sounds like the worst way to die. I'd rather burn to a crisp. At least it would be quick.

A knock at the door startles me out of my fantasies.

"Tiffany?" Anthony's muffled voice says from the other side. "Room service before we head down to the show. You want anything?"

"No, thank you. I'm not hungry."

Third row center at Cirque du Soleil and I'm feeling like bugs are crawling all over my skin, but trying my hardest to act cool, calm and collected. Thankfully, everyone's completely engrossed in the Playbill and not paying attention to me as I scope out the exits to this theater. If something happened, like one of those mass shootings where some crazed killer comes in with semiautomatic weapons and shoots up the place, I'd need to know which direction to run. But the theater is packed. Not an empty seat in the house. If *that* happened, it would be utter chaos! I'm not exactly dressed for mass hysteria. Black ankle boots, blue chiffon dress with a black suede belt and suede jacket to match. And it's not like Anthony's dressed for a rescue. White dress pants, pale pink shirt, brown leather shoes. How's he gonna drag me from a pack of screaming people in brown leather shoes and a pink shirt?

"Check this out." Nevaeh leans over, showing me the program. "Paul McCartney has come to the show before. Coolness!"

"Mmm. Nice," I say.

Please stop talking, Nevaeh. For the love of your Jehovah God. Stop talking!

The lights flicker and I jump.

London squeezes my leg. "That means the show's about to start. You okay? You seem on edge."

"I'm good. I'm great."

I look over my shoulder. There's another exit. Whew. Lots of ways to get out of this joint. Always gotta be aware.

The lights dim and the show begins.

Uggh, this *show.* I scowl. This show is what I'd describe as the Beatles music meets the circus from hell. It soothes my soul to hear the smooth stylings of the best boy band in the history of boy bands. But these freakishly frightening images? Pumpkin shouldn't be watching this. I'm no expert on autism but I *am* an expert on weird shit. Too weird for me, let alone an autistic two-year-old who's scared of water getting in her ears. Contortionists, trapeze artists dressed like ghosts, people spinning on their heads. *Clowns?* This is spine-chilling. An *awful* idea for a show.

When is halftime? I mean…intermission. Oh, I feel nauseous. I keep closing and opening my eyes, and each time I open them, fresh images of horror are on the stage. Finally, after what feels like an eternity of gymnasts on bicycles, trapeze artists soaring through the air to the tune of Beatles hits and men and women with painted faces who could easily pass for demons or devils and will surely haunt my and Pumpkin's dreams, the curtain closes on the freakishness that is Cirque du Soleil and the houselights come up for intermission.

"What do you think?" Margaret whispers to us, holding a sleeping Pumpkin on her lap.

I hate it. *Hate it!* "It's nice," I reply with a fake smile.

"So cool, Mom," Heaven and Nevaeh exclaim in unison.

"It *is* cool, huh?" Margaret gives her signature polite tilt of the head for the first time today. "I'm in awe of the acrobats. The things they can do. Astounding."

Astoundingly awful. People are scooting past us to get to the aisle. People are so annoying and impatient. Why are they touching me? "London, can I borrow your phone?"

She hands it to me and I stand. "Bathroom?"

"Yeah. Me, too." London grumbles like she's about to graduate from sad school in her sad black dress.

I don't wait for her. I scoot down the aisle and move out of the theater as fast as I can.

Standing in line for the women's restroom is literally painful. My feet are throbbing in my heels and my stomach is killing me. Why do I have this foreboding? Maybe it's Marcus. Maybe I'm becoming psychic after meditating for twenty-seven seconds the other day and I know he's dying. I whip out my phone and send him a quick text: Are you alive? It's Tiffany, texting from London's phone. Please tell me you're okay?

Marcus: The better question is, are you okay?

Me: Oh, thank God you're all right!

Marcus: What's wrong?

Me: Flew into Vegas this morning. Flying back this evening. Am I okay to make the second flight?

Marcus: What do you mean?

Me: Do you think our plane will land? Or crash? Can you meditate on it for me? I have this bad feeling it's going to crash. Use your meditation powers to check and see if our plane's gonna crash.

Marcus doesn't text back right away. The line inches forward. I'm almost next. C'mon, Marcus! Text me back. C'mon! I hear a toilet flush and the line moves forward again. It's my turn. Shit. I stuff the phone in the pocket of my jacket and move into the stall.

The lights are dimming, the second half of the not so greatest show on Earth is about to start and Marcus still hasn't texted me back. What is *wrong* with him?

"Tiffany?" London settles into her seat beside me. "Are you sure you're okay? Can I have my phone back?"

I turn to her as the lights fade to darkness. "Huh? I'm fine." Her phone buzzes in my pocket. Yes! I pull it out and check the message as the curtains open slowly and the blaring sound of guitars fills the theater space. I read the text from Marcus.

Tiffany...call me.

Oh, *no*. He knows. He knows the plane is set to crash to-night when we fly home after the show!

I stand. "Excuse me, please." I scoot out of the aisle and race out of the theater. I push open the doors and rush into the vestibule, dialing Marcus as I pace back and forth.

A moment later, Anthony pushes through the doors and steps out into the vestibule.

"Tiffany? What is going *on*?"

"I need to talk to Marcus. Something's weird." Crap. Voice mail. What the fuck! Who tells somebody to call them and then doesn't pick up the phone?

"Tiffany? Tell me what's wrong. Right now."

"I can't do it! Please don't make me get back on that plane. I can't do it!"

"Oh, not this again. You did good. We landed. We're fine."

"I feel it in my gut! Something bad is gonna happen after the show. I think it's the *plane*!"

One of the ushers is staring at us. Anthony glares at the man. "Do you have some business to tend to, so you can get out of ours?"

The usher scoots away.

"It's the same feeling I had before Mom told me. I didn't feel right. And—" My eyes burn as tears spill down my cheeks. "She came home and—" It's getting harder to breathe.

"It's okay, Tiff. Take your time. I'm not going anywhere."

"She came home and—and she told me she was going to die. But I knew we could pray. I had faith we could fight it! And I prayed. I swear I prayed so hard! But it didn't work!" I cry. "She still *died*. So how do we know what to *do*? Who *helps* us?" I pause to catch my breath. "I'm so scared."

I've never seen a deer standing in front of approaching headlights, but I imagine that deer would look something like Anthony looks right now. Eyes wide and filled with horror. A desire to run but not sure which way to go.

"Please don't make me get on that plane. I can't do it." He wraps his arms around me. I can feel his heart racing. Sense his confusion. Or maybe it's my racing heart and my own crazed confusion. "I don't wanna die. I'm *scared* to die."

"You're not going to die."

"Yes, I am! Why does everyone keep saying that to me? I will! One hundred out of one hundred people die. Everybody dies." I sob. "She *died*. Why did she have to die? What's the point of living, if all we do is die?"

He holds me tighter. "Shh. Tiffany, it's okay. I understand. I hear you."

I sob onto his shoulder, his crisp pink shirt wet and wrinkled from all my tears. "Please. Please don't make me fly."

He lifts my chin gently so that I'm staring into his bright eyes. He wipes away my tears with the back of his other hand. "Here's what we're going to do. Forget the rest of this show. We're going to go to the airport—"

"No!" I wail. "Please, no!"

"Tiffany, wait. Shh. Listen to me. Hear me out."

I cover my mouth to contain my sobs.

"We're going to go to the airport…and rent a *car.* We're going to *drive* home. Okay? How's that sound?"

"But what about Pumpkin? She can't do long car rides."

"The rest of the family will fly. But you and me? In a car. On the *ground*."

"Thank you!" I lurch forward and wrap my arms around

him. My body shaking, heart racing, head pounding. "Am I crazy? Am I like…insane-asylum crazy?"

"I had no right to take away your medication. I had no *right.* I'm sorry, Tiffany. You need a chance to get better. I'm here for you."

I lay my head on his shoulder and suddenly realize all those years I spent without a dad I needed one. All the days I've been here…I've *wanted* one. "You promise?" I cry.

"I promise." He holds me tight. "I'm here, okay? I'm here."

I rub my tired eyes and smooth out my wrinkled dress as we speed down the dark highway.

"Go ahead and sleep, Tiffany," Anthony insists. "Only a couple more hours left. When you wake, we'll be back home."

I could certainly *pretend* to sleep. But to ensure we make it back okay, I need to remain on task, staring out the window, watching the highway lines race by in a blur.

"You can't sleep, can you?"

"I'm sorry."

"Don't be. Whenever I'm driving with Margaret and the girls it's almost like a contest to see who can get to sleep the fastest. It's nice to have the company. Hey, let's play a game?"

My brow furrows. "Is it 'I spy with my little eye'? Cuz I hate that game."

He laughs. "I was thinking 'two truths and a lie.' Ever played before?"

I have. You give three statements. Your opponent has to guess which two are true and which statement is a lie. "Sure. You want me to go first?"

"Go for it."

This should be easy, since Anthony basically knows nothing about me. "Okay. I grew four inches the summer before the eighth grade. I was once featured on *Sesame Street* singing with Elmo. Mom and I got trapped in an elevator for five hours at the Waldorf Astoria after sneaking into a wedding reception to get free cake."

Anthony shakes his head. "You're not playing the game fair."

"Huh? Yes, I am."

"Nope. The game is two truths and a lie. You just told two lies."

"No way. I did not."

Anthony shakes his head again. "Yes, you did. You were once on *Sesame Street*. But you didn't sing with Elmo. It was a Word on the Street segment. And it was the summer before the *seventh* grade when you grew four inches."

I turn to Anthony. Holy crapoly. "It *was* the summer before seventh grade. I didn't mean to say 'eighth.'" My jaw drops. "How did you know that?"

"Your mom told me."

"She did? When?"

"We talked for about an hour every day leading up to her death. If I had questions, she'd answer them. And I had a lot of questions. She told me everything about you."

"Like what?"

"You name it. Your best friend is Keelah. Favorite color is gray. Your dream vacation is Ireland. You like superhero movies, favorite being *Wonder Woman*. In fact, you dressed up like Wonder Woman last Halloween. You—"

"Wait a minute." I scratch my head in confusion. "You

spent all this time talking to Mom about me? Why didn't you talk to *me*? I never heard from you. Except for the one or two phone calls to arrange my flight."

"That's because your mom asked me not to contact you."

"That makes no sense. She knew I was coming to live with you."

Anthony slowly switches lanes to pass a truck. I close my eyes and grip the side of my door.

"She wanted the last days of her life to be spent in peace with just you and her mom," Anthony says. "Had I been in constant contact, it would've been a distraction. It's why we both agreed not to tell you about your sisters."

I open my eyes. We've passed the truck. I exhale. "That's why she kept it secret?"

"You have no idea how bad I felt when I had to run and do an emergency surgery the *moment* you landed. I didn't want you to arrive at a house with sisters and a stepmom you didn't even know existed. Tiffany, I felt so bad about that."

"That really was the worst."

"I know. I'm sorry."

"What about after Mom died? I still didn't hear much from you."

"I thought it was best to give you time to grieve with your grandma. I kept my distance, Tiffany. But I certainly didn't want to. I thought I was doing the right thing. It was a mistake. I see that now."

It makes *some* sense. Knowing I had four sisters certainly could have been overwhelming information to get when my mom was dying of cancer. And it *would* have been a lot to deal with—getting to know Anthony, knowing there was a stepmom. "All this time I thought you just didn't like me or something."

Anthony laughs. "Tiffany, that's silly. You're my daughter. I love you."

Unless I'm not his daughter. Will he love me then? We continue down the road in silence. I return to gazing out the window, hypnotized by the blurry highway. Anthony breaks the silence by saying, "Is it my turn yet?"

"Hmm?"

"Two truths and a lie? We're still playing, right?"

"Oh. Right. Yeah. Your turn."

"Okay." He taps the steering wheel. "I got it. I am sorry for all you've been through. I'm *really* sorry I went to San Francisco. I'm a moron."

I turn my head toward him. Watching him nervously clear his throat and repeatedly rub his hand across his forehead like he has a mild form of Tourette's. I kinda feel sorry for Anthony as he sits there looking as lost as a little kid, trying so hard to properly manage this first attempt to really get to know me. "You're not a moron. That's definitely the lie."

"You sure?" He heaves a heavy sigh. "Because taking away your medicine was pretty moronic."

I nod in agreement. "True."

"You forgive me?"

"That depends. Are you giving it back to me?"

"I already texted Darryl. He's picking up the medicine from the house in Malibu and dropping it off in Simi."

"Cool. Then apology accepted."

"Wanna listen to some Black Sabbath?"

I toss him a disbelieving look. “You don’t strike me as a Black Sabbath fan.”

“What type of fan do I strike you as?”

I shrug. “I dunno. Poison, maybe.”

His eyes bulge. “Tiffany Sly. I will pull this car over and make you walk home, you say something like that again.”

I laugh. “What? Poison’s…okay. ‘Every Rose Has Its Thorn.’ That’s a good song.”

Anthony rolls his eyes. “That’s *so* deep. Just like every car has its wheels?”

“Or like…every chicken has its bones.”

Anthony starts to sing to the tune of “Every Rose Has Its Thorn.” “Every house has its dooooor.”

I crack up laughing. And as Anthony and I make up more silly Poison lyrics while cruising across the highway, I relax for the first time all day.

As we pull into the massive driveway of Anthony and Margaret’s home, I check the clock on the dash of the rented SUV—10:30 p.m.

“That was quite a drive.” Anthony turns to me. “Inside the pantry, in a giant box marked Gluten-Free Pasta, is a hidden bag of Cheetos. Wanna sneak it into the den and share it?”

“I would love that more than life.” I grab my bag from off the floor and sling the long strap over my shoulder. “Hey… Curington has an after-school music program. Could I maybe join?”

“Of course. That’s a great idea.”

As we both push open the car doors, Margaret steps outside the house.

"Hey, babe," Anthony calls out casually as he moves to rummage through the back seat, gathering up his things. "How was the flight back?"

Margaret doesn't respond. She only stands there, nervously wringing her hands together.

Anthony grabs his small suitcase and slams the door shut. "What? What's wrong?"

I cover my mouth in horror as Xavior Xavion, in the flesh, steps through the door to stand beside Margaret, towering over her like a Chicago skyscraper.

"Who is this?" Anthony asks caustically.

Xavior and I exchange looks. Of *course*. Somehow I wasn't paying enough attention. Somehow the time raced by. Hours like seconds. Days like hours. My eyes, head and heart seem as though they each weigh a hundred pounds, like it's taking all my strength to simply hold up my body weight and keep my internal organs from combusting.

"Perhaps we should discuss that privately in your office?" Margaret looks over at me and gives me a polite tilt of the head. "Tiffany, sweetheart, why don't you head upstairs and unpack and we'll be up to speak with you momentarily."

"Um…" I glance back and forth between her, Xavior and a very confused-looking Anthony.

"Tiffany, please go inside like Margaret asked you to," Anthony demands as if he senses something's not quite right and is eager to protect me.

I avoid looking at Xavior as I move past him and Margaret to step through the door into the house. I inch slowly up the spiral staircase, clutching my bag tightly to my side. The sad sound of crying startles me from my feelings of utter agony as I move into the bedroom I share with London. The bathroom door is cracked partially open. A soft pool of light spills onto the dark wood floor. I peek inside. London is kneeling over the tub, hands folded in prayer.

"Please, Jehovah," she cries softly. "Please forgive me, Jehovah God. Please. I beg You."

I quietly back away from the door, slumping down onto the mattress, remembering my own middle-of-the-night prayers.

Please, God, I'd pray. *Please don't let my mom die. Please. I beg you.*

Mom's iPad. Something about it calls to me, stops me from curling up and assuming my favorite position. I can hold it close. I can look through her ebooks, play all the games she liked, check her planner, scroll through her photos. Wait patiently while Anthony gets all the details of how I might not be his kid.

I slide my bag off my shoulders and reach inside to retrieve the device. Holding it tightly, I crawl into my bed and scroll aimlessly through the apps. I click the photo icon and hundreds of images load on the display. I stare at them, perplexed for a moment. Videos? I scratch my head. Where did all these come from? I've never seen them before and I used to borrow Mom's iPad all the time. I scroll. There are so *many*. I tap one of the images and the video bounces to life.

"Hi, Tiffany!" Mom happily waves at me from the iPad. "Today is March 23 and it's 5:00 a.m. You're asleep in your room." She runs her fingers through her hair. Mom had beautiful hair. She blow-dried it so it hung in fluffy bunches on her shoulders. Her dark brown skin looks vibrant and healthy. I wipe a tear. March 23. Two days after she got her diagnosis. Before chemo and radiation left her as a shell of her former self.

"Okay, so this is my third video diary for you. I'm starting to get used to making them. Even though it feels like I'm talkin' to myself and going crazy. I dunno." She giggles. Mom had such a girlish, youthful energy about her. "Oh, Tiffany, if you knew I was making you these videos you would be so mad. You don't wanna believe I'm dying, but that's okay. Death is okay. I have a peace with it. And these videos…you'll be able to keep them forever. You can always come back and talk to me. Let's try it. Hi, Tiffany." She pauses for a few seconds. "Tiffany Sly. This is where you say hi back. Say, 'Hi, Mom.'" She pauses again. "Girl, say hi!"

"Hi, Mommy." I cover my mouth to silence my cry.

"Hi, honey. See? Wasn't that easy? We can always talk like this now. For years and years until we meet again on the other side."

I pause the video, grab tissues from off my nightstand and blow my nose as quietly as I can. I tap another image. Once again, Mom bounces to life from beyond the grave.

"Hi, Tiff honey! You have no idea how weird it is for a parent to see their kid grow up. I swear it was just yesterday you were running around this apartment in your diaper." She fans her eyes. "I don't wanna get emotional. Let me stop." She takes a deep breath. Her warm brown eyes glisten as she repositions herself on her bed. "Okay, my dear. Today I want to talk to you about *s-e-x*. That spells *sex*. I know, I know. Gross. Mommy talking to you about sex? But it's bound to happen. So here are the rules. 1. You should be in a committed relationship…preferably married. 2. You should be old enough to deal with the responsibility behind it. 3. You should be with a man who you love and who loves you and who respects you and admires you." She smiles. "And finally... you should forgive yourself when pretty much none of that happens. If it turns out that you're not married, you're not old enough to deal with the responsibility, the d-bag doesn't love you and you get your heart broken, you come back and watch this video and listen carefully to my words, okay? You listening, Tiffany Sly? You ready?" She takes a deep breath. "It's *okay*. In the grand scheme of life, losing your virginity is like..." She presses her thumb and forefinger together. "This important. God doesn't care about most of the nonsense we be thinkin' about. God is love and understanding and sex is just a blip on the radar. Use protection. Be safe. I don't wanna see grandkids from heaven." She giggles again. "Not for at least a decade, girl. You hear me?"

"That's your mom?"

I turn. London is standing beside my bed. I blow my nose again and nod.

"She's so pretty." London climbs over me and sits beside me under the blankets. "You look like her."

"Thanks." London glances over my shoulder as I scroll through the videos. "She made these for me," I whisper. "I never knew. Not until now."

"That's amazing, Tiff. Now you can always come and say hi to her. It'll be kind of like you have her back, huh? In a way, I mean."

"In a way. I guess it will be kind of like that."

There's a knock on our door before it's pushed open. It's

Anthony, looking as disturbed as Margaret did a few minutes ago.

"Tiffany, may I see you in my office downstairs?"

Fuck my life, for real. I swing my legs out of bed. Countdown to ultimate destruction begins…right…now.

"Is everything okay, Dad?" London asks curiously.

"Yes, London. Go to sleep," he replies. "School in the morning."

I swallow and follow him out the door.

I squirm in the fancy leather chair across from Anthony in his giant home office. Xavior sits in a matching armchair beside me. Margaret stands beside Anthony, a hand resting on his shoulder. She smiles comfortingly and gives me a polite tilt of the head.

"Xavior is not a friend from school, Tiffany." Anthony shakes his head. "You lied to me. Why did you lie?"

"Don't accuse her of lying, man," Xavior says. "This is a lot. She didn't know what else to do."

"Excuse me?" Anthony's pissed. "Don't tell me how to talk to my daughter."

Margaret squeezes Anthony's shoulder. "Everything's fine. We're having a peaceful discussion. Right, everyone?"

Xavior sighs. Anthony rolls his eyes.

"Xavior's right." I hang my head low. "I didn't know what to do."

"How long have you known this man?" Anthony asks.

"This man has a name," Xavior cuts in.

"Uh…" I look over at Xavior. He gives me an encouraging nod. "Mom never mentioned him. I swear she didn't. He showed up at my door the day before I left. I didn't tell you guys because I was scared. I don't want to upset your home this way. I feel terrible."

"Sweetheart, don't feel terrible. You're not upsetting our home." Margaret politely tilts her head again. "None of this is your fault."

"You won't be going to school in the morning," Anthony declares.

"Are you sending me back to Chicago?"

Anthony looks up, frowning. "*What?* No."

"Tiffany, we would never do that," Margaret states. "We are your legal guardians. Your mom left you in our care. We hold that in the highest honor."

"Besides, we don't even know who this man is. He could be a local Chicago crackhead, for all we know."

"You know what, man?" Xavior stands in anger. "I've had just about enough of you!"

"Honey." Margaret turns to Anthony, irritated. "We have to take this seriously. Xavior has hired a lawyer to determine paternity. He has every right to know if Tiffany is his child." Margaret motions to Xavior to sit. "Please. We apologize. This is just...well, it's a lot. You understand, Xavior?"

An angry Xavior slams back into his seat.

Anthony calmly rests his elbows on the glossy wood of his massive desk, not seeming the least bit intimidated by Xavior. "Anyway, there's an express DNA testing facility in Los Angeles which Tiffany and I will go to *alone*." He glares at Xavior when he stresses the word *alone*. "Because we have a legal case on our hands, our family lawyer will facilitate. We can have the results same day. As quickly as eight hours."

"And then what?" I ask. Like what if it says I'm *not* a Stone? What will happen then?

"Xavior?" Margaret asks with her signature eerie calm. "Would you mind giving us a moment alone with Tiffany? You can wait in the den—it's right across the hall."

Xavior stands. "Not a problem." He reaches across the space between our chairs and squeezes my hand. "It's *really* good to see you again, Tiffany."

"You, too, Xavior," I reply softly, struggling to fight back the tears boiling to the surface.

As Xavior moves toward the door, Anthony calls out, "And we have cameras in the den and pretty much everywhere in our home. Don't get any ideas."

You can tell Xavior wants to lurch across the desk and choke Anthony until he loses consciousness, but he only shakes his head in disbelief and pushes into the hallway. A moment of silence passes after the office door clicks shut.

"We're going to prepare for a legal battle." Margaret breaks the silence. "We will legally adopt you if we have to. We won't give you up without a fight. Right, Anthony? I mean, this is what her mom wanted. This was her dying wish. That has to count for *something.* He can't come here and take her from us, can he? She's started Curington. This is her home now." Margaret's voice has risen to a fevered pitch, but Anthony Stone only sighs in response and a deafening silence falls over the room. Tragic.

"Tiffany," Margaret says ever so softly. "Perhaps you can walk Xavior out. I'm sure you're exhausted. I'm sure he's exhausted, as well, and would probably like to get back to his hotel. It's been a long day for everyone."

I stand, thank them both and move toward the door before the tears spring forth. *We won't give you up without a fight*, she said. And what did he say in response?

Not a fucking word.

I push through the office door, move across the hallway and step into the dimly lit den with all its rustic brown leather furnishings and floor-to-ceiling windows that overlook the sprawling backyard. Xavior stands when I enter.

"Um, they want me to walk you out."

"Tiffany, I'm so sorry I lost my temper in there."

"*That* was losing your temper? You should've seen me yesterday."

"What happened yesterday?"

"Let's just say it involved an F-bomb and a kidnapping." I motion with my hand down the hallway. "We should hurry."

Xavior follows me as I move across the dark wood floors of one hallway, turn around a corner and continue down another long hallway. When we finally make it to the front door, my hand rests on the bronze doorknob for a long moment. I turn to him.

"You flew all the way out here, Xavior? I can't believe you did that."

"That's nothing. You know I'm willing to move, Tiffany."

"I'm sorry?"

"If it turns out you're mine. I'll sell my home so you can be in your old school district and close to your grandmother. I won't be able to buy anything nearly as fancy as this, but you'll have your own room and office space for your schoolwork and we can get a pet. You like dogs?"

"Um—"

"And we'll start grief counseling. Together. I've never been a dad before, but I'm willing to give it everything I've got. I promise you that. I *want* to be your dad."

And the tears I worked so hard to hold back in Anthony's office crawl down my cheeks. I should say, *I want you to be my dad, too, Xavior.* Something deep within me says he's a good man and actually would make a great dad. I want to squeal with excitement at the chance to have my old life back. But all I can manage to say in response to Xavior's heartfelt expression is "Yeah. I know you do."

No matter what I try I can't seem to fall asleep. I've counted sheep. Imagined every happy thought imaginable in the universe. Invented a new alphabet. Nothing. I glance at the digital clock on the dresser—4:00 a.m.—and I haven't slept a wink. Today will be hell. I grab Lucky and squeeze her tight. Weird. I feel a hard object that I hadn't noticed before. Normally Lucky is as soft as a basket of socks fresh out of the dryer. I sit up. London is sleeping soundly on the bed beside me. I squeeze Lucky again. There it is! I can feel some sort of…object underneath her fur. I twist the stuffed animal around and lift up her T-shirt. A zipper? My brow furrows. That definitely was *not* there before. I pull the zipper down and reach inside. My fingers wrap around something hard and rectangular. I pull it out and gasp. It's my *phone.* There is a note wrapped around it with a rubber band. I pull off the band and open the folded paper. It reads:

Because a girl deserves some privacy. Keep it secret. Love you. Grams

I cover my mouth to mute my squeal of delight and power it up. My phone is back and fully charged! Grams rocks. I could call Keelah. Tell her the happy news. Or I could call Xavior to make sure he made it back safely to his hotel. Thanks to Tommy Tutone I know his number by heart: 867-5309. He'd want to talk to me. He'd be thrilled I called. He'd stop anything and everything for a few seconds of conversation with me. I mean, he flew all the way to California for me. But instead, I tap the movie app icon on my phone and do a search for *Cinema Paradiso.* I click the link to purchase. Anthony said if I watched it, I would have a window into his soul. I'd like that very much.

I pull the covers over my head so I won't wake London. The movie is subtitled but I don't mind reading. It's about true love and leaving home and never being able to come back again. I don't know why it touches my heart so deeply, but it does. After the credits roll, I cry about a million tears and drift into a somber sleep.

21

"I need coffee," I confess to Anthony as we approach the freeway toward Los Angeles. "I couldn't sleep last night."

He frowns. "I don't allow my girls to have caffeine until they're—" He pauses. I see his fingers tighten around the steering wheel. "I'm sorry you couldn't sleep, Tiffany. I couldn't, either." He sighs. "How much sleep do you think you got?"

"Forty-five minutes. Maybe."

"Ouch." He makes a sharp turn into a parking lot with a Starbucks. "We'll keep this between you and me."

He pulls into the drive-through, and within a moment, we're both sipping on caramel Frappuccinos. Caffeine begins to course through my veins, lifting the fatigue. After I slurp down the last bit of my grande, sugary goodness, the car ride to the express DNA facility becomes excruciatingly quiet. Like the kind of quiet you'd expect when our sun finally explodes and Earth implodes thus reducing billions and billions of years of evolution to random particles of dust floating through space. Yep. It's basically that quiet. Maybe he's relieved at the prospect of me not being his official offspring and all he can do to contain his excitement is be deafeningly nonverbal.

"Could we listen to the radio or something?" I finally ask after a half hour in bumper-to-bumper traffic on our way to Los Angeles.

As he moves to click on the radio, his phone rings. The voice of an Indian lady with a heavy accent booms through the car speakers. I try to pay attention but the conversation is way over my head. A lot of legal mumbo jumbo like legal custody versus sole custody versus physical custody versus blah blah blah. Also, he's cursing...a lot. Not a good sign for his Jehovah's Witness-ish-ness. Margaret would be all kinds of not pleased. Pumpkin would be scarred for *life*.

"What do you mean he would have a right? So we keep the kid and *pay* him?"

The *kid*?

My phone chimes. A text from Xavior. I exhale nervously and lift it to read: You guys headed to the express DNA facility yet?

I text back: En route.

His reply: Good. I found something late last night I wanted you to see.

A photo comes through via text. I click on the screen. It's an old photo of my mom. Her face is so young, bright and happy. She's sitting on the edge of a bed, holding her guitar, eyes closed, playing. A Happy New Year party hat on top of her head. I raise an eyebrow as I study the photo. She's holding the guitar in her right hand. But...Mom played left-handed guitar after she broke her hand. My head instantly starts aching. Pressure building. Combustion…*imminent.*

I turn to Anthony. Traffic has started to move again and we've begun to pick up speed. He's no longer on the phone with the lawyer lady. Just staring straight ahead, concentrating on the road.

"Anthony?" I say, placing my hand over my heart as if that can somehow stop it from beating so fast.

"Hmm?"

"When did you meet my mom?"

"January? Yeah. It was right after the New Year."

I sit up, palms profusely sweating. I wipe them dry on my Curington khakis. "Are you sure?"

"I'm sure. Yes. Why do you ask?"

But before I can answer, the lawyer lady calls back. She and Anthony get back into another discussion of big words.

I text Xavior back: Do you remember when my mom broke her hand?

A moment passes. I wipe my sweaty palms on my khakis again. The seconds passing are absolute *torture.* C'mon! Text me back!

Finally, after what feels like an eternity times infinity, Xavior replies: Can't say that I do. She broke her hand?

Omigosh! *Omigosh!*

Mom wore a cast for almost *two* months after she broke her hand. Xavior would have known that if they were dating around the time I was conceived. But they weren't! They *couldn't* have been.

I turn to Anthony and imagine us both on the stage of the *Maury Povich* show. Maury peels open the manila envelope.

The crowd is eerily quiet. Anthony biting his nails. Me biting mine.

"Anthony Stone," Maury says slowly. "You *are* the father!"

And he is. I *know* he is.

The DNA testing facility looks and feels like your average doctor's office. I'm sitting in the waiting area while Anthony's in the back getting his portion of the DNA test. Whatever that is. Blood draw? Brain scan. I want to talk to him. I have to talk to him. Tell him what I know. The dates don't add up. Xavior definitely dated my mom but I'm sure it was *before* she met Anthony.

"Tiffany Sly?" A pretty blonde woman is standing at the doorway that leads into the facility, holding a clipboard. "We're ready for you now."

The DNA test is pretty chill. The lady with the clipboard puts gloves on, reads something to me about information being admissible in a court of law, then takes a long Q-tip and swabs the inside of both my cheeks.

"And that's that. All finished." She stuffs the Q-tip into a plastic bag and seals it shut.

"You don't have to take blood or anything?"

"Buccal swabs are preferred over blood samples these days. A few seconds and you're done. Easy peasy." She stuffs the plastic bag holding the swab into what looks to be a small express mailing box and seals that shut, too.

My phone buzzes.

It's a text from Anthony: One of my patients has a postsurgery infection and needs an emergency hysterectomy. Darryl is on his way to pick you up and take you back to school. I have to run. We'll talk about the results when I get home. Don't worry about anything. Have fun at school. Dad.

Have fun at *school*? Is he insane? I want to scream at the top of my lungs. Throw stuff. Shout obscenities.

"Are you okay?" the blonde lady asks me, and politely tilts her head the way Margaret does.

A giant lump forms in my throat. I try to swallow it away but it's no use. Sobs erupt out of me. I attempt to muffle my cries as much as I can, ashamed that I've been reduced to public wailing, suffering and humiliation. "I'm so sorry."

"Oh, sweetheart." The lady looks like she wants to hug me or do something to help me. Finally she says, "Maybe you should call your mom?"

I sniff. Ashamed to admit I'm mom-less.

"Call her, okay? I'll give you some privacy." The lady quickly exits the room, leaving me to suffer alone.

With shaking hands, I dial the closest thing I can think of to a mom.

"Hello? Tiffany?" Margaret answers sweetly.

"Margaret," I start. "Um, I know Pumpkin doesn't like long car rides. I know that you're probably really busy. But is there any way you could pick me up at the DNA testing place?"

"Tiffany, sweetheart? What's wrong?"

"Margaret? C-can you p-please take me to the airport?" I sob.

"Airport? Tiffany, why? What's going on?"

"I wanna go back to Chicago," I cry. "Please, Margaret? Let me go back home."

"Tiffany, I'm on my way, okay? Let me call our sitter. Hold tight, my love. I'm on the way."

I'm sitting outside on the curb, backpack strapped tightly to my shoulders, when Margaret arrives sans Pumpkin, her wet hair pulled into a messy bun, suggesting I called her at the exact moment she'd gotten out of the shower. A simple pair of gray lounge pants, a T-shirt and sandals manages to look classy and very rich on Margaret. I stand as she approaches, clutching her cell in one hand. Without so much as a word she rushes for me and pulls me in tightly. Holding me. Rubbing my back with her free hand. The everlasting lump in my throat breaks free once again and I cry on her shoulder, grasping on to her like my life depends on it.

"He doesn't want me, Margaret. He doesn't really want me."

"Tiffany," she says soothingly. "Don't say that. Anthony loves you."

"He doesn't." I cry. "He probably thinks Mom was the biggest mistake of his life. Wishes he'd never cheated on you with a random woman and almost destroyed your family."

"A random woman?" Margaret pulls away and stares at me, perplexed. "Tiffany Sly, where did you get that idea? Anthony was madly in love with your mom. Did he not tell you that?"

I shake my head.

She folds her arms across her chest. "Well, then, *I'll* tell you. You deserve the truth. It's your right, Tiffany. Anthony was madly in love with your mom."

"He was? Did you—" I wipe my eyes with the bottom portion of my polo "—know he was cheating on you?"

"Cheating?" She shakes her head. "Anthony is many, many things but a cheater he is not."

"Why does London think he cheated on you?"

Margaret shrugs. "Why does London think she has to brush her hair at least eighty-seven strokes a day so it can be super-shiny?" Margaret sits on the curb of the parking lot and I sit beside her.

"So then he didn't cheat on you?"

"We were on a break while he was in Chicago. He and I started dating when we were in high school and got engaged our senior year in college, but during his residency, we both decided we wanted time to make sure this was the right thing. We were still close. Best friends, to be honest. We talked every day and kept in touch while he was away, but everything changed when out of nowhere he started talking about one of his patients *all* the time. She went from patient to friend in a matter of days. Next thing I knew, he and his new friend were basically inseparable."

"So my mom wasn't the other woman," I say more to myself than to Margaret. I knew she wouldn't have been the other woman. I *knew* it.

"I mean, to me she was. But technically, no. He had every right to date. I was dating, too. Here and there, but nothing serious. His was serious." She gets a faraway look in her eyes. "And then I got the call that your mom was pregnant."

"Wait. You knew about that, too?"

"Of course I knew. Anthony would never keep something like that from me. Terrified I'd lost him, I flew out to Chicago and asked him to make a choice. Her or me. No more 'on a break.' Engagement back on. Anthony reassured me it was *us* he wanted, too. Told me he'd already broken things off and had asked Imani to get an abortion." Margaret heaves a heavy sigh. "Tiffany, I have replayed that conversation in my head every *day*. Relived that moment. Every day. For *years*. I could have said, 'No, don't do that. Call her, support her, be there for her.' I should have demanded that. But I was overcome with jealousy. So you wanna know what I said?" Tears spill down her cheeks. "Nothing. I said nothing."

"Don't cry, Margaret," I say as kindly as I can, even though I'm crying, too, imagining a young mom, all alone, the guy she'd loved completely deserting her in her time of need.

Margaret wipes her face and looks over at me, warm brown eyes red and pained. Face tear-streaked. "Can you imagine how Anthony and I felt when Imani got in touch with us? Can you imagine our joy? I cried every day. I would turn on the bathwater so the girls wouldn't hear me cry, but I was so *happy*. It was like Jehovah God was giving us this beautiful blessing. This chance to right our wrong. To complete our family. Jehovah God has a plan for everything."

"Don't say that," I snap. "Don't make it seem like 'God' *killed* my mom to complete your family. God had nothing to do with my mom dying. She just died. Because that's what people do. They die."

"I'm sorry," Margaret replies softly. "I didn't mean it that way."

"But it all worked out." I shrug. "You got the guy. You *beat* my mom. And now she's dead and you get to keep her kid, too."

"Tiffany..."

"Here's a thought." I stand. "Maybe Anthony's so damn

miserable because he missed out on the chance to be with the girl he really loved. Maybe he can't get over the fact that he made the wrong choice. You ever think about that?"

I see all remaining color drain from Margaret's pale face and immediately wish I could push a button, which would allow time to rewind about thirty-five seconds, so I could take back what I just said. She looks young and vulnerable in this moment and I can't help but now imagine a young Margaret, her "on a break" fiancé calling her and telling her that his new patient/friend is pregnant with his baby. The pain she must have felt. The agony.

"Margaret," I whisper. "I shouldn't have said that."

"It's okay, Tiffany. You're upset with me. I understand."

"Omigosh, no. Margaret, you've been nothing but *amazing* to me. I'm not upset with you." I wipe my eyes. "That was so wrong what I said. Please forgive me."

"Forgiven. Forgiven a thousand times over and over again." She stands and reaches for my hands. Squeezes them lovingly. "Now will you forgive *me*? Sixteen years ago I said nothing when I should have said something. Tiffany, *I'm* sorry. You could've had a dad. You *should* have had a dad."

"I wanted one." I'm crying again because I know it's true. "All these years I really wanted a dad."

"Tiffany, you've always had one. Anthony and I, we didn't know if you'd have been a boy or a girl but we talked about you. Constantly. When the girls played, we imagined you playing with them. And I promise you, at night when we prayed, we prayed to the soul that we *thought* was on the other side. We have *always* loved you. He's always loved you."

I stare out into the parking lot. Cars come and go. "Maybe

you love me. You're a good person. But who does he love? Seems like the only thing he cares about is his job. And his rules."

"He wasn't always like this. He's changed. Maybe part of the reason you're here is to help him find his way back."

I turn to her. "Why do you put up with it? With him?"

"Because sometimes people lose their way. And it's up to the people who love them to help them find their way back. Love isn't some warm and fuzzy feeling. It's action. It's work. It's commitment." Margaret's phone buzzes. She checks the caller ID. "Give me one second?"

I nod.

She slides her finger across the phone to answer it and takes a few steps away for privacy, though I can still hear her quite clearly. "Hi, Karen, everything okay?...*What?* Ambulance?"

My heart starts to pound in my chest. I swallow, imagining the worst. "Is Pumpkin okay?"

Margaret gives me a reassuring nod as she listens intently. "Jehovah God, have mercy...Okay." She nods again. "Thank you so much for calling. I'm gonna take Tiffany to the hospital. Would it be okay to stay a few more hours?...Oh, thank you, Karen. We'll see you soon. Kiss Pumpkin for me." Margaret turns to me, her eyes clouded with worry.

"What's wrong? Why are you taking me to the hospital?"

"Tiffany..." Margaret starts slowly. "An ambulance just rushed Marcus away."

I cover my mouth. "Is he okay? Margaret, please tell me he's okay."

"Karen only saw them from the window. She said it looked dire."

"Omigosh. Is he dead?"

"Sweetheart, I don't know."

"Can we go now? Please?"

"Yes, of course, Tiffany. Let's hurry."

22

By the time Margaret and I make it to Genesis West in Simi Valley we find out that Marcus has been helicoptered to Children's Hospital in LA. We immediately hop in the car and get back on the freeway.

It's an hour and thirty minutes before we make it into LA and exit the 101, an additional fifteen minutes before Margaret actually pulls up to Children's Hospital Los Angeles and exactly six minutes on top of that before we make it to the front counter at the check-in. By this time, Jo has been in touch. I reread some of our text exchange as a kindly Hispanic woman prints visitors' passes for Margaret and me.

Jo: Marcus is in surgery right now.

Me: What happened?

Jo: Heart too weak to pump blood effectively. Surgery is to install a left ventricular assist device. Called an LVAD for short.

Me: So, then he'll be okay?

Jo: If he makes it out of surgery.

I reread her last text. *If he makes it out of surgery.* One very important word—*if.* Jo's ever so subtle way of letting me know that today might be the day we say goodbye to Marcus McKinney.

Margaret listens to instructions on how to follow the green lines on the hospital floor to the elevator and I glance around. There are sick children in wheelchairs, that signature "I'm fighting for my life" bald head that Mom used to sport. Some walking around slowly, pushing IVs, loving family members standing in support with them. I remember being that family member. Helping Mom take painful steps. Lifting her spirits as much as I could, even though when you're dying, death is always in the air. Every thought ends with death. "Wanna go have a snack, Mom?" I'd ask. She'd nod and I'd picture her gravestone. "Tomorrow it's supposed to rain, Tiff." She'd speak barely above a whisper and I'd imagine it raining as they lowered her casket into the ground. Everybody would send messages on Facebook and email. Flowers. Precondolences. "Please know we're praying for you!!!" They'd add a gaggle of exclamation marks to seal their point, an emoticon of praying hands added at the end of the sentence for good measure. But when it came to being by Mom's side, to cleaning up the sick that erupted out of her body, to wiping away her tears…

"You ready, Tiffany?"

"Hmm? Oh, yeah. Ready."

Margaret thanks the lady behind the desk and we move on.

★ ★ ★

The hospital has strict rules about the ICU visiting area, so Margaret and I are waiting in another waiting room on an entirely different floor. I keep checking my phone every second and a half, hoping to get another text from Jo. I don't dare text her, knowing she's in her own personal hell and truly doesn't need distractions from me.

"Your dad's here. He's parking." Margaret breaks the hours-long silence.

I check my phone again. Still nothing from Jo.

After a few minutes, Anthony rushes into the waiting room, still in his hospital scrubs, looking frazzled, tired and anxious. Margaret stands to greet him and they hug.

He sits beside me, squeezes my leg. "How you holdin' up there, Tiffany?"

He smells like a mixture of alcohol and that pink bathroom soap they have in public restrooms. "They're installing an LVAD. Is that a dangerous surgery or something? I feel like Jo was hinting that he might not make it."

"Medicine has advanced tremendously. People can live for years with an LVAD. He'll have a little backpack. The device will reach from his heart and out his stomach. He'll carry it with him wherever he goes and plug into a machine at night." Anthony squeezes my leg again. "Tiffany, let's go home. There's no reason to be here. If he makes it out of surgery, he'll be placed in an induced coma until his body heals and revitalizes. He won't wake up for days."

"But I want Jo and Monique to know I'm here. I don't want them to feel alone. I always felt so alone when Mom was dying."

"Trust me," he tosses out casually. "They're not worried about you being here."

"Correction. They're not worried about *you* being here." *Asshole.* "I'm staying."

"We'll stay with you, Tiffany." Margaret gives Anthony the same look I gave Aric right before I dislocated his nose from his face.

"Well, then, let's be proactive and not just sit here." Anthony leans back in the chair beside me. "I think it would be a good idea for us all to pray together."

"Great idea, honey," Margaret replies.

A few chairs away from us a baby starts to wail. Her mom pats her on the back and paces around the small waiting room.

"I'm not going to do that. You guys knock yourselves out."

"Tiffany, c'mon," Anthony urges. "Let's pray together. As a family."

"What exactly is the point? I prayed for my mom and look where that got me."

"The point of prayer is to ask for Jehovah God's help," Anthony states.

"And what if Jehovah God doesn't offer one bit of help?" I ask. "Like, what if we all hold hands and pray and then Marcus dies? What then?"

Margaret and Anthony exchange looks. Disturbed, confused, mystified looks. Almost as if the thought never occurred to them. What happens when "God" doesn't answer prayers? Hell if we know, they seem to say without saying.

I think back to when Marcus and I talked on the balcony in Malibu. "When is the last time God ever physically helped anybody?" he asked me. "In so many ways, Tiffany, you are the God you seek." I so wish that were true. If I *was* God, like if I really and truly were like...a *god*—I would make an awesome one. I'd create a place where people like my mom and Marcus got to live long, happy lives.

"I have an idea."

Anthony and Margaret perk up, hope sprung back to their dead, crazy eyes.

"What if instead of praying for God to save Marcus's life and then being disappointed if that doesn't happen...what if *we* saved a life. Someone who needs saving. Someone we *can* save."

Anthony's brow furrows. "I'm not sure I understand."

"Marcus's family has money, right?" I say. "They can afford health care. What if somebody didn't have insurance and they had Marcus's issues? What would they do?"

"That would be a rough road." Anthony shakes his head.

"Sadly, it happens all the time," Margaret adds.

"What if we... I dunno...started a GoFundMe page to help victims of heart disease who don't have health insurance. Is that lame?" I ask.

"Not lame at *all*," Margaret replies.

"I like this idea, Tiffany." Anthony squeezes my leg again. "But instead of a GoFundMe page, what if we started a non-profit organization? I can help you get it started."

"You'd do that for me?"

"Are you kidding? I'd be happy to." Anthony sounds genuinely happy to be of some use to me.

"Thank you, Anthony. This will be my prayer. This *is* my prayer."

"I like it. It's *active* prayer. Let me make some calls. See what I can do to get the ball rolling for you."

"I want to help, too," Margaret adds. "Tiffany, can I be a part of it?"

"Definitely. I need all the help I can get."

It's after 4:00 p.m. when I get a new text from Jo. Margaret, Anthony and I are in one of the hospital cafeterias eating a snack when my phone buzzes. With shaking hands I read the text.

"Read it out loud, Tiffany," Margaret urges.

"'Marcus is out of surgery,'" I read. "'Praise God! He's in a medically induced coma, but—'"

"See, I told you," Anthony interrupts.

Margaret glares at Anthony. "Anthony, shh! I want to hear this."

"'But things are looking good.'" I continue reading. "'Might be days before he wakes. Please go home, Tiffany. We love you so much and will be in contact. Thank you for being here. It means so much to us.'"

As I look up and breathe a sigh of relief, Anthony's phone buzzes loudly on the table. He grabs it. A look of sheer terror clouds his face.

"What's wrong?" Margaret asks.

"It's Rachel calling." Only he says, *It's Rachel calling*, like he really said it's the devil calling. "I can't answer it. I can't."

"I'll do it." Margaret grabs the phone.

Anthony's head is lowered, eyes closed, and he's breaking his plastic fork into tiny pieces like a crazy person. Is that because he wants me to be his kid or he doesn't? I can't tell.

"Hi, Rachel," Margaret says weakly. "Right. Okay." She nods. "What are our options at this point?" Margaret gives me a polite tilt of the head.

That polite tilt of the head says it all. It's written all over her face. Etched in the lines of her frown. But how could Anthony *not* be my father? It doesn't make sense.

"Right but..." Margaret trails off, listening. "I do understand that, but—" She sighs. "Right. Then what's the next appropriate step?" Margaret sighs again. Heavier this time. "I'll talk to Anthony and see if he wants to move forward with that. I doubt he will, though. We just want to move on. Get back to our lives. Thank you, Rachel. I will speak with Tiffany and let her know her options. We'll be in touch." She hangs up and Anthony throws his crumpled bits of plastic fork. Fork bits fly everywhere.

"What is *wrong* with you?" Margaret asks as she dodges an airborne shard of plastic.

"We'll take another test!" he bellows.

"Why would we do that?" Margaret sounds exasperated. "These tests have no gray area. They're ninety-nine percent accurate."

"I don't believe it! I know she's my daughter! I know she is."

"Of course she's your daughter!" Margaret shrieks so loud a few people in the cafeteria look over at us. She ignores the stares. Speaks pointedly. "You *are* Tiffany's father. You are. That's what Rachel said. You *are*."

I exhale. Relieved. I knew it. I knew it!

"But what was all that 'We'll see what our options are from here'?" Anthony asks. "And you sounded so sad."

"That was Rachel wanting us to sue Xavior, which I don't think we should. He's a nice man. He meant well. That was what she was asking me about." Margaret beams. "Turns out Tiffany Sly...*is* a Stone. Perhaps you two could do with some privacy." She slides her chair back, stands and quickly makes her way out of the hospital cafeteria, a satisfied smirk plastered across her face.

Anthony and I sit in silence for a long, long while. A rewritten version of Peaches and Herb's "Reunited" plays in my head. *Reunited and it feels so awkward.*

"I don't want you talking or texting with that guy ever again," Anthony finally says. "Are we understood?"

"That's what you want to say to me? A DNA test confirms I really am your daughter and your response is 'Don't talk to that guy ever again. Are we understood?'" I shake my head. "Dude. You're unbelievable."

"Dude?"

"Oh, I'm sorry. Was that on the house rules list? Do not call your father a dude?"

"Tiffany, look. I didn't need a DNA test. I already knew you were my daughter."

"Well, I *didn't*. Can you imagine what I must have been feeling for the past several days? Do you know anything about empathy? Or is your goal in life to be mean and awful and never think about how other people feel? Are you a sociopath?"

"Is that what you think? You think I've been awful enough to be a sociopath?"

"And mean. Don't forget mean."

"Jesus." He leans back in his chair. "That hurts when you say that."

"Talk about hurt? You made me play basketball. I *hate* basketball."

"Why? It's a great sport."

"So is rugby. Doesn't mean I want to play it. And you made me take out my braids."

"So? Your hair looks lovely."

I pull at my hair. "It's not mine! It's a weave. Jo gave me a weave because my hair is a mess."

He sits up, angry. "Why would you go against my rules like that?"

"I have *alopecia*. I don't care about your stupid rules when it comes to me looking like a troll doll or a human girl! The braids were strategically placed to cover up the bald spots on my head."

He leans back in his chair again, grabbing a plastic spoon. I imagine him breaking it up into bits and throwing it like he threw that fork. But he doesn't. Thankfully he sets it down gently in front of him and stares ahead. Blue eyes as dead as the deadest dead man in dead town.

For some reason I mumble, "I watched *Cinema Paradiso*."

He tosses me a side eye. "Really?"

"I watched it last night. I've decided you're Salvatore. But instead of loving filmmaking, you love helping women and delivering babies. And Chicago is the home you never wanted to return to. And Mom—she's Elena, the girlfriend from your past, and—"

Crazy happens. Like, absolutely insane *transpires*. Anthony Stone starts to cry. He lowers his head over his tray of hospital cafeteria food; his shoulders shake and he *weeps*.

My eyes bulge and I stare at him in shock. Holy. Baloney. What do you do when a grown man starts to cry?

"You're right, Tiffany," he sobs. "You're right. This has

been *so* hard for me. Seeing you. Having you here. Reminds me of what I lost. What I walked away from."

"What?" I whisper.

"When I was a kid, we had these books." He looks up at me, eyes pained, tears streaming down his light brown cheeks. "When you finished a chapter it gave you a choice. Turn to this page if the hero goes through the door. Turn to another page if he…climbs the mountain or whatever. I used to *love* those stories. Mostly because I could always go back and make another choice. See what happened on the other page. But in life you can't do that. You make a choice and you don't get to go back and…see." He lowers his head. "You show up and you remind me of those pages I can't ever read. What would our life have been like? Maybe I might have noticed the signs of the Hodgkin's. Perhaps Imani would still be alive."

I close my eyes and imagine just that. My doctor dad dropping me off at school in Chicago. A happy, healthy mom at home. We would have visited a lake house on the weekends. Mom and Anthony would argue playfully on the long drive up. Maybe there would have been siblings. Little brown-skinned brothers and sisters that looked just like me. My heart aches at the thought.

"You called me a runner at the beach house," Anthony continues. "It's true. I have been running. You think growing up in Englewood was easy? I made a vow when I left Chicago. One…to never return. Two…to be better than all the horrors I saw growing up. I wanted to be *better.* But I spent so much time working to be a cut above… I suppose I forgot what I was working for. I forgot about my family. I'm so sorry I didn't even have the common decency to come to her funeral." Anthony cries. "I was a coward—I couldn't face what I did. I loved her. I have always loved her."

I sit in a stunned silence.

"I love you, too, Tiffany."

I sit up, baffled. "I don't believe you."

"What? How could you think I don't love you?"

I quote Margaret. "Love is not a warm and fuzzy feeling. Love is action. Work. Commitment. You've been gone for my whole life. And the day after I get here, you leave for San Francisco. Lame."

"Which I admitted was the wrong thing to do."

"But then you try to isolate me from the McKinneys, even though they actually *have* shown me love. Even lamer. You—"

"Tiffany, stop." He groans. "Please don't point out everything I've done wrong. I'm sorry. Look, I can't fix everything overnight. I can't rewind time. So tell me something I *can* do? Name one thing I can do to make things better."

I don't even hesitate. "Accept who I am."

"Of course I accept who—"

"I won't ever be a Jehovah's Witness."

"Tiffany." He shakes his head. "I can't accept that. You're sixteen. Traumatized by the death of your mom. God will reveal Himself to you again. I know He will."

"Maybe," I admit. "Or maybe not." I lean forward. "But this is where I am right now."

He drums his fingers on the table. "I can *respect* where you're at. I won't force church and religion on you. I'm sorry I tried to do that."

"Apology accepted. Next. Stop judging the McKinneys because they're gay."

"What? Tiffany Sly, I am *not* judging—"

"I wasn't born yesterday. I know you are. You know it, too."

He picks up the spoon again. Another long moment passes. "Fine. I can work on it. It's hard for me. I can admit it. I don't approve of their lifestyle. I think homosexuality is a sin."

"See?" I say with a sigh. "Doesn't it feel good to be honest?"

He chuckles. "It feels bad actually. Really bad. I feel like a jerk. Tell me something, though. Why does Marcus paint his face white? How can you not be creeped out by that?"

I tell him everything about Marcus and why he wears white makeup on his face. Anthony shakes his head in wonder. "Jehovah God. I owe that kid an apology."

He's right. He does. In fact, Anthony Stone owes an apology to his whole family. Margaret and Pumpkin, London, Heaven, Nevaeh…and me, too. "What is keen-wah?"

Anthony laughs. "It's spelled *q-u-i-n-o-a*. Beyond that…I don't know."

"It's pretty gross. Maybe we can kindly tell Margaret I don't eat that?"

"Done."

"Hey, I know something else you can do to make things better."

"What's that, Tiffany Sly?" Anthony asks with a sad smile.

"You can give me a hug. Like a real hug."

He kneels at my side and embraces me. This time the hug doesn't feel like the hug from the principal at my old school. It feels like the way Mom used to hug me. Like she was never going to let me go.

23

As I'm stepping into my pajamas, my Stone family cell buzzes. Anthony's decided to no longer confiscate it at night. Another attempt to make things better. Though internet is still not allowed. But what are you gonna do? Rome wasn't built in a day. London's in the bathroom taking a shower, so I quickly grab it from off the nightstand. *Xavior X* scrolls across the screen.

I sit slowly on the edge of the bed and press the answer button. "Hey."

"Tiffany." He's still saying my name like it's the most important name in the world. I can hear the hustle and bustle of the airport in the background. "I hope you don't mind me calling. I won't keep you. I just wanted to say I'm sorry."

"Why? You had a hunch. I don't blame you for wanting to know the truth."

"Maybe all this happening is the universe guiding me to get my act together. Meet a nice girl. Fall in love. Have some kids. I'd really like that."

"Make sure you make them listen to *Sgt. Pepper's.*"

"And *Ziggy Stardust.*"

"*Spiders from Mars?* Best. Ever." I hear the shower click off in the bathroom. "I...better get going."

"Hey, listen. If my kids turn out to be half as cool as you, Tiffany Sly...they will be the greatest ever. Rock on, my little homey."

I smile. "Rock on, Xavior Xavion."

It's six days before we get the call that Marcus is awake. An additional three hours and twenty-five minutes before Anthony is able to extract me from school and drive me back to Children's Hospital Los Angeles. And another eleven minutes before we make it to the front counter at the check-in.

The same Hispanic woman I remember from before prints visitors' passes for Anthony and me.

"Excuse me?" I say to her.

She glances up. "Yes, miss?"

"May I get an application to volunteer here?"

She reaches into a drawer beside her and hands me a packet of papers. "Filling these out is the first step. Then there's a mandatory eight-hour information session. We only do them once a month on a Saturday. If you miss it, you'll have to wait until the next month before you can move forward to orientation."

I place the packet inside my backpack. "Thank you."

Anthony thanks the lady, as well, and we move off.

"Hey," I start. "Would you mind if I went up alone?"

He shifts. I can tell he does mind but rather than object

he replies, "Sure. Not a problem. I can visit the McDonald's here."

"You can't eat McDonald's. Everything is covered in gluten."

"I'll spit out the gluten. Follow the green line to the elevator. Eighth floor."

"Okay. Thanks, Dad." I freeze. Holy. Baloney. Did I just say what I *think* I said?

Anthony grabs my hand. "Dude. You just called me Dad."

"Um, well..." I run my fingers through my long extensions. "You just called me dude."

He squeezes my shoulder. "You can call me Dad. Anytime, okay? Tell Marcus and the family I'm here if they need anything."

I nod and move off. I called Anthony Dad? What are the *odds*?

When I push into Marcus's ICU room, Jo and Monique are sitting in chairs beside his bed. They both stand when I enter.

"Tiffany Sly," Jo says softly.

"Hi, Tiff," Monique whispers.

The tone of the room is quiet and peaceful. Zen for Marcus.

I follow their lead. "Hello, you guys," I whisper, pulling idly on the sleeves of my Curington polo.

Marcus is hooked up to an assortment of machines, the honey-brown skin on his face scrubbed clean of makeup. I stand speechless for a moment. Not sure why I didn't think that I'd be seeing him this way—without the white face. He looks so gentle, kind and soft...like his voice. His green eyes sparkle. I don't even realize I'm crying until Jo hands me a tissue and I wipe my eyes.

"Hi, Marcus," I whisper.

He waves from his hospital bed.

"He's got a dry-erase board," Jo explains. "So he can communicate with you. Won't be another few days until they can take out the trach tube. Then he can continue spreading wisdom and being his ol' incorrigible self."

Marcus writes on his board. We all wait for him to finish. A moment passes and he turns the board over. It reads, *I'm not incorrigible.*

We all smile.

"Yes, you are, honey." Jo moves to his side, kisses him on his cheek. "Yes, you are."

"Let's grab some food, babe," Monique says. "Give the kids a chance to chat."

Jo wrings her hands together as if the thought of leaving Marcus for even one second is making her uneasy. "Okay." She kisses Marcus's forehead. "Okay. Tiffany, you press this button right here should Marcus need anything at all, okay?"

I nod and the two leave. The door shuts quietly behind them.

"Marcus McKinney." I sit beside him. "I never realized how *attractive* you are. Without all that makeup I can see it now. Jeez. We might have to rethink this cousin/family pet relationship."

He writes on his board. I wait patiently for him to finish. He turns it over to show me. *I thought you liked thirty-year-old white men?*

"See? Incorrigible." I unzip my backpack and present to

him the folder and articles of incorporation for our new nonprofit. "It's a nonprofit that not only helps victims of heart disease who don't have insurance and money for the care and medication they need, it also teaches victims of HCM meditation techniques so they can learn to keep their heart rhythms under control. But I know nothing about meditation, and neither does my dad…so we're hiring *you* to help get things started."

Marcus gives me a thumbs-up.

"Do you like it?"

He writes on his board, *I'm proud of you, Tiffany/God.*

I grab his hand; a jolt shoots through my body. I quickly release it. "Whoa…"

He writes, *Without the makeup, energy coming through me is so strong. I'm sorry.*

"Don't be sorry. That's freaking cool. I'm tellin' you, you need to be on a morning talk show." I take his hand again. This time the jolt doesn't shock me as much. It does make the hair on my arms stand straight up, though. "London's not pregnant, by the way."

He nods as if he already knew that.

"And Anthony *is* my real dad."

He nods again and writes, *Duh.*

"You're totally psychic. Just admit it!" We sit for a while. Holding hands and listening to the sound of his many beeping machines. "You know, back in the olden days, before they had Wi-Fi, people used to read books out loud for entertainment. So I was thinking we could pretend we don't have Wi-Fi and I could read you this new book I got. What do you think about that?"

He releases my hand to write on his board. *I like books. You think it's gonna be good?*

"I don't know," I say. "Quite honestly, I've been a little bit scared to read it. But not anymore. I think I'm ready. Actually, I know I am. Maybe it'll even help me find my way back."

I reach into my bag and extract *The Boy Who Lived Before.* I hold it up for Marcus to see. He smiles and writes, *I'm all ears.*

I flip the book open to the first page, where a simple quote is italicized and read out loud.

"Everybody wants to go to heaven,
But nobody wants to die."

I close my eyes and take a deep breath. Thoughts of death immediately rush in. I strain to push them out, trying to imagine the sound of Marcus's soothing voice. *It's okay, Tiffany,* he'd say.

I know it is. But I also know that I am going to die someday. Marcus will, too. But one thing's for sure. We probably won't die at this minute. Everything happens. But for now what's happening…is a very special moment with my very special friend.

Thump-thump, thump-thump:

And for the first time in so very long, the foreboding of my rapidly beating heart says nothing.

I smile and turn the page…

★★★★★

ACKNOWLEDGMENTS

It was my own experience with depression and anxiety that compelled me to create the world of Tiffany Sly, but I could not have brought this story to life without the guidance from superamazing people that I know, love and admire.

First up, my fabulous team of agents at Triada US, with special thanks to Dr. Uwe Stender. You are, quite simply, the best. Thank you for your honesty, love and incredible work ethic. I'm sure I've known you for a billion years. I hope we stay friends for a billion more. Times infinity.

Mallory C. Brown…you're lovely. And thank you for always being down to read early drafts and give feedback. Your honestly is invaluable. I appreciate you.

To Brent Taylor. One phone conversation with you and Tiffany changed forever. I will be eternally grateful for you.

Thank you to my amazing team of editors at Harlequin. Extra special thanks to T.S. Ferguson for your genius. I'm so grateful to have landed under your care. I admire you. Thank you Natashya Wilson for your insight and for seeing the beauty in Tiffany.

Thanks to copy editor Christine Langone and cover design team Bora Tekogul and Erin Craig.

To my early readers, Sarah Skilton, Kevin Richmond and Gregory Schwartz, thank you for your insight. Additionally, thank you Gregory Schwartz for the crash course in geography. And thank you Travis Lee Stephenson for guiding Tiffany's love of music.

In addition: Martha Davis, Carmen Price, nurse extraordinaire, for your vast medical knowledge (all mistakes my own). My Electric Eighteens and Bree Barton for your love and support during this whirlwind debut experience.

Thank you to my family, who supported my writing. A trillion thanks to my mom, Candra Cheers. The drive that I witnessed in you has become the foundation of my life. I could not have spent so many hours laboring over this story without the values you instilled in me. You were my first example of active prayer. Thank you. Thank you.

To my darling daughter, Cameron. This story could not have come to life without you and our journey thus far. Thank you for choosing me. I love you so much.

To my aunt Margaret Stone. I know you're reading this from the other side. I love you and miss you.

A very sincere thank-you to my readers, especially those who can relate to the complexities of tackling life after trauma. I hope you enjoyed taking this journey with Tiffany.

Until next time,
Dana L. Davis